Kyles Reveal

My Brothers' Keeper Series

Blue Saffire writing as Royal Blue

Perceptive Illusions Publishing, Inc.

Bay Shore, New York

Royal Blue /Perceptive Illusions Publishing, Inc.
PO BOX 5253
Bay Shore, New York 11706
www.AuthorRoyalBlue.com

Publisher's Note: This is a work of fiction. Names, characters, places, and incidents are a product of the author's imagination. Locales and public names are sometimes used for atmospheric purposes. Any resemblance to actual people, living or dead, or to businesses, companies, events, institutions, or locales is completely coincidental.

Ordering Information:
Quantity sales. Special discounts are available on quantity purchases by corporations, associations, and others. For details, contact the "Special Sales Department" at the address above.

Kyle's Reveal/ Blue Saffire writing as Royal Blue . – 2nd ed.
ISBN 978-1-941924-56-3

Love has a way of catching you when you fall.
Especially when there appears to be no safety net.

– Royal Blue

Heartbroken

Kyle

"Sing to me," my sister whispers.

She licks her dry lips, before giving a labored swallow. Every breath has become a challenge. I remember the days when I thought my sister was a superhero. Nothing in the world could defeat her. Now she looks so small and fragile.

My heart aches. I've wished this day away with everything I am. Yet the ash-gray of her rich brown skin, the yellow of her eyes, and the scent of nearing death tells me that all the wishing in the world won't hold this off much longer. So with a throat filled with emotion, I give in to her request.

I begin to sing one of her favorite songs—"Misty Blue," by Dorothy Moore. Our mother played it in our home when we were little. We'd sing right along with the record player and giggle, while our mother cleaned the house with her scarf wrapped around her head. It's one of the few memories I have of my mother.

I breathe through the line about not being about to forget. I know I'll never forget my sister. The words hit home, almost choking off the notes I'm crooning.

I belt the song out with my soul. My heart squeezes, when tears start to roll down Savanna's cheeks. I stand to my full height beside her hospital bed, unable to sit still any longer. I need to do something with my body.

I pound my chest in defeat, but never once do I stop singing. I sing like it's my profession. Through my own tears, I see the looks of awe from the nurses that have gathered. I'm sure none of them expected Kyle Tyson to be able to do more than dribble a basketball.

That doesn't stop me from granting my sister her last wish. My voice fills the room, my vision clouds, and my entire being feels like it's coming apart. All the money I've made, none of it will save her in this moment. I'm losing my rock, but the burning fact in all of this has to be the little boy waiting at my house.

Mason is probably in my living room playing with his toys, thinking this is just another one of Mommy's trips—the ones she has returned from in the past. Savanna has loved my nephew with every breath she's had. She has fought so hard to be here for him.

"I'm tired, Kyle," she whispers on the last note I croon out.

I drop to my knee beside the bed, clinging to her already stiff legs. The last breath she takes shatters everything I know. I was too young to mourn my mother the way I'll mourn Savanna. This… this has the power to destroy me. I know the only reason

I have to push forward now is the part of her heart that she's left behind for me to care for.

"I'm so sorry. I'm so damn sorry," I sob. "I'm so sorry."

"You did everything you could, man. This isn't your fault. She fought as hard as she could," my best friend, Beau, says, while wrapping an arm around my shoulders.

"No. No, I didn't. I'm so sorry." I continue to beg my sister's forgiveness.

I should have been here more. I should have worked harder to find a cure. I should have done better, more, something.

She's gone. She's really gone. Savanna, I still have so much I want to say. So much to explain.

Beau leans down, placing his lips to my ear. "I know what you're thinking. She was proud of who you are. You don't have to apologize for any of it. She loved you for you. Don't do this here. Let me get you home."

It's as if he has heard my thoughts.

It takes a few more moments before I'm able to move. Slowly, I shift to kiss my sister's forehead. My tears dropping onto her cooling skin.

"I'll do right by your boy. I promise," I whisper. "I'll raise him to be the man you want. That's my word on my life."

I Need More

Kyle

"It's been months. The season is over. Why can't we go to this dinner party?" Michael huffs, placing his hands on his hips in exasperation.

Perched on the edge of my bed, I rub my temples. We've had this conversation a million times over, in a million different ways. Michael is an openly gay New York attorney. He and his family know everyone that's anyone. When his brother and sister-in-law throw a dinner party, you can expect A-list guests, including folks I'd rather not get wind of the fact that Michael and I have been dating the last five years.

One news reporter in the room and I'll wake up to a shitstorm in the morning. I'm just getting back to feeling like

I'm living life instead of barely moving through it. I don't need to add anything else to my plate.

"You and I both know you're not going to take me to this dinner as a friend. Everyone there will know I belong to you. You can't help yourself. All of that is cool at Club Refuge or around our friends. It's not outside of that," I reply, not able to keep the frustration out of my voice.

"Why isn't it? Five years, Kyle. I think we are past this invisible threat you think is waiting outside the closet," he tosses at me bitterly.

"I want you to stop and think about some of the things you tell me. You have seen what it's like for me, your colleagues, and your clients as black men. You rant about it all the time. Tell me, how many times have you admitted that it's ten times worse for a gay black man?"

I stand folding my arms over my chest. I'll wait. I can see in the red of his cheeks I hit the nail on the head. Michael has seen my world up close. He's been in the car with me, when I've been pulled over for nothing more than being black while driving a nice car.

"You know I'd never let anything happen to you or your career. I'd bury those sons of bitches if they tried to come for your livelihood." His words come out so passionately I believe them.

Still, Michael can't fight the world for me. I have too much responsibility to my team and my nephew. I can't just go and make decisions that could turn my world upside down.

"Wanting something and knowing the consequences of having it has to mean something. You're too educated a man to think with your emotions. I have my nephew to think about now," I say.

Sighing, I run a hand over my low waves.

"We've done nothing but think of your nephew for a year now. I rearranged everything to be here to help you with Mason, even before the end. I missed your big win in the playoffs because I've been here playing Mr. Mom," he seethes.

"Keep your voice down," I hiss, looking at the bedroom door. "You've complained about the playoffs every year we've been together. Besides, you're the one that said it would be best not to disturb his life any more than necessary. You said you wanted to stay behind and get him settled into school."

"I hate the fucking playoffs because I have to stand on the sidelines and watch as groupie after groupie throws themselves at you. That shit makes me sick. You smile and play right along with it in my face," he says.

"Name once when I've left with one of them. When I leave, I leave to go home with you," I retort.

"In separate fucking cars!" He pushes a hand through his thick locks as his chest heaves.

I swallow hard. I don't know if I have it in me to fight about this any longer. After losing the championship game, I had plans to return home to grieve in peace and raise my nephew. He needs more time with me, more stability.

Michael knew from the beginning that I wasn't ready to come out. I had reservations about our entire relationship. I knew Michael wouldn't be satisfied with concealing our connection. He promised he would be able to deal with it—I knew it was bullshit then, and he's proving me right.

"What would you have me do?" I sigh, sitting on the bed once again.

"Take the next step with me. I want the world to know how much I care about you. That you belong to me. I'm tired of living a lie," Michael says.

"A lie you promised you could be a part of. You don't know what the locker room is like. You don't understand the culture. Not just the basketball culture. My community is not like yours. I don't have the circle you do.

"You saw how my aunt wanted to take Mason from me, thinking I was single and too busy for him. If I come out now, she'll fight me tooth and nail to take that boy away from me. I promised my sister I'd take care of him. I won't fail her again," I say, pleading for him to hear me.

Michael moves across the room, sitting on the bed beside me. He cups my cheek, turning my face to him. I search his dark eyes. His cologne soothes my anger and hurt. His comforting scent is one of the things I've come to love about him.

"When did you ever fail her? Savanna knew who you were. God, Kyle, you can't keep blaming yourself for her death. She had stage-four cancer when they found it. She fought hard for longer than anyone expected."

"We promised to protect each other after my mother died. She was the first person I ever came out to. She has protected me all my life. She just needed me once, and there was nothing I could do," I reply, my voice breaking.

My brows draw as I search his face. How can he not understand this? That cold look in his eyes speaks volumes. I start to vibrate with anger and frustration.

"Protecting you by telling you to hide?" Michael says with a hint of anger.

"Don't," I warn, seething.

I shift away from him. My jaw tightens. It's like I float above the room and start to truly take this relationship in from the view of a painter. I watch the canvas before me and the colors become so much clearer.

"It's the truth. She drilled it in your head you had to be hard, you had to hide who you are to make it. You're even a different person with your nephew. He's five, but he'll have questions about us someday. What do you plan to do then?"

My jaw ticks. I've asked myself this question repeatedly. I want to be a role model for Mason. The type of role model my sister shaped me to be. I haven't figured out how to balance that. I don't know what I plan to do. Maybe it's time I made some changes.

"Just as I thought," he says tightly. "You're willing to give us up for this bullshit façade you've built. I can't do this. I won't do it."

"What do you want from me!"

"Nothing." He shakes his head. "Nothing at all. I'll send for my things. I'm done."

CHAPTER TWO

If I'm a Good Boy

Andy

"Mason, do you want to tell me what happened?" I say gently.

I asked the principal to allow me to have a chat with Mason, before his guardian arrived, given that the boy had shut down and wouldn't speak to anyone.

I care about all of my students, but this little boy has taken up a special place in my heart. He has been through so much in a short lifetime. He did well in the beginning. I've talked to Beth Ann, his teacher from last year. I remember him being a bright, outgoing student from the after-school program, but after the death of his mother he started to pull into himself, which is totally understandable. He's five and has had such great loss. My heart bleeds for him.

"I don't want to talk about it," he pouts.

"Your uncle will be here soon. It would be helpful if I understood so I can explain things to him from your side."

He turns his dark brown eyes up to me. His expression is almost pleading. He nods. I wait him out. Mason speaks so carefully for a small child, intent on selecting all the right words.

"Sean pushed me on the playground. My... my mommy wouldn't like if I got in trouble for fighting. I need to be good. If I am, then maybe heaven will let her come back," he explains, hope blooming in his voice.

It's like someone just punched me through the heart. What do I say to that? I'd give anything to make this better for this sweet child, but I can't help him with his ultimate wish. In my moment of silence, trying to find the right words, he continues instead.

"I tried to be the bigger man, like Uncle Beau taught me. But Sean pushed me again and started calling me names." He shrugs his small shoulders. "So I put the brakes to him like Uncle Kyle would do."

I bite my lip to keep from laughing. This is not the time to let my professionalism slip. Mason indeed put the brakes to Sean Novak. That little kid is a troublemaker and deserved the beatdown Mason gave him.

I've been trying to get Sean's parents up here to the school for months. It's funny how they appeared once their son became the victim. I don't doubt that Mason's uncle being Kyle Tyson had something to do with their sudden interest.

A loud groan sounds, pulling my attention. I lift my eyes to see *the* Kyle Tyson standing in the doorway of my classroom. I hadn't thought about the chance of Kyle coming here, to my little classroom. I thought I'd have Mason back to the front office by the time of his arrival.

I've seen the man in passing a few times. Even at this distance his presence seems all-consuming. That deep, rich brown skin and those dark brown eyes are something to admire. The way his brows and lashes frame the windows to his soul displays something else entirely.

I feel like I'm being invited into a secret. Something dark and mysterious that only a precious few are able to get a glimpse of. I lower my eyes to his lips and have to keep myself from licking my own.

I'm five nine, but I've always been a sucker for taller men. Kyle has to be six five, maybe even six seven. His body reads every bit of the story of an athlete. Even the slight gaps to his stance send my pulse racing.

I shake my head clear. Kyle Tyson is like Jason Momoa—I'll always have fantasies of him, but I'll never have a shot.

Kyle moves into the room, squatting beside his nephew's desk. His cologne is the second thing to engulf me, after his overwhelming presence. I watch silently, as Mason jumps into his uncle's arms.

"I'm sorry. I didn't mean to mess things up," Mason sobs into Kyle's neck.

"You didn't mess anything up. I'm proud of you for trying to be the bigger man. You did what you needed to defend yourself in the end," Kyle says softly.

"She's not going to come back. I was a bad boy," Mason whimpers.

Kyle's dark eyes lift to meet mine, his thick brows knit. I can feel my eyes soften. Clearly he didn't hear the beginning of our conversation. I place a soothing hand on Mason's small back, as he sobs on his uncle.

I'll explain, I mouth, not wanting to repeat the conversation in front of Mason. I think it's something Kyle should have time to digest.

"Hey, buddy, I want to talk to Mr. Connor," Kyle says. "Emma's out in the hallway. Why don't you go and say hi?"

I'm surprised by the feeling of irrational jealousy that hits in the pit of my stomach. I don't know where it comes from. I mean this is Kyle Tyson, NBA player. I'm sure he has plenty of women in his life.

"Okay." Mason sniffles, before taking off.

I shove my feelings back. Straightening in the little chair I suddenly feel ridiculous for sitting in, I turn my attention to Kyle.

Only you can manage to look silly in front of a god like this. Just great, Andy.

Kyle

I've seen Mr. Connor a time or two, and each time I've thought the same thing. This man should not be teaching children. He should be on someone's magazine cover.

He has the most striking blue-gray eyes. His square jaw is the only thing that keeps him from tipping over into pretty. His dark hair contrasts against his lightly tanned skin that yields to those full pink lips.

There's something about the way his long lashes cast a shadow over his cheeks, even with his lids open. His straight nose that's slightly pointed at the tip. He's a work of art.

Pushing that observation to the side, my mind turns to Mason's words. My brows furrow. Mason hasn't smiled as much as he used to in a long time. Still, the image of that long face and his sad eyes peering nervously at me tells me I'm going to be gutted when I get the answers I'm seeking.

"Just give it to me straight," I blow out.

"Mason feels if he's a good boy his mother will come back," Mr. Connor says slowly.

I stagger to the side, bumping into the tiny desk next to my leg. It's like I've just had my soul torn out. I've been trying to do everything I can to ease things for Mason.

"I… I don't know what to do." I voice the secret I've been holding since I lost my sister.

"You're doing the best you can. He's five. In time he will learn to understand she's not coming back. I can suggest a counselor or two, if you like. I think the best thing you can do for him is be there," he says soothingly.

I snort, drawing my hands down my face. "I've started camp for the season already, and preseason starts next month. I've thought about a traveling tutor and homeschooling, but he's so little he needs friends, he needs to socialize. What was my sister thinking?"

I purse my lips, biting back the rest of my words. This man doesn't need to hear my life story. I don't know why I'm telling him all of this.

"It sounds like she was thinking of her son and who would care for him best. You sound just like a good father. Those are all the right things to be concerned about."

Mr. Connor's eyes light up as he looks at me. I tell myself he must be a fan. There's no way that look is the type of admiration it feels like. I've been lonely and confused the last few months.

"What kind of trouble is he in?" I clear my throat and ask.

"Mason doesn't give us any type of trouble. From what he tells me, it's Sean's parents that we need to have a long talk with." His face tightens. "In all honesty, I think you should take Mason and go home. You don't need the stress of dealing with the Novaks. I'll handle things from here."

"Are you sure? Can you make that type of decision?" I ask cautiously. "The principal called me personally."

This is one of the top private primary schools in New York. Michael pulled all kinds of strings for Savanna to get Mason in here. I don't want to do anything that could jeopardize his enrollment.

"It will all fall on me. I got this. Go home," Mr. Connor replies with a warm smile.

Gratitude washes over me. I nod my head, holding my hand out to shake his. When his tanned fingers rest in my palm a spark shoots between us. Our eyes meet and hold. The moment is arresting, leaving me speechless.

"Kyle." Emma's voice breaks the connection.

I turn to find my assistant holding a sleeping Mason in her arms. She silently tells me it's time to go. I have an interview in an hour. I blow out a breath and send her a nod.

"Thanks again, man," I say to Mr. Connor, backing away from him slowly.

I look him over, frowning to myself. His fine ass has a shorty laid up somewhere. There's no way he's down for this D, but he'll do for a few of my fantasies. That's for sure.

CHAPTER THREE

Sweet Recitals

Kyle

I've been making as much of an effort as possible to be there more for Mason. It's been brutal on my schedule, but I make it happen whenever I can. Which is the reason why I'll be taking a red eye to meet my team tonight. I had to be here for this.

"You look so nervous," Emma whispers.

I turn to her and frown. She's stating the obvious. The sparkle in her eyes and the teasing tone in her voice aren't not helping.

I am nervous. Mason is going to sing a solo in front of his entire school. Emma made his little costume, and he asked me to listen to him rehearse every time he got a chance to. I can tell this means a lot to him.

The kid can sing, I know that. Singing has always been a thing in my family. I think we get it from my mother. However, this is different. He's about to sing in front of a bunch of strangers.

"Man, he's a better kid than I was at his age. I would never have done this," I murmur back.

"That's because you're not awesome like he is," she says.

"Whatever."

Emma nudges me with her arm and winks at me. I'll admit, I'm glad she's here. Emma goes above and beyond being an assistant, but I know that's because of our family bond.

"Stop stressing. The kid's got this," Jordan, one of my closest friends, says, drawing my attention.

"Yeah," I huff the simple reply.

Looking down the row at the men I consider my brothers, I'm grateful for my support system. The fact that they've taken time out of their busy schedules for Mason means a lot to us both. I'm sure he'll be excited to see so many of my friends here to cheer him on.

"Daniel, you all right, bro?" I whisper over Jordan to my other friend frowning down at his phone.

He looks up with clouded-over eyes. "Yeah, I'm good."

I can tell he's not from the dazed look on his face, but this isn't the time to pry. Making a mental note to check in on him later, I turn back toward the stage. My knee bounces with nerves.

I spot Mr. Connor in the corner of the stage. He's squatting while talking to someone out of sight. Again, I note how attractive he is. The fact that he's so good with the kids makes him more alluring.

It seems he's been giving Mason extra attention in the past few weeks. My nephew can't stop talking about him. I'm still grateful to him for all he did the day Mason got into that fight.

"Oh, I think they're going to start," Emma says, pointing to the curtains that begin to open.

Sitting up straighter in my seat, I watch as the first group of kids comes out. They all look so nervous. I can only imagine how they feel.

I spend the next hour on the edge of my seat, waiting for Mason to appear. My row roars to life when Mason steps out dressed as a Greek god. I chuckle to myself—him and his mythology. It didn't matter what he chose to sing he was going with that costume.

"He changed songs," I mutter when the music starts and Mason begins to sing.

"Yeah, he wanted to surprise you," Emma says.

I swallow the lump in my throat as Mason's voice carries the lyrics to "Wind Beneath My Wings." He sounds amazing. I'm so proud of him. So many emotions overcome me, tears stinging the backs of my eyes. I swallow the lump in my throat; my chest swells with pride.

"Wow," I hear Jordan breathe.

All of my friends are aware of my ability to belt out a tone, but not many know Mason can as well. My chest puffs out some more. That's my little guy up there.

From my seat, I can see his eyes searching the crowd. Placing my fingers in my mouth, I whistle through the crowd. His little eyes find me and light up. I know he didn't think I would make it.

The look of joy on his face is priceless. I haven't seen him smile like that in so long. Mason's voice grows clearer, and he begins to loosen up. He takes the crowd by storm, earning a standing ovation.

"That was phenomenal," Jordan says, shaking his head.

"Yeah, Savanna would have been proud," I say, clearing my throat of emotions.

The recital ends after Mason steals the show. I'm still in awe of him as we start to file out of our seats. The families are invited to stay for an after-party. I know all of my friends can't stay. I'm not the only one in season. They'll be rushing off to catch flights as well.

"I hate I have to go. Tell the little guy how proud we are of him," Jordan says, patting me on the back.

"Sure thing. Thanks for showing up."

"Always," he replies.

My other friends begin to say their farewells as the crowd shifts around us. I can't wait to get to Mason to give him a big hug. Emma grabs my arm, leading me to the cafeteria where they announced the repast would take place.

Mason locks on me the moment I walk in. He flies across the room into my arms. Lifting him into a hug, I put everything into the embrace.

"You were amazing, buddy," I croon.

"Thanks, Uncle Ky," he chimes. "Did you like the song?"

"Yeah, it was great. You're amazing, little dude."

"That was so awesome," Emma says. "So proud of you, squirt."

"Thank you. Everyone loved my costume," he says to Emma with bright eyes.

"Why wouldn't they? You're killing it."

Mason makes a muscle and wiggles his brows at me. I throw my head back and laugh. He's a trip, but it's good to see him showing so much personality tonight.

"You have to say hi to Mr. Connor."

Looking around for Mason's teacher, I find him midconversation with some of the other families. I decide to wait our turn. Mason's little tummy rumbles, confirming that decision. He looks at me sheepishly, giggling when I tickle his belly.

"We'll get you something for that monster in your stomach first," I tease.

"There's not a monster in my stomach," he says.

His stomach growls again, causing me to lift a brow at him. He tucks his head into my shoulder and his giggles fill my ear. I breathe a little easier seeing his happiness.

"Excuse me."

I turn to find Mr. Connor at my side. Damn, he's just as fine as the last time I saw him, if not more. I don't think I got to appreciate him as much then, with Mason in the middle of a breakdown.

At the moment, I take it all in. From his eyes, his hair, and those lips—it's a package worth admiring. There's something about him I can't put my finger on. I don't realize I'm staring until he clears his throat nervously and continues.

"I just wanted to come over and say I thought Mason was extraordinary," he says.

"It was a great show. All of the kids did amazing," I reply, placing Mason on his feet.

"That's nice of you to say." He lowers his voice and leans in. "But you and I know he was the star of the show."

We both laugh. I like a dude with a sense of humor. Mr. Connor is checking off a lot of boxes. That shyness that exudes from him is a turn-on, all day.

"Hey, Mason. Let's go get something to eat," Emma says.

I know that sound in her voice. I'm here for Mas, not to hit on his teacher. That's not my style anyway.

I watch Mason and Emma walk over to the refreshments table. Again, I note that Mas seems to be having a great day, causing my smile to grow. This will be worth the late flight out.

"He adores you."

I turn back to Mr. Connor to see his eyes glued on me. I'd like to stare into those eyes while finding out what that mouth tastes like. I shake off my lust-filled thoughts and focus on what Mason's teacher is trying to tell me.

The last thing I need is to drool over my little guy's teacher. Besides, I believe the thoughts I had the last time I was here. He has to have a girlfriend at home.

"He's a great kid. I adore him too," I reply. "I wanted to thank you for all you've been doing for him. He talks about you nonstop."

His lids lower, and I think I even see a blush forming. However, before I can see if it forms fully, Mason's squeal draws my attention across the room. I turn to see him running around with some of the other kids. Emma is busy stuffing her face and making new friends.

A hand touches my forearm, causing my head to snap back in Mr. Connor's direction. He pulls the hand back quickly. From his reaction he felt just what I did.

Electricity zapped up my arm, warming my body from the touch. I look down at my arm—the hairs are standing up.

Forcing myself to ignore the humming that's spreading through me, I lift my head and I clear my throat.

"I only wanted to say have a good night. I need to go say something to the other parents," he rushes out.

My eyes run over him. I tell myself I'm tripping. I think to press him and see if he reacts, but I remember myself and where I am. Letting the thought go, I nod.

"Right, thanks again," I reply.

"No problem, anytime," he says and takes off.

Andy

I can't stop looking across the room at Kyle. He is magnetizing. My fingertips are still sizzling from touching him earlier.

I've dared a few times tonight to imagine that he felt what I did. I've also brushed those thoughts away. I've seen Kyle in countless photos with nothing but gorgeous women surrounding him.

The brunette with him tonight being one of them. She's the same woman that accompanied him the day he entered my classroom. Clearly they are an item or something.

"Mr. Connor," a voice says, finally tearing my attention away from Kyle.

"Oh, hello, Mrs. Stevens," I say with a smile.

"You're doing such a lovely job with the children. I think your future here at the academy is a great one. You keep up the good work, dear," the older woman states.

She's on the board of directors and pulls a lot of weight around here. Her sons and grandchildren were all once students here. Her approval is golden and goes a long way.

"I love what I do. Glad things turned out so well," I reply.

She leans into me, beckoning me closer with her hand.

"You're a fine young man. We could use more role models like you. Don't say I told you, but you're in line for the vice principal position. You already have my vote," she says and winks.

My chest expands. This is just what I've been working for. I put my application in for the promotion, but I didn't think I had a serious shot. Some of the older teachers have their hats in the running.

"Wow, thank you for your vote."

"It's time for new blood. I know what's going on with the Tyson boy. That performance was amazing. I don't think he would have done something like that a few months ago," she says with a bright smile. "You're a keeper."

Mrs. Stevens walks off, leaving me smiling from ear to ear. When I look across the room and see a smiling Mason waving as his uncle carries him out, my heart is full. I've come a long way.

CHAPTER FOUR

We Need To Talk

Kyle

"You know you guys are going to eat our dust this year," Ray taunts. "I can't wait to hand you that ass on the court."

"Here you go. Always talking shit." I shake my head and take a pull of my beer.

I look around the backyard of Javier's home as Ray and I stand poolside. Smiling faces can be found everywhere. A few of my friends have gathered around with partners, engaged in animated discussions about this or that. Tons of laughter flows, while music plays in the background.

It feels good to be out with friends. Emma insisted on taking Mason for the weekend so I could come to this barbecue to relax with familiar faces. I'd been reluctant at first. When Michael and I dated, this would have been the type of event we could chill and be ourselves at. Javier has these inclusive parties just for that purpose. Sort of like a monthly gay pride event as Javier calls it.

I wasn't sure if Michael would be invited or if he would show up. Javier assured me that not only would Michael not be here, he wasn't invited in the first place. I should have known I could count on my friends.

"I talk shit because I back it up." Ray shrugs.

"Fair enough, but I'm not going to make it easy on you," I say with a chuckle.

"Never that. I don't expect you to. I live for the challenge you bring. I swear you need to leave that weak-ass team and come play with some winners. You're a free agent next year. You know we'd take over the league on the same team." I see the same spark in his eyes that he gets every time we have this conversation.

"I might have thought about it a year or two ago. I don't know now. I don't want to change anything else in Mason's life," I grumble.

"Man, I'm sorry I missed the recital. Heard he did his thing. How's the little guy holding up?" Ray's demeanor shifts to one of a big uncle.

My nephew has been lucky there. I have a great circle of friends that would give the shirts off their backs for me and my nephew.

"He's hanging in there." I look down at the bottle in my hand. "He misses his mother. I'm doing everything I can to be there for him."

"Is that you, Tyson?" I hear come from behind me in a singsongy voice.

My lips tug up in the corners. Not all of my friends are living a secret life. Darwin is as flamboyant as they come. He lives his life without a care and loves hard if he likes you. He has become sort of a mother hen with me. Just hearing his voice picks up my spirit.

"Damn, who is that with Darwin? He's fine as fuck," Ray murmurs, shifting my attention.

When I look to find the source of his comment, the smile falls off my face. I freeze in horror when I see the man walking beside Darwin. It isn't his gorgeous face that has my heart pounding so hard I feel it in my throat.

I can't lose my nephew. If this man runs and spills that I was here, I could have the fight of my life on my hands. I know Javier trusts everyone that comes to these parties—whether straight or gay—but I can't bank on that trust when my nephew is involved.

My mind races. People see things differently when children are involved. The bullshit I've heard people say. I get pissed just thinking about it.

With a scowl on my face, I hand Ray my beer. Grabbing Mr. Connor's arm, I tug him from the poolside back into the house. He doesn't protest as I step into one of the guest rooms, slamming the door behind me.

His blue-gray eyes are wide, his full lips partially open. I watch the heaving of his chest. It's clear the lack of protest comes from shock.

The blood drains from his face. His lips flap as his eyes bounce across my face. He almost looks lost.

Several emotions race across his features—fear, confusion, and uncertainty. His pretty ass blinks up at me a few times, as I tower over him. Seeming to snap out of it, he tugs his arm out of my hold.

"Listen, I haven't disclosed that I'm gay to the school. I love my job, and I'd never do anything wrong to the children. Being gay doesn't make me a pervert. Whatever you're thinking, please don't put my career at risk because of your bias," Mr. Connor says through tight lips.

My brows draw in, my mind moving a mile a minute. I think back to looks he gave in that classroom and the night of the play. I notice the buzz still running through my hand from dragging him into this room.

I don't think. Rather, I move on instinct. I step into his space, tugging him forward by the back of his neck, and crush my lips to his. I should be ready for the instant sparks that fly, but I'm still stunned by them. I'm even more stunned when he curls his fingers into my T-shirt, pulling me to him.

Andy

All I could see when Kyle turned in my direction was my career ending. Rage radiated from his eyes; his jaw was clinched tight. I was sure he planned to tell the school board that he found me at a barbecue full of gay men. It never once dawned on me that he, too, happened to be at the same barbecue.

My brain short-circuits from the moment he tugs me into his kiss. His mouth is searing me with his heat. His soft but firm lips have melded to mine. I'm putty in his hands. A groan slips free from my throat, when his teeth nip at my bottom lip, coaxing me open to him. The moment his tongue slips into my mouth, a flavorful burst of beer and mint nearly buckles my knees.

His fingers move into my hair, drawing me nearer. I'm too shocked to move my hands even an inch from the lock they have on his T-shirt. Kyle deepens the kiss just as a knock sounds on the door.

"Andy? Kyle? Is everything okay?" Darwin's concerned voice comes through the door.

Reluctantly, I pull away, clearing my throat. I reach to touch my now swollen lips. Kyle looks down at me with such intensity. I can see the rise and fall of his harsh breathing. I look away, feeling my shy side rear its head.

"Yes, Dar, we're fine. Just give us a minute to clear something up," I call out.

"O-k-kay," Darwin drags out in his singsongy way.

I roll my eyes. There's sure to be an interrogation later. When Darwin went on and on about his friend who just broke up with someone not too long ago and wanting to set us up, I had no idea he was talking about Kyle Tyson. It hits me like a ton of bricks now, as all of the pieces fall into place. He brought me here to meet Mason's uncle.

Kyle places his fingers under my chin, turning my face toward him. I lift my eyes to his, searching for what he must be thinking. I'm met with unrestrained passion.

His tongue darts out as if his searching for my taste on his lips. He swallows hard, causing a shiver to run through me. I can only imagine the thoughts behind the hunger in that gesture. The heat coming from his eyes mirrors the desire warring inside of me. I'm still trying to catch my breath and wrap my head around all of this.

"We need to talk," he says.

"Yes, I think we do."

His eyes follow my tongue. It seems like he plans on kissing me again, but he just pulls me in close. I look up at him expectantly.

"This is not a talk we can rush through here," he says as he searches my face.

I nod. "That's for sure," I breathe. I shift nervously. "Do you have time to sit down or something? I know camp has started."

His lips turn up and his eyes light. The smile on his face warms me from within. I'm actually excited about the upcoming season. I'm a fan and I follow his team.

"I'll be free at the end of the week. We can have dinner then. Will that work for you?"

"Yes," I say much too quickly.

I want to groan at my own eagerness. Kyle's smile broadens, showing his teeth. It's a breathtaking smile, one that beckons you closer. It has me under its spell.

"We can get together then to have this talk in detail," he murmurs before dipping his head and capturing my lips.

I mean, he doesn't just kiss; he consumes me. Kyle takes and gives at the same time. It's the hottest thing I've ever experienced in my life. He's completely frying every brain cell I have.

I've officially forgotten my name. If I were asked, I would say Kyle Tyson. At the moment, he is the only thing I know.

CHAPTER FIVE

Non-Kyle

Kyle

The barbecue is in full swing, but I'm glued to the same spot with the only view I want for the rest of the night. The little group standing about three feet away from me is where my focus lies. The pool lights have come on, providing somewhat of a spotlight on the center of my attention. Standing off to the side by myself, I probably look crazy to everyone else.

I'm banking on the fact that most don't know how to approach me after all I've been through. I'm not in the mood to talk about my feelings. Honestly, I've switched into research mode. I want to see how this Andy dude moves.

"So you live in the city?" someone asks Andy in the small group he's standing in.

"Yeah, it's an easy commute to work, and I love my apartment." Andy's reply floats to my ears.

"I used to live in SoHo before I moved out to Jersey," the other guy says.

"I love that new Thai fusion place down in SoHo," Darwin adds.

"I have to try that place out. I love Thai food," I hear Andy reply.

I note that fact for later. I've been earhustling for a half hour at this point. I have no shame; it is what it is. I'm learning details about my nephew's kindergarten teacher. I've always found Mr. Connor attractive, but I'm seeing him more closely now.

"I don't mean to pry, but that's a nice neighborhood on a teacher's salary," someone in the group says.

I frown. That is very personal. The protective part of me wants to tell them to mind their fucking business. The side of me that wants to learn more leans in to listen closely.

Andy gives a small laugh. "I actually work at an upscale private school. I'm doing pretty well. Although, I work there by choice—"

"And that was too much of an explanation," Darwin cuts him off. "Learn some tact, honey, will you?"

I chuckle to myself. You have to love Darwin. He said exactly what I was thinking.

"You guys have some great bars and lounges," the guy from Jersey notes.

"Yeah, I don't go out to those much. Unless my sister drags me." Andy chuckles softly.

I love that quietness. I bite my lip as my mind goes back to that last kiss I took before walking out of that guest room earlier. I wanted to leave him with something to think about. It's going to be a long weekend now that all I have on my mind is our date.

"What has that look on your face?" Beau asks as he walks up with two beers.

"Nothing," I reply, taking the offering he holds out.

Beau's the one person here that knows me enough not to care how standoffish my body language might be. I don't mind. Beau and I understand each other. He's the brother I wished all my life for, right up until the moment I got him, and I wouldn't trade him for another.

"I've seen nothing, and that ain't it. You were coming out of the house with that guy when I arrived. By the way you've been watching him—not that I blame you, might I add—I'd say nothing is a whole lot of something, all right," he says, nodding in Andy's direction.

"Yeah, I know him," I reply nonchalantly.

"From...?" Beau draws out with a questioning gaze. "Better yet, are you sure you're ready?"

I blank-stare back at him. Beau has known me long enough to know I'm not going to open up here around all of these people—if I were going to open up at all. Which is still highly unlikely to happen.

"Fine," he murmurs, before taking a pull of his beer. His twang comes through as he speaks.

"Country ass," I tease.

"Some things ain't never gonna change. What's your point?" he tosses back.

"Don't have one. You stopped asking me questions, though. Didn't you?"

Beau grins around his beer. We both fall into our usual comfortable silence. It's exactly what I need at the moment.

Time with my thoughts and enough quiet to overhear Andy's conversation.

It might seem a little stalkerish, but it's my way of learning the details I need to know. Details give insight, and insight always gives you a hand in the choices you make. Choices are important, and to make the right ones you need every crumb that falls into your lap.

"Mm, you're about to do something non-Kyle. Be careful," Beau says and walks away.

Something non-Kyle. That entire scene back in that room was not me at all. I think it's time I do exactly that. Something non-Kyle it is.

CHAPTER SIX

Nervous

Andy

I drop my brush in the bathroom sink and curse. I've been jumpy all day. I came out of my skin every time someone stepped into my classroom unscheduled.

It seemed like I had more visitors today than ever. Like the Universe was out to expose me. I can't begin to number how many times I thought my secret would explode before me at any moment.

I've been waiting for someone to jump out and say I'm on some type of reality prank show. It's been over a week since the barbecue, and I still can't convince my mind that Kyle asked me out on a date. I'm not sure where this all is going to go. I think that's what has me spinning in circles.

Or it could be that kiss he laid on my lips before leaving me in that guest room to fall into a puddle of goo. I haven't been able to function without thinking about it since. I just want to shout it out to someone. I kissed Kyle Tyson, and I have a date with him tonight. However, there's the mental slap and stern voice that keeps telling me to get a grip.

Startled, I look down as my phone rings. I roll my lips and send it to voicemail. It's my sister, Tara.

"Not now," I mutter.

I'm avoiding her. She knows me best. She sees everything, even the things I choose not to tell her. If she were to hear the nerves in my voice, she'd be relentless. I'm not ready to share what I hope is the beginning of a relationship.

"Get it together," I grumble into the mirror.

Plucking the brush from the sink, I place it aside and roll my shoulders back. I run a shaky hand through my locks. When I pull my hand from my hair, I stare at the tremble in it. I'm always nervous before a date, but not this nervous. I swallow hard, lifting my eyes to look at the mirror again.

The doorbell rings and I jump as a yelp bursts from my lips. "Jeez!"

I blow out a breath and roll my eyes at myself. Smoothing down the front of my shirt, I take one last look at my outfit. A blue button-down, khakis, and a pair of brown loafers are what I settled on. I'm not sure where we're going, so I went with the safest thing I could think of.

I shake off the nerves, turning to leave the bathroom. I take deliberately slow steps to the front door. I don't want to seem anxious, although I'm sure he'll smell the anxiety on me as soon as I open the door. I check my armpits to make sure I haven't sweat right through my shirt.

Phew, you're fine.

I let that thought pass, rolling my neck on my shoulders. Stopping at the single barrier between me and this date, I take one last deep cleansing inhale. Releasing the breath, I reach to unlock and open the door. I tip my head back to look up into those dark eyes. A small smile plays at the corners of Kyle's lips.

He makes everything he wears look picture-perfect. He is groomed to perfection. His barber takes love and care to have him camera ready even on his off days. The way his skin is glowing makes me envy his flawless complexion. Kyle is a work of art. One that has my breath whooshing from my lips.

"I brought dinner," he says, holding up a bag before me. "Do you plan to let me in?"

Disappointment hits me almost as hard as the delicious aromas. I should have known someone like Kyle wouldn't want to parade around with someone like me.

I suck it up and step back out of the way. Kyle enters the apartment slowly, but not without his watchful gaze taking me in. I can feel his eyes on my skin as mine remain aimed at my shoes while I sort through my feelings. Closing the door behind Kyle, I lock it.

His hand reaches beneath my chin, a soft gesture, but the roughness of his fingertips makes my belly flip. He turns my face, lifting it to look up at him. His soulful eyes search mine, pulling all of my secrets to the surface—like some unknown force with the power to possess me. I touch my suddenly dry lips with my tongue, drawing his eyes to them.

"What is it?" he asks.

"Nothing," I reply.

His brows dip low, and a frown takes over his mouth. He's too handsome for the scowl that now covers his face. Kyle is a man who should always have that God-given smile in place.

"I'm not about that life, Andy. I don't lie, and I don't like being lied to. Something is wrong. What is it?"

His words come out gentle but firm. The authority in them sends a shiver down my spine. I wonder if he has any clue as to how his mere words and presence captivate and draw me in.

His thumb caresses my bottom lip. His eyes remain on mine. His soft touch eases me just a bit, enough to loosen my tongue.

"I just thought we had plans to go out on a date. I didn't think we'd be dining in. I mean, staying here," I reply.

Kyle drops his hand, taking a step back. He shifts the bag with the food in his hands, lifting his now free palm to pull it down his face. We lock eyes, and he searches my gaze, nodding his head to some unspoken thought.

"First, you're way too gorgeous of a man to be insecure. I had my doubts, but I'm seeing that I'm right. That's exactly what I'm picking up on. We'll get to that later tonight. I want to know all about you and your past relationships.

"Second, I'm very private about my love life. We can start with that discussion. It's important to me that you can agree to what I'm willing to give," he says.

I open my mouth, but I don't know what to say. He hit the nail on the head. I've had a rough go of it. I haven't always been the man that's standing before him. He might not be here if he knew more about me.

Kyle cracks that big smile. Reaching for my hand, he laces our fingers together. The rest of my anxiety floats away. He gives a gentle tug, prompting me to lead the way. I start for the living room, thinking of the more intimate setting. It sounds like we're going to need to get comfortable for the discussion he has planned.

Kyle sits on the couch in front of the coffee table. I take a seat on the floor across from him. I smile when Kyle starts to unpack Thai food, including plates and utensils. I'd mentioned liking Thai at the barbecue. Kyle had been standing nearby, but he wasn't a part of the conversation. I had no idea he was listening. From the smile on his lips, he knows exactly what I'm thinking.

"When I decide I want something, I pay attention to all the details," he says.

"I see." I smile back.

"That blush is sexy. I'll make sure to make it happen more often," he says, causing me to blush more.

I focus on the food he's placing on the plates. It's all I can do not to turn into the awkward teenager I'd once been. When Kyle pauses in the middle of his actions, I lift my gaze again.

He narrows his eyes and tilts his head. You would think he was trying to figure out how to tug something free from just the right angle. I don't realize I've stopped breathing until he speaks.

"I think I changed my mind. There is a story behind those eyes. I want to know it first. Tell me, Andy. Why so shy?"

I watch my hands smooth over the hardwood of the mahogany coffee table. This isn't a conversation I'm used to getting into on a first date. Yet I want to share with Kyle. It feels right to do so. I'm more than painfully shy when it comes to men.

I purse my lips, as my stomach twists in knots. I've come a long way, but it has taken so much time. I'm still a work in progress.

"I gained a lot of weight in my teens...." I pause and look up at him. "Up until my freshmen year in college I was extremely overweight. I'd spent so much time eating my emotions and secrets. I also had it in my head that if people focused on the obesity, they wouldn't zone in on me being gay."

I pause, thinking about my past. Food was a shield for me. I tried to become invisible and almost killed myself in the process. Back then the doctor said I had the organs of a seventy-year-old.

"Go ahead, continue. I'm listening," Kyle coaxes.

"It took a family intervention from my father and sister to help me through breaking the cycle that was making me sick, literally. My body had started shutting down on me. Everyone started to fear for my life," I explain.

"An intervention. Like a drug intervention?" he asks with furrowed brows.

"Yeah, Tara knew something deeper was going on with me. I wasn't hiding as well as I thought." I snort. "My parents were concerned as well."

"Sounds like you have a loving family," he says.

"Yeah, I do." I take another pause, needing a moment.

Holding up a finger, I gesture for him to hold on. I get up to go into the kitchen for the bottle of wine I have in the refrigerator. I grab a couple of glasses and a bottle of water in case Kyle's not drinking, with it being the season and all.

When I return he's waiting patiently. I like that about him. He's direct but patient.

Holding up the offerings I have, I wait for him to pick one. He reaches for the water, brushing my fingertips as he takes it. A shiver runs through me. I relish in that spark that passes between us. It's a much-needed comfort. Reclaiming my seat, I pour myself a glass.

"I.... Hearing my father tell me he knew my sexual preference all along and he accepted me no matter what—it went a long way. His words meant a lot. Even now, saying this out loud to you reminds me of how much I needed to hear that then.

"I grew up in a proud Irish home. My father had always been the alpha macho male of the household. My older brothers fell right in line with that same persona.

"A part of becoming obese was to stop my brothers from dragging me into their antics. It worked with Mitch, my oldest brother. John, the younger one, not so much. John and Tara, my sister, wanted me around no matter what. They have always coddled me. I know they were the reason I never gave up. They all looked out for me. Mitch is my biggest protector. If I'm happy, he's happy."

"So you have three siblings?" he asks, taking a sip of water.

"Yeah." I nod, followed by a gulp of wine.

I think through my words. Placing my wine back down, I shove some food in my mouth to give me a moment. When I finish chewing I continue.

"With my family's help, I essentially learned not to care what others thought. My sexuality nor my weight define me. I'm a great person. I stopped wanting to harm myself just to hide. Despite all of the things going on inside my head, I never wanted to die. That last scare, I passed out on campus. It was an eye-opener for us all. Eventually, I started living for me.

"I worked hard and got my health back, but a lot of damage was already done mentally. The insecurities were very real for me. I started dating and getting out to meet people to boost my confidence. It worked for the most part, but those insecurities still surface. Especially after being in a few relationships that tapped into those dark places and drilled them further into my brain." I drop my eyes again.

Silence fills the room. My own breathing filling my ears. I'm afraid of what I'll see if I look up into his eyes. All of this is my truth. I know that, but others don't always understand it. I only lift my head when I hear his rich velvety voice offering words to close the gap between us.

"My sister, Savanna, was the only one that listened to me when I said I love basketball. I didn't want to do anything else. I was good at other things, but I loved balling. Because I was so lanky, my uncle said I didn't stand a chance," he says with a hint of bitterness.

Suddenly, he gives a wistful smile. His eyes glisten a little. I find myself leaning in to listen more closely.

"I was going to the ninth grade that next school year. She got me up at five in the morning every day that summer, with a protein shakes and egg yolks. That shit was disgusting." He makes a sour face. "But she pushed me through.

"She would have me do suicides until I felt like I was going to throw up, and I lifted weights until I was sore all over. By the end of the summer, I put on weight and had built up muscle. All that running and those nasty-ass drinks changed the course of my life," he says quietly.

"Sisters are lifesavers," I say softly.

I don't comment on the tears he quickly wipes away. I know the wounds are still fresh from his loss. I admire his strength.

Reaching across the coffee table, I touch his hand. When his eyes meet mine, I smile reassuringly. He turns his hand over and squeezes my fingers. A sense of a bond has begun with our sharing.

I release his hand, and he tucks into his food without a reply. I watch as he gets lost in thought. I can see in the set of his brows he's gone somewhere else.

I start to think back to those darker times. I was unsure of so much. My thoughts so misguided because I kept them to myself.

However, I'm grateful for those days. I learned a lot about myself through them. I took control, and now, I'm a survivor. I've proven that to myself repeatedly.

I reach for my own fork and begin to eat. I moan as the flavors melt in my mouth. I don't know where he went, but he'll have to tell me. This will definitely make it onto my cheat list.

"I don't date publicly," Kyle says, breaking into my thoughts. "I like you. I think we have something between us. But I need to know you understand I'm not that guy. I will never be public about who I'm dating or that I'm gay. It has nothing to do with being ashamed or not wanting to show you off. You're a gorgeous man. I'll be happy to show you affection in settings like this, at Javier's club or one of his exclusive parties. Outside of that, I need you to know that I won't… I can't go there."

I take a moment to process his words. I hear them. I just need another second to absorb them. After a beat or two, I nod my understanding, while rubbing my palms on my lap.

"My family knows. I have a few friends that I've shared with, but I still fear coming out at work. When you work with children, people can be narrow-minded," I reply.

"Yeah, pretty much. I mean, the shit I hear in the locker room. Some days, I stick my earbuds in just to block out the bullshit. Some people will never understand. Then there's my family. Everything that's not to their liking or understanding makes you the devil." Kyle shakes his head.

"I do my best to be a loving person. I'd give the shirt off my back to a stranger. I pray every morning and night." His jaw tightens, as his words get caught in his throat.

"I have questioned God in my life. I've had reason to, but when I look at my nephew. When I think about how much my sister loved me and took care of me. When I think of the things I've been through and lived through. I know He's there. To say I'm a child of the devil because I find comfort in the arms of a man is...

"I'm starting to question the world, not God. I am Kyle Tyson. Someone's son, brother, uncle. I love to play basketball. I love to buy and drive nice cars. I enjoy sitting on the beach in the middle of the night, while listening to the waves. I hate shopping for clothes, but I like to dress nice." He gives a small chuckle. "Savanna used to be my personal shopper.

"I love to see people win. I love music. Those are the things that make me who I am. The things that help others know me. The things that shape my personality. When you share too much about the intimate parts of you, people forget those things. Who I love, it's none of anyone's business because that belongs to me and me alone."

I sit speechless. I've never heard anyone explain their choice to remain private like that. I don't think I could have said it better, but I can totally relate. At the end of the day, I just want to be loved. I don't care what the world has to say because it'll be a treasure that's been given to me, no one else.

"I'll take it," I say when I finally find my words.

Kyle's eyes light up with a smile. For the first time today, I don't feel like I'm coming out of my skin. I'm content. Kyle is just like me in so many ways. I think I've found my perfect match.

Kyle

"Thanks for dinner," Andy says as we reach the front door of his apartment.

"You're welcome. I enjoyed talking to you. It was refreshing," I reply.

He gives me that shy smile. Moving closer to him, I reach to cup his jaw. My thumb takes a pass over his skin. I can feel he shaved before the date.

"What did you find refreshing?"

"I don't like dancing around what I want. You win points with me for being so straight up," I say. "It's something I can get used to."

"I don't want to be played with. It's only fair I treat you the same."

"True. I feel you. Like I said, I respect that. I like it." I nod. "I can tell your words have been genuine. I need that more than you know."

"Sounds like you have a past to share. Maybe next time?"

He says the words so cautiously. As if I'm not going to call him after this. I decide to show him my answer.

Backing him into the door, I tilt his head back and take his lips. He opens up to me and I deepen the kiss, pulling a groan from us both. I can taste the wine and spices from our dinner flavoring his mouth.

Reaching for his hands, I pin them to the door above his head. If a kiss could scorch, we'd both be on fire. What I meant to be a simple show if my interest in him turns into a make-out session. I'm not sure how long I have him pinned to the door as I devour him.

My phone buzzes in my pocket, bringing me back from the edge of sanity. Releasing Andy, I take a small step back. I grin at the dazed look on his face. The dreamy gaze in his blue-grays is adorable.

"Things are about to get crazy for me, but I'd like to see you again," I say.

"I'd like that," he pants.

"Cool, we'll talk soon." I peck his lips one last time before I walk out the door.

Kyle

I have a little time before we board the bus for the arena. I pull out my phone with thoughts of Andy circling my head. Bringing up his number, I long to hear his voice. In fact, I haven't stopped thinking about him since I left home for this week's schedule.

"Tyson, you coming down?"

"Nah, I'm going to check in at home and get my head right," I reply to Rick Knight, one of my teammates.

"Okay, cool. See you on the bus," he says, heading out of the room.

I nod, waiting until he's out the door before turning my attention back to my phone. I hesitate for only a moment before I start a text to Andy. I read it three times before sending it, as if it isn't a simple text.

Me: *Hey. How are you?*

Andy: *I'm great. Was just thinking of you.*

His reply comes back quickly. I look at the clock, noting where I am and the time difference back home. I smile when I think of Andy sitting with a stack of papers, grading spelling tests, looking over finger paintings or something—whatever kindergarten teachers do.

Me: *What are you up to?*

Andy: *Just got in from dinner with my sister. Waiting for the guy I'm seeing to come on TV.*

My smile broadens. So much for my assumption. Andy stays surprising me in good ways. This light banter is just what I need. Something to relax me before I get into the zone.

Me: *Oh yeah? What's he doing on TV? You sure we should be texting? I don't want to cause no problems.*

Andy: *You'll be kicking ass on the court. I miss you that's the only problem you've caused.*

Damn, this guy has me in my feelings. I'm smiling so hard my face hurts. I wish I could actually talk on the phone. I just don't want to chance getting too comfortable and Rick doubling back to listen at my door. He's one of the nosier players on the team. No one likes to talk in front of him.

Me: *Yeah. I miss you too. It seems like it's been forever.*

Andy: *I thought it was just me. Didn't want to sound whiny. Damn, I miss you.*

I laugh out loud, shaking my head. Looking at the clock again, I see I don't have time to talk too much longer. I'm going to have to cut this short. I wish I had longer. It's been a while since I've been in a relationship with someone as easygoing as Andy. Michael and I had a clash of wills often.

Me: *LOL. Listen, I have to get ready to go. Just wanted you to know I've been thinking of you.*

Andy: *Give them hell. Watch that temper.*

I laugh aloud again. I'm known around the league for my temper on the court. I push my team, and I'm not afraid to get in their faces about it. I've also been known to challenge players from other teams. Those moments can get heated. Although, it takes a lot to bring that out of me off the court.

Me: *Got it, baby. I'll think of you when I'm about to lose it. That should keep me calm. Have a good night.*

Andy: *Good night.*

I stare at his reply a few beats, before swiping the text closed. Putting my phone away, I get up off my bed and grab my earbuds and duffel bag. I head out for my game, feeling on top of the world.

Andy

I'm falling so hard.

I bite my lip as I stare at my phone, rereading my text exchange with Kyle. Today has been a great day. After making it through dinner with my sister without her prying into my love life, I'd say this day has been a win. Getting a text from Kyle was unexpected but more than welcome.

Prying my phone from my own hand, I get into my nightly workout. It seems to go quickly as my mind keeps circling our little exchange. Thirty minutes later, I'm hot and sweaty, but not for the reasons I wish.

I undress to take a long shower before the game. It's getting late, but I had planned to stay up to watch. Thoughts of Kyle fill my head as the warm water cascades over me. My mind drifts to our last kiss. I have to shift the water to cold just thinking of it.

I step out of the shower and towel off before throwing on sweats and a long-sleeved sleep shirt. I pad to the kitchen to pop some popcorn. Looking at the clock, I see I still have about forty-five minutes before tipoff.

My phone rings as soon as I get the popcorn in the microwave. I run for it, stubbing my toe on the kitchen island. I curse under my breath. I don't know why my heart is racing or why I think it might be Kyle in the first place.

I know he's getting ready for the game. Which is exactly why I shouldn't be so disappointed when Tara's name comes up on the screen. Hopping on one foot as the pain really bites in, I answer.

"Hey, Tar. What's up?"

"Hey, everything okay?"

"Yeah, just banged my toe trying to get to the phone," I huff.

"Sorry," she says.

"Wasn't your fault. Everything all right?"

"I was just thinking. We were so into planning Mom and Dad's party, I forgot to ask you how things went with the guy Darwin wanted you to meet," Tara says.

I roll my eyes. I don't know why I thought I was going to make it through the day without her prying. I begin to hobble back to the kitchen as I decide how much I want to share.

"It went well," I reply, failing terribly at hiding the smile in my voice.

"*Oh,*" she drags out. "Sounds like this is a good one. Tell me more. How does he look? How old is he? Why the heck is

Darwin being so secretive about this one? I can't get that blabbermouth to spill anything."

"He's twenty-five—"

"Oh, so he's younger than you. That's a bit new," she says.

"Yeah, but I find him very mature for his age. He has an old soul, but I think his life can be attributed to that," I muse aloud.

"Oh, really?" she says, her interest seeping into her words.

"I love you, Tar, but we're not getting into specifics. I like him. I want to see where this goes. I think sometimes I share too much too soon," I reply.

There's a brief pause on the other end of the line. I pull my popcorn from the microwave as I wait my sister out. I know she's not going to let this go easily. I truly value her words of wisdom. I can feel them coming on along with more of her prying.

"You take all the time you need. I sort of didn't ask at dinner on purpose. You seemed so happy. I thought I could get more out of Darwin, but that was a total bust.

"Anyway, you deserve to be happy. I hope this guy is as deserving of someone like you. Just remember to be you, Andy. None of that breaking yourself down to please everyone else. Okay?"

Her last words come out gently. My brows jump to my forehead as she throws the towel in so quickly. I expected to have to fend her off a lot harder.

Still, I hear her. I compensate for what I'm not given, and I always come out with the short end. Yet when I'm with Kyle I don't feel the need to do so. He gets the shyer side of me. I think he actually likes it.

I've watched him see through to core of who I am. I like that he can see me in a way no one else can. At twenty-nine, I've dated older men that haven't had the type of perception Kyle has when it comes to me.

"Yeah. I've come a long way. I think I'm ready this time, and I think I have the right one to try with," I say before clamping my lips shut.

"Good. You're beautiful, Andy. Inside and out. Anyone that can't see that isn't worth it," Tara says with so much love in her voice I start to get choked up. Then she takes me home, her accent turning on. "Aye."

"Aye, I hear you."

If anyone knows how deep my damage runs, it's my sister. She's been there when I was ready to give up, when I thought happiness was in on a cruel joke to elude me. The one time I tried to handle it all myself, Tara was the first person I called when I realized I wouldn't make it on my own.

Silence fills the line. I know we're both taking our time to collect our emotions. Feeling a bit overwhelmed, I think it best to end the call.

"I love you, Tar. Call you tomorrow?"

"Aye, love. You know how much I love you, And. You can call me tomorrow or whenever you need," she replies before hanging up.

Thankfully, Tara knows to stop prying. It's been a good day. I don't want to dwell on the things I can't change. The last thing I want to do is think about the things that most likely will send Kyle running for the hills.

CHAPTER EIGHT

Thinking of You

Andy

"Mr. Connor, Mr. Connor." That's all I heard as the day came to a close.

Bridget ran around the classroom, making buzzing sounds with her lips. Jeff was in the corner rocking and crying over his brother's baseball card that Jeff traded at lunch. A group of the other kids were dancing and singing cleanup time, but they weren't cleaning a thing.

"Is it time to go home yet?" a voice whined.

"Eww! Mr. Connor, someone didn't flush," Mason called from the classroom bathroom.

Just one of those days. Staying up late to watch Kyle's game didn't help one bit. I don't regret it. Kyle put on quite the show last night. His team won by thirty points. I just wish I'd gotten at least an hour or two more of sleep.

I swear the kids were feeding off my drained energy. By the end of the day, we were all climbing the walls needing to get out. Today I had one of those moments when I wished I would've gone into antiquing like I'd dreamed of in high school.

I push into the lobby of my building spent and ready to fall facedown into my bed. A nice glass of wine before passing out wouldn't hurt either. I have a nice red I've been wanting to get into.

"Oh! Mr. Connor, sorry I almost missed you," the doorman calls at my back.

I turn to find Jimmy rushing toward me with a large bouquet of roses in his arms. It's a gorgeous arrangement of reds and whites in a tall glass vase, wrapped with a black satin sash. Jimmy seems to be struggling a little under the weight.

"Hey, Jimmy. Need some help?"

"No, no, I was going to bring these up to your place for you. I know you get in around this time. Got sidetracked by Mrs. Feltman in 5G. She's hearing things in the closet again," he whispers, rolling his eyes up to the sky with a shake of his head.

My brows pitch in confusion. Why would he be bringing these flowers to my place?

"These arrived for you about an hour ago. Maybe one of those moms at the school wanted to send you a special thank-you," he says and winks.

I chuckle, reaching for the bouquet. Jimmy is in his midfifties. There's no need for him to lug this upstairs for me. Just as I thought, it's heavy.

"I'll get the elevator for you and ride up. I can help you to your door before I go check on Mrs. Feltman," Jimmy says, rushing around me for the elevator.

I nod. I'll need the help juggling my briefcase and this massive bouquet. Today would be the day I decided to use the vintage case my sister give me, instead of my messenger bag. I should have taken my keys out.

My mind whirls. These can't be from who I think they are. I refuse to make that assumption. Yet I don't have anyone else that could be sending me roses. I mean, why would *he*?

Jimmy and I exit the elevator on my floor and head for my apartment. The vase gets heavier with each step. Not because of its size but because of the questions swirling in my brain.

"I can hold that while you fish out your keys," Jimmy offers.

I grunt, handing the vase over. Shifting my briefcase in my hands, I dig my house keys out of my pants pocket. I get the door open, and Jimmy starts inside with the vase. Although I appreciate his helpfulness, he's clearly being nosey. He wants to know who the flowers are from. I can see it in his eyes when he places the vase down on the table in my entryway.

"Thanks, Jimmy," I say, holding the door open for him to leave out. "How did your wife like those tickets last week?"

"Oh, she wanted me to thank you again. I can't stand that theater stuff, but she was over the moon. Nearly peed her pants when we got to go backstage to meet the actors. Thanks again," he replies, starting for the door as he catches the hint.

"You're welcome. Maybe I can get you some tickets for a game next time. Something more your speed." I smile.

"Oh, you don't have to do that," he says, but his eyes light up. "Excited for the season this year. Hoping the boys bring us a chip."

"They're looking good. We just might have a shot," I reply.

"Tyson was looking good last night. If he keeps that up and the boys get behind him with some good defense, we should be A-OK." Jimmy nods.

"Yeah, he sure was looking great last night." I chuckle. "Have a good one, Jimmy."

"You too, Mr. Connor. Enjoy the flowers," he says, giving one more glance in their direction.

I close the door, drawing in a deep breath before I turn for the roses. I move toward them as if they're poisonous. I tug the card free and flip it over. The small envelope is sealed shut.

"Ah, you couldn't be nosey," I mumble to myself, while laughing at Jimmy.

Prying the envelope open and pulling the card out, I read the message with shaky hands. The roses are from the one person I didn't want to assume they were from. A smile takes over my face, as I read the message again. Brushing the initials at the bottom with my thumb, I bite my lip, reading it a third time.

Last night's win was because of you. Thank you for being on my mind. Can't wait to see you soon.
Thinking of you,
K.T.

I run my hand through my hair. Kyle is definitely showing himself to be in a league of his own. This is a first for me. I've never gotten flowers from someone I was involved with. I feel my cheeks blush.

Reaching for my cell in my pocket, I forget all about being tired. I think about calling, but I'm not sure if he can answer, so

I send a text instead. My face hurts from grinning as I send off the text.

Me: *Thank you for the flowers. This was very sweet of you.*

I wait a few minutes for a reply. My shoulders sag a little when one doesn't come. I know he's a busy man or he could be resting. I suck up my selfish thoughts and start for the kitchen to make dinner.

I have salmon searing in a pan and a salad in the works when my phone pings. I put down the wine I've been sipping to snatch up my device. My smile returns when I see Kyle's reply.

Kyle: *Not as sweet as you taste.*

I nearly choke. The butterflies in my belly take full flight. I feel his words like a caress. It's almost as if I can hear them in my ear. I decide to go for it and play along.

Me: *Is that a taste you remember?*

Kyle: *Now that you mention it, I wouldn't mind a reminder.*

Me: *Anytime. I'm just waiting on you.*

I suck on my lip as I stare at my sent reply, palming my forehead when I see him replying back. I stop breathing waiting for his response. It seems to be taking longer for him to type. I seriously have to wonder who's younger here.

Kyle: *I'll be back home for a hot second. Need to spend time with Mas but hoping I can get in some time with you.*

Me: *I'd like that.*

Kyle: *No promises. I'll do what I can.*

Me: *No worries. I know you will.*

Kyle: *Going into a meeting. TTYL*

Me: *Okay. Later.*

I go back to making dinner with a smile on my face. How quickly a day can turn around. I think I'll head to the gym after this so I'm not staring at my phone waiting around for later.

CHAPTER NINE

Deserve Better

Kyle

"It's good to see you looking so happy," Beau says from across the booth.

Beau has always been straight with me about everything. The fact that he's here says a lot about him. He could have easily involved our lawyers and let them do the legwork on all of this, but that's not his style. He wants to look you in the face as a man and know you're on the same page with him. We're alike in that respect.

"What's not to be happy about? We're about to close a multi-million-dollar deal and I get some time with my best friend. Life is great," I croon.

"You know that's not what I'm talking about. But since you brought it up, everything looks good. We get all five lots and the construction company we wanted to go with came in with the lowest bid. We sign and it's a done deal," Beau says, while taking the contracts out of his backpack and sliding it across the table.

"You're sure you're good with overseeing all of this? I know it's a lot to undertake. I'll carry my load during the off-season." I look him in the eyes to gauge where he is on this.

Beau has been through a lot. I think this project will be great for him, but I want to make sure he's ready for such a big undertaking. We're building an entire complex after all—apartments and training facilities. The properties span five blocks. We've also discussed adding a school. I've thought a lot about what families would need since Mason has been in my life permanently.

"I'm more than good. We'll have this thing done right. It will bring some life into that community and show what we're capable of. They'll be coming to us to do the next one," Beau says with a bit of that old spark back in his eyes.

"All right, I looked over the contracts and things you faxed over. It all looks good," I say and go to sign the papers before me.

Beau's hand shoots out to cover mine, halting my action. I look up into his gray eyes. His face couldn't be more serious.

"Although I appreciate the trust and respect you have for me, you know better. We have time. Read it again. Then sign this copy. We've been around too many snakes for you to be signing anything you haven't read in person," Beau says sternly.

I nod. He's right. Beau learned that the hard way with so-called friends we couldn't trust. His old promoter screwed him in every direction he could, turning his life upside down.

I put my pen down and start to read through the pages as Beau sits quietly sipping his beer. Everything is in order just as I thought, but I still comb each page, noting the changes I had my lawyer add in and a few Beau suggested in our last meeting.

"Looks good," I say and sign when I get to the end.

"Now, about that smile you walked in here with. What's new? Who's the lucky soul?" Beau quizzes.

"Remember Javier's last barbecue?" I say.

"The brunette with the blue-gray eyes? The one you couldn't keep your eyes off. *Nothing*, as I remember you saying." Beau nods.

"Yeah, that one."

"Total opposite of you know who. Seemed cool, though. Darwin's friend, right?"

"Yeah, Darwin called himself hooking me." I chuckle.

"Looks like it worked. This one good with the rules? That other one was an asshole and not worth the time you invested. You knew from the beginning your preferences weren't going to be respected." He twists his lips in annoyance.

I had reservations with Michael from go. Beau warned me to take heed to them. For one, Michael initially tried playing a beta role. It was only after we were in the relationship that his more dominant side came out. That switch-up was a big problem for me. Yet, as always, I allowed him to smooth talk his way out of a breakup.

I was like a moth to a flame. I fell for all the tricks and sweet talk. Things I regret in hindsight.

"Don't remind me. You live, you learn. Andy and I have an understanding. I made things clear from jump," I reply.

"Good. You deserve better. Fairchild was a predator, and I've never known a snake that backs away without biting someone first. You mark my words that one's coming back for another round," Beau grumbles.

"But I'm not entertaining that bullshit this time. I'm done. I don't have it in me to deal with the self-indulgent crap and the games. Nothing about that relationship was healthy for me. Everything, including helping to take care of Mason, had a motive. Always some agenda to trap me into feeling indentured to the relationship," I say bitterly.

"Finally!" Beau throws his hands up. "Five years and you're finally seeing the truth. You deserved better than that."

"At the time I thought it was what I needed," I say and frown.

Beau lowers his voice, leaning into the table, that country accent coming further to the surface. His eyes locked on mine.

"You're a grown man. You have made every decision in your adult life. Good or bad. You be proud of that. Your choices have shaped the man you are.

"That asshole knows how to sway your decisions when it comes to him. The time for needing a daddy has come and gone. Heck, Darwin steps into that role for many of us. You don't need that in a relationship. Michael took advantage of that need while you were younger. This Andy needs to be the complete opposite of that. You deserve someone to love you, not manipulate you through your needs. You feel me?"

"I got you. Honestly, I think this will be different. It's new, but we'll see," I say.

"You deserve better. I'll keep reminding you that," he says, then flags the waitress.

I know my friend and I know he will. Still, I've already been telling myself the same. Life is too short and unexpected to settle for unhappiness.

CHAPTER TEN

Homesick

Kyle

I'm lying facedown in bed, with one hand hanging over the side. My mind and body are exhausted. All the more reason for the frown on my face when my phone pulls me from my sleep. Too tired to lift my arm to answer, I ignore it at first. However, it rings again, letting me know I'm not getting back to sleep without addressing whoever's on the other end.

Reaching out, I search for the annoying device on the nightstand beside my head. When it's in my hand I answer, not bothering to fully open my eyes.

"Hello," I rasp, tiredly.

"Hey there, you sound like you haven't started moving this morning." Michael's voice comes through the line.

My head whips back, a sour expression crossing my face. In true Michael fashion, he's acting as if nothing ever happened between us. This is his thing. Wait around for me to start feeling lonely, knowing how closed off I am to dating and that I just don't have the time for it to begin with.

Usually if we break up, I don't get back into dating right away. He relies on this, giving me enough time to miss having someone in my life so he can have his way when he reappears.

Nah, not today. I'm not in the mood. With my jaw set tight, I open my eyes and hit the end button. It's time I close the door on Michael. Enough is enough. I'm not falling back into his web.

"Fuck you," I mutter, tossing the phone back onto the nightstand.

I take my ass back to sleep, hoping to get a few more minutes at least before my alarm goes off for practice. I punch the pillow under my head, when the alarm comes to life not that much later. I groan, knowing that single interruption is going last all day.

I wish I could say that call was the end of my shitty morning. It was just the beginning, and the day has spiraled out, leaving me in a funky mood.

Two of our starters got injured during practice. It wasn't even a full practice. We had a game tonight. The season hasn't started, and we're down some of our best players. It only places more of a demand on me. A demand and attention I try to avoid at all costs.

We were looking good up until this morning. We bombed tonight's game. My team's morale has dropped way down. They've thrown in the towel. I couldn't be more pissed.

I decided to go out with the team to see if I could help spark our chemistry. Sometimes all the guys need is a little time together off the court to gel again. However, tonight it just doesn't seem to be working.

It could be because these fools chose a strip club to party at. Half of the married guys looked lost, guilty, or scared out of their minds. The other half are in the middle of something they'll regret at some point, if not by sunrise. Then you have the single guys partaking and encouraging it all.

Me, I've been off to the side feigning interest, while stewing in the fact that this team is falling apart before my eyes. The foolishness some of these guys are getting themselves into tonight is bound to show up sometime in the middle of the season or, God forbid, during finals.

"Listen, sweetheart, can you give a minute to answer this call?" I say to the stripper dancing in my lap.

Shorty is nice. We've been chilling in the cut while I keep the money flowing. Having her here has kept attention off me as well as serving to keep her coworkers at bay.

I've learned she's the mother of two, trying to pay her way through school. She has a little girl Mason's age. Her soft-spoken voice has had a soothing effect during our conversation in the last few hours.

She looks over her shoulder and nods, getting up from my lap. I pull out my phone that hasn't rung since before I walked into this place, when Mason called me to say good night. I stare at it in my palm. I miss my nephew's little face. He was excited about a field trip at school tomorrow.

I wish I could be there to go with him. One more reason for the lie I just told. I just can't sit in here anymore. My nephew is without me, and this is what I'm sitting in the middle of?

My life has been so crazy the last few weeks. Andy comes to mind. I never did get to see him when I made it back home. Between meetings and spending time with Mason, there just wasn't a right time.

I pull up the number to the person I really want to talk to. I just need to hear his voice for a little while. I start for the door of the club.

"Hey, Tyson, where you headed?" one of my teammates calls from under a pair of breasts in his face.

"Need to check in at home," I reply.

"All this pussy and you worried about home? Come on, man," someone else slurs.

"Grown man business. You handle yours. I'll handle mine," I reply, not even looking to see who made that dumb-ass comment.

I've reached my limit and the team's tension hasn't eased since we arrived. If you ask me, it's brewing to a boil. Too many selfish members involved. We're not a family at the moment.

I push my way out of the club heading for the parking lot. I rented a car for the night, knowing there was a bigger chance than not that I was going to leave this place way before any of the other guys decide to.

I never drink when I go out with the team. I always order a vodka, no ice for my first drink along with a glass of ice and water. I never touch the vodka. By the time the guys are good and wasted, they never know the difference.

I sink into the driver's seat and press call. Staring out the car window to the street before me, I wonder how I got here to this point in my life. I fist my hand over my heart and rub.

I've never been this homesick before. Sure, the preseason and season schedule can be hard. City after city, sometimes not a day in between games. Still, this ache is fierce.

"Hello."

When a groggy-sounding Andy picks up the line, I groan. I totally forgot about the time. I feel like such a dick. He has to work in the morning. He'll be taking his class on that field trip Mason's so excited about. Again, I wish I were home to join them. I blow out a breath and make a sour face he can't see.

"I'm sorry. I wasn't looking at the time. I'll call later," I say.

"Hang up and I'm not talking to you for a month," he says on a yawn.

I smile. It's been a few days since we've been able to text or talk. Our schedules have clashed nonstop. It's good to hear his voice, even if it is tired.

"You sound off. What's going on?" he says, the sound of him shifting muffling his words a bit.

"I'm so tired of this life," I say more to myself. I'm also thrown when the words slip free. With Andy I always feel safe to express my thoughts and feelings. "If it's not one thing it's another. I worked so hard to get my head right in time for this season. Savanna would want that. Now, it's like my team is just giving up."

"I'm sure your guys are just taking those injuries hard. That had to be a huge hit this morning. I'm sure it will work out," he tries to reassure me.

"Those injuries were bullshit. Mack was horsing around, shit talking, and not watching where the fuck he was going. We're all too old for this shit. Do you want to know where I am right now?"

"Where are you?" Andy asks, sounding more awake.

"I'm outside a strip club. I just spent two hours with a dancer in my lap. My plan was to bond with my team, but all that ended up happening was an out-of-body experience. I could see us all in the room taking this life for granted. I can't tell you how many of the guys are just happy to be playing and getting a check. The win means nothing to them," I huff, shaking my head as if he can see me.

"Wow, um...."

"I mean, none of this shit matters to me. The parties, being a celebrity. I play to win. I'm not about being mediocre. Why should I be when I can strive to be great? For me, being great isn't just about me. It's a team sport. I do what I need to protect my team and help make them better—them not so much," I continue to vent.

"I see it in the way you play. You're one of the best players on your team, but you don't hog the spotlight or the ball. I've always admired that about your game," Andy replies. "I think it's a great way to be a leader."

"It's how I know to make the right moves on the court. Everyone is an option. If we all become strong together we never have to put it all on one person's shoulders. No one has to take the burden for the team. Our decisions on and off the court affect that. I don't bring my life on the court. You know how Baker got hurt?"

"They said he broke his wrist during practice," Andy replies.

"Yeah, after our teammate tripped him for fucking his wife. Some of those guys are older than me and this is the type of shit they pull. I'll never lead this team to the playoffs, fuck a championship. They're all too selfish. Looking for someone to rise as a star instead of us rising together as a team. Looking for someone to point the finger at. It's bullshit. I'm not getting any younger. I just wish they'd stop and think about their actions sometimes," I huff.

"The worse part of your job is that you rely on a team. The best part is that team has to come together at some point. You're a great leader. Your ability to look at the situation from the outside in makes you a great leader. This is just the preseason, plenty of time for things to shake up," he says.

I sit silently. Do I want the leadership role? I don't know. On one hand, it would allow me to take the team forward. On the other hand, I've been leading all along from arms-length. I let others take the shine while I play the game and do what's necessary. I fix the problems, pick up the slack.

Yet I question it all. Stepping up calls for new demands, new attention. I have Mason to think of. I think twice about all of my decisions now.

"Yeah, I feel what you're saying. It's just sometimes I wonder if chasing a trophy is worth the time I'm giving up with my nephew," I admit.

"You're not just chasing a trophy. You're securing your nephew's future. You should hear the way Mason talks about you. You hang the stars and the moon to him. He works harder in class just to please you and be like you," Andy says, with a hint of a smile in his voice.

"I love that kid."

"I know. He loves you too. I'll say it again. You're doing a great job. Your sister was lucky to have someone like you to take care of Mason. You're making this easier for him. You may not see it, but you are," he murmurs.

I stare out of the window, my brows dipping. I don't know how I could be doing a good job when I'm never there. Mas sees my face more often through a phone screen than in real life.

"I hope so," I scoff, not totally believing I am.

"Trust me."

I smile. Trusting him is happening faster than I thought it would. That's big for me, but I keep that information to myself.

Pulling a hand down my face, I mull over his words some more. I'm lost in my musings, falling silent. After a few beats his voice brings me back to him.

"So, a stripper was in your lap for two hours. I'm so jealous of her," he purrs into the phone.

I laugh. It's a welcome change of topic. I push thoughts of my team and my worries with my nephew to the side, for now.

"She had nothing on you. I'd rather have your scent all over me," I croon back.

"I can't dance to save my ass." He chuckles.

"Don't worry. I'll help you with all the rhythm you need," I reply, licking my lips. "I have a question for you, Andy. How far can I push you? I aim to please. Are you open to all I can give?"

Andy

Air whooshes past my lips. I learned from Kyle's kisses that he can be demanding and passionate. I have no doubt that he knows how to set the sheets on fire. I'm just a bit out of my depths trying to have this phone conversation that I've steered left.

I'm in no way ready to dive into a physical relationship. I like Kyle. I'm hoping we can build more of a connection before I have to unveil my biggest secrets. Intimacy is a sore spot for me. I run a hand through the front of my hair, trying not to let my insecurities show in my voice.

"I don't know. I think we'll have to see what you're giving before I decide how far I can open up," I say as confidently as I can muster.

He chuckles on the other end. It's a husky sound that makes my stomach flip. I'm fully awake now, with images of Kyle's sweat-soaked body in my head. I watched the game earlier and couldn't keep my eyes off of the play of his muscles beneath that smooth skin. Although his face remained frustrated most of the game, something sexy emitted from the intensity in his features.

"Baby, I have a whole lot to give. When you're ready for me, I'll show you just what pleasure truly is. I leave nothing untouched," he says back.

I clear my throat and shift in my bed. I'm grateful for the headboard at my back. I might have toppled over if I couldn't sag into it. My eyes fall to the tented sheet. I start to feel brave. After all, he's on the other side of the phone and country.

"We shall see," I quip.

"Yeah, you're playing with fire, Andy. I promise, I'mma bend that ass over and teach you how to sing my name," his voice rumbles back. "On that note, you get some sleep. I'll see you this weekend, good night."

"Good night." I clear my throat again. "Kyle?"

"Yeah?"

"Stop taking on the world. It's going to get better," I say.

"I hope you're right. I'm counting on it," he replies.

The line goes dead, and I pull the phone from my ear. Closing my eyes, I take a breath. I swallow hard. It's settling in that this relationship is a reality. The time to be awestruck has passed.

What will I do once my truth is out?

Old hurt and the feeling of depression try to roar at me. I won't let them. I'll keep the lid sealed on them as tightly as I can. I start to chant repeatedly in my head.

You're a great person, Andy. Someone will love you for you. If it's not Kyle, it will be someone.

CHAPTER ELEVEN

Making Time

Kyle

"Look, Uncle Kyle! I'm running," Mason squeals as he does a slow jog on the treadmill with Andy's assistance. He turns his face up with a beaming smile at Andy. "I can go faster, Mr. Andy."

"I think we're good right here. Slow and steady wins the race, pal," Andy says to him.

I smile at them both. I asked Andy to come over and workout with us today. It's the only time I could fit in to spend time before I'm off again. Mason was excited to have his "favorite teacher" arrive.

"Well, well, well, looks like a party in here. I'm feeling left out. How come I wasn't invited?" Emma says as she enters my home gym, feigning a pout at the end.

I put down the weights I've been curling, going over to give her a sweaty hug. She frowns, holding a hand against my chest to prevent it. My reach is longer than hers, so I win out, tugging her in.

"Ew," she squawks.

I look up to find Andy watching us. He has a smile on his face, but it's tight. I can see a hint of unnecessary jealousy. It dawns on me that I've never officially introduced the two. I drag Emma over to the treadmill with me as she tries to wiggle free.

"Emma, I want you to meet Andy. Andy, this is my pain-in-the-butt assistant, Emma."

Andy's face softens. He stops the treadmill and reaches out his hand for Emma's. Mason jumps down and wraps his arms around Emma's leg.

"Hey, Aunt Emma," Mason sings.

"Hey, handsome. You're looking good. Let me see those muscles," she replies, reaching down to squeeze the little arm he curls up for her.

"Did you see me running?"

"I sure did." Emma nods. She turns her attention back to Andy. "It's nice to meet you. I wish I could say I've heard a lot about you, but this one is so tight-lipped about his special friendships. My hands hurt from trying to pull teeth."

"Don't see how knowing any of that helps you do your job," I reply.

"Whatever." She rolls her eyes.

"I'm sure there's not much to tell about me." Andy blushes.

"Ha! You're here around the little guy. That's says a lot," she says. "Speaking of which, should we get lost and go play some video games?"

"Yeah!" Mason woots.

"I promised to kick your butt. You sure you're ready?" she teases.

"I got this. You're going to owe me ice cream." Mason giggles and takes off running.

"God, that kid owns my heart," Emma says before she follows after Mason.

I watch them leave before I turn to face Andy. His cheeks are red again. Those blue-gray eyes search my face. I reach for the front of his zip-up—it's a bit warm in here for it—tugging him toward me. Ducking, I place my forehead to his.

"You have no idea how much I've missed you," I croon.

"I think I have a bit of an idea. I'm glad I get to see you this time," he says back.

"Em is going to wear him out. He usually takes a nap after playing video games with her for a few hours. Tell me what you want to do. We can get in the jacuzzi or sit in the sauna," I offer.

When I pull back, a nervous look crosses his face. I'm taken aback by it. I thought some time doing either would allow us to relax and talk.

"What if I cook us a little lunch and we take some time to relax?"

"That sounds good too. I'm not sure what's here, though," I admit.

"No worries. I'll pull something together."

I dip in for what I mean to be a quick kiss. That fails. It's been so long since I've felt that undeniable spark between us. It draws me in, begging me to take more. I devour his mouth, searching every corner with my tongue. When his arms snake around my neck, I wrap mine around his back, dragging him into my body. My arousal makes itself known without question.

I can feel the smile that takes over his lips, bringing one to my own. My hands slide down his back to his tight ass. I won't lie. I had been checking him out on the treadmill. His ass and legs are sculpted nicely beneath his jogging pants. I knead his cheeks over the soft fabric as I deepen the kiss.

It takes everything in me, but I break the lip-lock. We don't have the time I need to finish this, and it's too soon for that anyway. We have an insane connection beyond the physical. I want to explore that.

"Wow, you know how to make me forget everything." Andy's words come out as if he's confused.

I laugh and kiss the tip if his nose. I nearly forgot myself as well. Needing to find my thoughts, I shake my head clear.

"Wanted to get missing you out of my system," I respond. "You sure you're not hot in this?"

I pull at the front of his zip-up. Andy steps back out of my reach. Wrapping his arms around his middle. I hone in on his stance, causing him to drop his arms.

"No, I'm fine. I haven't really worked up much of a sweat," he says.

"All right, come on. Let's get that food. I'm starving now," I say.

Andy

This has been one of the best days I've had in a long time. After Kyle and I turned the heat way down, we had a fun lunch and talked about everything under the sun. Kyle has a brilliant mind. He has a way of putting things that makes you think.

For a twenty-five-year-old, it's impressive. I'm still learning some of the things he seems to have a clear grasp on. While I admire the trait, something tells me his upbringing has a lot to do with it. "Adapt or die," he once said.

I wish we had more time together. He and Emma had a party they needed to attend for a charity. Knowing he was taking her along would have made me jealous before today. However, after getting to know her, I see we have a lot in common. Seeing Kyle happy being one of those things.

I flip through my planner for work, trying to focus on the task before me. It's useless. My mind keeps running through my day.

When my phone rings, I lift my head. My brows shoot up when I see it's Emma calling. We exchanged numbers before I left Kyle's place. I reach for the phone and place it on speaker.

"Hello," I say into the device.

"Hel—lo, Andy." Emma's voice greets me, dragging out the word hello. I'm more curious now. "Listen, I was thinking. Kyle flies out in the morning. I'll have Mason this time around. I'll be staying at the house with him. We have this project we've been working on. Mas wants to do something special for Ky— oh, wow, would you look at that. Did she have a mirror at home before walking out the door? Humph, what people will do for attention." She snorts, then continues. "I was thinking that you could help us out."

I grin at her very entertaining conversation with herself. Must be a showstopper. I can't imagine what she's looking at.

"Sure, anything I can do to help," I reply.

"Great, sorry about the late call. I just wanted to ask before it slips my mind. Besides, this thing is totally lame. Beau and

Kyle are in their element. I, on the other hand, darlin', can't wait to get home," she giggles and hiccups.

"No worries. I'm still up," I say, rolling my lips to prevent laughing out loud at her.

"You know, it was nice meeting you. This project will be fun. Okay, enough of me talking your ear off. Champagne may or may not be in my system. Just get used to my drunken calls, now. It happens," she says and hangs up.

I look at the phone on the table and release the laugh I'd been holding. Yup, I like Emma. She will make life more interesting for sure. I finish my planning with a smile on my lips.

CHAPTER TWELVE

Lucky Charm

Kyle

"Emma needed to make a stop, but we'll be there in just a few. Did you need anything?" Andy says through the phone.

"Okay, just you and I'm good," I say. "See you in a bit."

I hang up with a smile on my face, while I finish putting my dishes from breakfast in the dishwasher. I have an appearance today, and Andy and Mas are going to come along. I just can't remember what the appearance is for. Emma has told me a million times, but my brain has been too tired to retain the information.

"Finish up, buddy," I call over to Mason, as I start to run through emails.

"Okay," he says back as he eats his snack.

It's been over two months since I've started seeing Andy. He still has his shy moments and times when he seems uncertain about himself. It's adorable most of the time, but I feel like there's something I'm missing. Something that has the potential to be a roadblock or a turning point in our relationship.

There are a few variables that I've turned over in my head. I've had mostly away games so far. I haven't really been home. There are still so many questions about how he will settle into my work world. That part of my life can put a strain on any relationship.

As for my home life, Andy has slipped right in like he's been there all along. Mason seems to be happier with the stability Emma and Andy have provided. I'm not sure what they've been up to, but I know Emma has had Andy around a lot while I've been gone.

I still feel the need to offer more to that equation. Missing out on time with Mason is taking more and more of a strain on me. With the season in full swing, it's hard to divide my attention as much as I would like to.

I look forward to coming home more than I ever have in my life. The way Mason's face lights up whenever I return to him makes me eager to step through the door each time. It also makes it harder to walk out of it to board a plane that will put way too much distance between us.

I don't think I resent my career, but I do question the effects it's having on my nephew. I lie awake at night in my hotel room exhausted but too concerned with the little person that's most important to me. I worry about whether he misses me, if he had a good day at school. Are his friends the right ones for him? Is he developing the way a boy his age should?

I think of all the things Savanna would have done right for Mas and wonder if I'm even getting close. All of these things are important to me, but I don't know if I've made them as much of a priority as I need to. It's not easy when traveling is a mandatory part of my work.

"Uncle Kyle," Mason says from the kitchen table.

I look up from my phone to see a wide smile on my nephew's face. I chuckle to myself. I know the little monster is about to ask me for something. I've learned that smile and I love it. He's such a good kid. I love when I get to spoil him.

"What's up?" I reply.

"I was thinking. You started the season, right?"

"Yeah, buddy. That's right."

"Shouldn't you have, like, a lucky charm or something?" he says with a hopeful gleam in his eyes.

I tap my chin in thought to play along. I can't wait to see where his little mind is going with this one. The things that come out of his mouth floor me most of the time.

"I guess you're right. What do you think I should do about this?"

"You see, I was thinking. We should get a puppy," he says enthusiastically.

I can't help the laughter that erupts from my belly. I can see that he has put a lot of thought into asking for this. The sparkle in his eyes is everything and more.

When a pout takes over his lips, I round the kitchen counter to reach him at the table. I stand over him, dipping my head to kiss his forehead. Tickling his tummy, I cause him to laugh.

"You think a puppy will bring us luck?" I chuckle.

"Yup," he giggles back.

"Okay, I'll see what we can do about it. I think you have something here," I reply.

"Yes!" he squeals, pumping his little fist in the air.

"What's all the happiness about?"

"Aunt Emma," Mason says, wiggling to get out of his seat. "Mr. Andy!"

I've lost the kid. Mas runs right into Emma's arms, hugging her around the neck as she bends to get down to his level. Andy holds his hand up for a high five.

"I'm getting a puppy," Mas says excitedly.

"I thought *we* were getting a puppy," I laugh.

"Oh yeah, it's a good luck charm for Uncle Kyle, but he'll need me to take care of it for him. You know, because he has to go away all the time," Mason explains.

My heart pangs. I know he means no harm by his words, but they sting nonetheless. I look to Andy to see his eyes soften.

You're doing your best, he mouths.

I nod and swallow hard. I bottle up the emotions to deal with later. I have a lot of those bottles waiting as it is.

"I think it's great that you're going to take care of the puppy for your Uncle Kyle," Andy says to Mas.

"Of course." Mason nods firmly. "Uncle Kyle takes good care of me. He read my favorite book last night and played video games with me this morning before and after breakfast. He's my best buddy."

Andy's face lights up as he turns back to me. I nod again, too choked up to say anything.

"Well, how would you like to go ride in some go-carts with your uncle today?" Emma says.

"That fundraiser is today?" I groan.

"Yes, sir," she replies. "I told you that last night."

"I was dead on arrival last night," I blow out.

"Tell me about it. I have no idea what you were trying to say in your text." Andy chuckles.

I wink at him. "I'll clarify all of that for you later."

I love the blush that covers his cheeks and the way his lashes lower to fan over his cheekbones. I want to move over to him and pull him into an embrace. I hold back, reminding myself we have all weekend. Emma is having a sleepover and taking Mas to Sesame Place along with her other godkids.

"I'm going to get my new sneakers Uncle Kyle brought me from Denver," Mason says, freeing himself from Emma's hold.

Emma turns to us, beaming, after Mason runs out of the kitchen. Her eyes bounce between Andy and me. I roll my eyes at her, already hearing her words before she sings them.

"You two are my favs. I just want you to know that," Emma gushes. "So adorable. Love it."

"We'll see if you can say that after he sees my bed hair and gets a whiff of my morning breath," Andy says nervously.

I reach to tug Andy a little closer, running my hand up and down his arm. He visibly relaxes under my touch. It will be the first time we spend the night together. There are more things I have to learn about Andy. I know for a fact tonight has his nerves on edge, but I haven't pinpointed why.

I'm not going to rushing him into sex. I think I made that clear. I'm looking for a real relationship. I think we both need time to build that before we throw the complications of sex in the mix. Not that it hasn't crossed my mind or played a part in our flirting. I have some very vivid fantasies of Andy.

"I think I have a pretty good idea of what your bed hair looks like. I did catch you knocked out after Mason wore you out in the park," I tease.

It was one of the moments I felt myself falling for Andy. I returned from a game to find him and my nephew passed out in front of the TV in the living room. Mason had curled right into Andy's side just like he does with me. I've never seen him do that with anyone else. Not even Michael.

That speaks to the trust Mason has for Andy. It goes a long way in aiding my own trust. It took a long time for me to allow Andy to watch Mason without Emma or someone else I trust around. Actually, it only happened within the last week.

Andy palms his face. "Don't remind me," he groans. "So embarrassing."

I shrug. "You were sexy. You know how many men would kill to wake up looking like a supermodel?"

"I would," Andy snorts.

"You did, babe. Trust me," I croon into his ear.

The tremor that rolls through him brings a smile to my lips. Goose bumps line his skin. Those eyes turn to me revealing his desire.

"Totally my favs," Emma says with a goofy grin, releasing a dramatic sigh.

I shake my head, kissing Andy's temple quickly before taking off to get ready. It's going to be a long day before we get to relax and kick back. The sooner we head out, the sooner we can be done.

"You shouldn't sell yourself so short. He's falling for you already, believe me," I hear Emma say in her version of a whisper, as I walk out.

I grin. The girl couldn't whisper if her life depended on it, but she's right. Andy shouldn't sell himself short, and I'm most certainly falling.

CHAPTER THIRTEEN

Revealing Scars

Andy

"I work with kids five days a week, and I've never been this tired," I groan as we settle on Kyle's couch.

"Welcome to my life. Those kids had more energy than should be legal." Kyle laughs.

"That was a great charity event. Go-cart races and basketball—kiddie heaven. Those kids are going to benefit so much from the new rec center," I reply. "You're great with kids."

Kyle shrugs. "They're people. I'm a people person. Most of those kids are just like me. I was once their age, just needing to know someone cared. What sucks is that I only get to show them that for a day. They have to go back to whatever struggle is going on in their life."

"I know what you mean. I worked in the inner-city school system for two years. It nearly killed me. Those kids had so much going on. You want to help to change all of their lives, but in the end there's only so much you can do. I realized that I had to work with the hours I got each week. If I could make a difference within those hours, then I was doing the best I could," I say, remembering how tired and sad I'd been back then.

"I can remember a few teachers that made that difference for me. Sometimes it was just the little things. Needing to hear good morning or being asked if I was okay. I wasn't, and I never told them any different, but being asked meant something," Kyle says quietly.

I reach to lace my fingers with his. He lifts my hand to his lips. I love moments like this. It's been two months and I still find myself a little awestruck every now and then. Yet this… I'm beginning to live for these moments.

"It's tough to watch some of the situations those kids dealt with. What's harder, the lack of care some of the staff had. Some because they just couldn't relate, others because they lost faith in the system and were to the point of just showing up to collect a check," I huff. I can hear the bitterness in my own voice.

"What made you leave?"

My lashes lower. I suck in a deep breath and let it out slowly.

"I left for a few reasons. The children and environment weren't among them. It was… it was the beginning of my career. I was more trusting back then." I release a humorless laugh. "I thought some people were my friends that weren't. It was the first time… my first time being drawn into the in-crowd." I pause, blowing out a breath. "Long story short, I started dating the vice principal.

"He learned about my family's connections and my past struggles, then turned into a different person. It was my first serious relationship, so I took the verbal and mental abuse from him until it started to bleed into the workplace," I respond.

I turn to catch Kyle watching me, his brows drawn in. I can see the millions of questions in his eyes.

"How did it bleed into the workplace?"

I look away from him, my stomach rolling. My mouth waters as anxiety and bile rise. The backs of my eyes sting.

"Patrick was like a ring leader in the staff clique. All the other teachers took their cues from him. Others started to sling harsh words my way. Making reference to my eating habits and questioning why I worked there in the first place when I could go anywhere I wanted. It turned into gossip and rumors behind my back. When I broke things off with Patrick, it got worse.

"In the end, I left. I couldn't give those kids what they needed when I had all of that drama surrounding me. I hated getting up in the mornings and felt sick every time I walked into the building," I explain, becoming aware that I've been rocking with my words.

"You, Andy, are tougher than you think."

Kyle tugs at my hand, bringing me into his side. His arm wraps around my shoulder, and he kisses the top of my head as I lean against him. The comfort I feel in his embrace spreads through me from head to toe. I also note that ever-present hum between us.

"Are you seriously going to get Mason a puppy?" I ask.

"Why? You don't think I should?"

"No, I think it would be great for him. Another connection to you when you're away. I was only asking because my sister has a friend who breeds dogs and has connections to a whole community of breeders. I'm sure she can help you get whatever you're looking for," I reply.

"Oh, cool. Can you set that up for me? I want to get him one as soon as I can."

"No problem." I yawn.

"Ready for bed?" Kyle asks and I involuntarily stiffen.

I groan internally because I know the moment he feels it happen. It's the moment I've been dreading. I'll find out tonight exactly how Kyle sees me, and then I'll know where we stand.

Kyle

I'm tired and I should let this slide, but I wouldn't be me if I did. My instincts tell me Andy's reaction goes deeper than sex. It's one more piece to his scarred past. That Patrick dude sounds like he needs his ass beat. That asshole better pray we never cross paths.

"Are you not ready to stay over? I can take you home," I offer.

"No, I want to stay," he replies.

I can tell he's trying to sound confident, but it falls a little flat. I watch as he rubs his palms over his thighs. When he reaches to run a hand through the front of his hair, he completely gives himself away. It's also one of his huge tells.

I release him, turning to face him. I smile inside when he straightens his shoulders, attempting to give off an air of confidence. I like Andy. I want to be patient and understand him. However, I'm caught off guard the moment I see his eyes mist over.

"We've worked out together a few times. Have you noticed I never wear short sleeves or shorts?" he says.

My brows draw. I comb my thoughts and he's right. Whenever he joins me for a workout, he wears sweats or jogger pants. I've never seen him in short sleeves, but we're well into fall. That's not unusual.

"I guess."

I nod. My mind turning the question over, trying to figure out where he's going with this. Andy shifts reaching for the hem of his shirt. I go to tell him we don't have to rush things, but my words are caught in my throat.

Andy's body is toned and sculpted from working out. Exactly what you would expect to see from the way his shirts mold to his body. Though I can see that his torso is a lot paler than his face and neck. However, that's not what stands out most.

He has scars on his stomach and upper arms. They're not gruesome, but they're noticeable. However, given what I know about Andy, I bet these scars look ten times worse to him.

"Tell me about them," I reply.

I can see the relief that covers his face. Another note that I'm right in my assumption. He was sure I was going to run. Knowing this tugs at my heart.

My determination to see this relationship through builds. My shoulders grow heavy knowing he has been waiting for me to make an exit on him. He has no idea that with each imperfection he reveals to me, he endears himself to me more and more.

"At my heaviest, I was three hundred and seventy-five pounds. The doctors made it clear that I make the necessary changes or… I… I was dying. The fainting, the headaches, the sciatic pain… I had to do something.

"I worked out so hard to lose the weight and I did, but then I was left with the excess skin. I was hiding again but for a different reason," he whispers, wrapping his arms around his center.

As I watch him, so much begins to become clear. The pieces click into place. I listen intently as his pain flows through his words.

"I didn't want to fall down the rabbit hole like before, but this time I chose not to involve my family. My oldest brother was promoted to detective. Tara's career had taken off. The family was in such a good place. I didn't want to be a burden again.

"I also didn't want to ask for the financial help. I couldn't touch my trust at the time. So I went to an affordable plastic surgeon that made it all sound so easy. No scars, recovery would be a cinch. Nothing went the way it was supposed to. I flatlined twice on that table, and as you can see everything else was botched. My legs aren't as bad, but they have scars as well.

"My inner thighs and my right calf. I've felt like the never-ending freak show. People are so taken with my face, but when the clothes come off, it's always a different story." His words trail off, and he turns his head. "I… I've never had the courage to go back and try to fix it again."

I reach to turn his face back to me, leaning in to take his lips. It's time Andy learns that I'm committed to this, to him. It's going to take more than the scars he carries—on the inside and out—to scare me away. I have scars of my own. If I were that superficial, I wouldn't love myself. My own scars run deep, deeper than losing my sister and feeling like I lost my way.

I kiss him with everything I am. All the love I can give here and now, I let it thread and weave a healing tether between us. I get the sense that both our healings start right here.

"Neither one of us is whole, but I've been feeling myself come back to life piece by piece with you. If I can give you just an inch of that, I will," I say against his lips.

Andy groans, slipping his arms underneath mine, reaching up to latch on to my shoulders. I lean in until his back falls against the couch. Shifting, I nip at his chin before licking the sting away and continuing a trail down his throat.

I pull back and look down into his eyes. The trust and admiration there tighten my stomach. *This is real love.* He has become a friend I can trust, a partner I look forward to spending time with. Andy takes what I give. I never question his motives or when the other shoe will drop.

My only question is whether or not I have enough love to heal his open wounds. If this flame burning within is any indication, I believe I do. I sure intend to try.

Andy

The fire in his eyes burns for me. Even after I've revealed my biggest secret. He hasn't once looked at me in disgust. I reach to cup his face as he stares into my eyes.

I know I've fallen for Kyle. I've just been hiding behind my worry and fear. However, now, I can see it, I can feel it.

"Every single scar has helped to make you who you are. My present and my future. I'm not perfect, baby. I'm just like you. Finding my way and needing to be loved along the way," Kyle says before capturing my lips again.

I open to him, surrendering to what has become us. My safe place. The words may not have been officially spoken, but I can feel the love.

Kyle starts another slow trail of kisses from my face down the center of my body. My breath hitches when he stops at the largest of my scars. The one that crosses over my stomach. His lashes flicker up. Kyle watches me through them as he places a gentle kiss to the marred skin.

I bite back the sob that wants to surface. In the past, I've been asked to cover up or to turn off the lights. To have this man look at me with such lust, my heart aches in a way I've never known, and it's not the hurtful ache I've become so accustomed to.

His tongue peeks out to trail the path of the scar. A tear does slip free. I allow my tense body to relax beneath him, all except for my pulsing arousal trapped in my jeans. Kyle grasps my sides as he kisses and explores my torso.

My back bucks off the couch when he sucks a smooth patch of flesh into his mouth. My fingers strain against the tight grasp I have on the edge and back of the leather couch. I become tense all over again when he reaches for the button of my jeans and pops it open.

Kyle makes sure to keep his eyes on my face as he tugs my pants down my hips. I close my eyes as my thighs are exposed. Another tear slips free when his lips caress the long scar on my right thigh. My mouth falls open in a gasp when he shifts a few inches away from the scar, testing my sensitivity there before pulling the skin into his mouth. His teeth graze me gently when he ceases the sucking motion.

I slowly lift my lids again as he turns his attention to the other side. I feel cared for and cherished. With each kiss and caress, the hurt from past lovers seems to shrink.

My heart races when his warm breath fans against my tightened groin. I'm ready to come through my boxer briefs. Yet he doesn't touch the one place that's reaching for his attention.

He makes his way back up my body, kissing me tenderly on the lips. I grab his ears to hold him to me. Kyle settles his body between my legs, and I can feel his length pulsing against me.

I reach for his belt to unfasten it, but my action becomes halted by the ringing of Kyle's phone. Frustration lines his handsome features as he backs away and reaches for the device he placed on the coffee table when we settled in. He sits back, placing the phone to his ear.

"Hey… wait. Buddy, slow down. What's wrong?" he says into the phone, concern taking over his entire being.

I begin to straighten my clothes and redress as he listens. His face turns sad as he nods. I can just faintly make out Mason's little voice on the other end.

"It's going to be okay. I'm coming to get you," Kyle says reassuringly into the phone.

After a few more minutes of talking Mas down, Kyle hangs up. He rubs a hand over his low waves. His shoulders sag.

"I'm sorry. He needs me," Kyle's huffs, rubbing his temple.

"It's okay, I understand. Don't worry about it," I reply, reaching to massage his shoulder.

CHAPTER FOURTEEN

We'll Be Okay

Kyle

I tuck Mason into my bed and settle in beside him. He's much calmer now he's home with me. I'm still not clear on what all happened. He was crying into the phone earlier as he tried to explain to me why he was hysterical. When I arrived at Emma's, she looked as confused as I felt.

I watch my nephew fidget in bed next to me, bracing myself for what may come out his mouth when I ask him what happened. Mason has a way of gutting me with his words. I'm sure this time will be no different.

"Hey, buddy?" I start.

He turns his head up to look at me expectantly. His little eyes so innocent but troubled. I want to turn back time to when happiness was all I saw in those eyes.

"Hey," he says.

"You want to tell me what happened?"

He turns onto his side and nods. His eyes get big, and he holds up his hand. Before I can ask what's going on, he jumps up and runs out of the room. I can hear his footie pajamas hitting the hardwood floors.

It takes about two minutes before he runs back into my room, climbing back into the bed beside me. He scoots his little body close to mine and looks up at me. He holds up his right hand, showing me the chain and locket I gave him almost a year ago. It has a picture of his mother and myself inside it.

"You said as long as I have this with me, I'll always have you with me," he says. "I left it here because I didn't want to lose it in the park. I wanted to keep it safe."

He takes the chain and tucks it under his pillow. He turns back to me to get comfortable, placing his head on the edge of the pillow as close as he can get to me but still on his own pillow. His hand reaches for my face.

"You're always with me in my dreams, when Mommy comes to talk to me," he says. "This time you weren't there."

He wraps his arms around my neck in a tight embrace. I return his hold, engulfing his small body in my arms. I hold on to him so tight it feels like I might break him, but I can't let go.

"Mommy told me to hold on to you. She said we're all we've got right now. I need you and you need me. She said that I have to hold on tight." He continues drilling at my heart. "It's why I woke up scared. You weren't in the dream, and I didn't have my necklace. You weren't with me."

"I'm always with you, buddy. I'm right in your heart, but if you need me you call me. I'll be there. As long as there's breath in my body, I'll be there. And when all the breath is gone, I'll still be in the ethers ready to make my way to you if you need me," I choke out.

"We'll stick together like Mommy said, right?"

"Always. You're my best buddy. We'll always stick together," I reply.

He loosens his hold and scoots down to curl into my side. I toss a protective arm around him. If only I could protect him from the world forever.

"Uncle Kyle?" His sleepy little voice pushes through my thoughts.

"Yeah."

"She said we'll be okay. Not to worry. We're going to be okay," he murmurs, already on his way to dreamland.

Tears roll down my cheeks. That's sounds like my sister. Savanna was a force all of her life. Of course she would have the strength to reach out to Mas beyond the grave. Always taking care of us. I'm banking on her words being true.

We'll be okay.

CHAPTER FIFTEEN

Meet My Sister

Andy

If I run my hand through the front of my hair one more time I think I'm going to pull it right out at the root. Sweat dews on my upper lip. When I told Kyle that my sister could help with finding a puppy for Mason, I didn't think she would see right through me and ask to meet him.

I also didn't think Kyle would agree to meet my sister for a lunch date. He's such a private person. When I tossed a snarky comment out about my sister being nosey and wanting to meet my boyfriend before helping to find a puppy, I thought he would laugh it off and move on.

No such luck. Of course, I would set this train wreck in motion. My stomach reels as I think of all the things that could go wrong at this lunch. My sister's opinion means the world to me. A single comment from her could sway the way I see Kyle. Her words could completely wash away my rose-colored glasses.

"Andy, you're making me nervous," Emma hisses at me from the seat beside me.

I jerk my head up from my menu, turning to look at her. I should have known there was a possibility she would be joining us. I was surprised when she arrived with him but also relieved. Emma has a way of easing a room with her presence and sharp wit.

"I've just been watching, waiting for him to combust," Kyle snorts.

I turn to look at him across the table, sitting back in his seat relaxed, with his arms spread over the top of the booth seat. He has a smile on his lips as his eyes roll over me. A shiver runs through me just before he conceals the heated look.

I push my hand through the front of my hair again, before rubbing my palms in my lap. I go to respond to them both, but my words die before they hit the air as my sister appears. She's moving toward us with a big smile on her face.

"I'm so sorry. I had to drive in, and the attendant in the lot was moving like a snail," Tara says as she pulls me into a hug.

Emma and Kyle stand to greet her as well. I relax a bit as both Tara and Emma each take one of my hands and squeeze. I'm grateful for their strength.

"This is Emma, Kyle's assistant." I start with introducing the two that are trying to anchor me.

"I'm more like his brain and the little sister he's always wanted but just didn't know it until my family adopted him into our awesome lives," Emma says.

"More like the annoying little sister that I haven't been able to get rid of," Kyle teases.

"Why would you want to get rid of me?" Emma bats her lashes.

My brows draw. My curiosity is piqued. I never knew Kyle was adopted. I bank the information to ask about it later.

"'Cause you're crazy," Kyle mutters under his breath, but a smile is still on his face.

The rest of my nerves evaporate. Definitely grateful that Emma came along. I turn to Kyle and feel the blush that raises to my cheeks.

"This is Kyle," I say to Tara.

"The boyfriend," Kyle leans in to say low enough for Tara to hear, while winking at me.

My chest swells. It's the first time I've heard him claim the title. I smile from the inside out.

Tara beams up at Kyle, pulling him into a hug. When she releases him, Kyle gestures with his hand for her to slide into the booth beside him. My sister takes the seat without question.

"Is he always like this?" Kyle asks Tara teasingly, nodding his head in my direction.

"Oh my gosh. Yes and no. I mean, he is always nervous to introduce me and the family, but never like this," my sister laughs.

"Can you blame me? Last time I introduced you to someone you told them to their face that they weren't good enough and to stop wasting my time," I say incredulously.

"You act like I was wrong," she deadpans.

I shake my head and purse my lips. She wasn't; she was actually very right. I just didn't see it until after she pointed it out.

"Honest. I love it. I'm a straight shooter as well," Kyle says.

I tilt my head to the side and look at the two sitting next to each other. *Oh boy.* I groan internally. I can absolutely see traits of my sister in Kyle. How the heck did that happen?

A smile creases my lips.

"So about this puppy," Tara says to Kyle.

Instantly, the two of them have fallen into a full conversation about Mason and the puppy.

I exhale. There was no reason for me to be so riled up after all. My face hurts from smiling so hard.

"See, he can charm the pants off anyone," Emma leans in to my ear to whisper.

I turn and wrap an arm around her shoulders, pulling her in for a hug. Emma kisses me on one cheek. Her eyes sparkle with mischief when she pulls away.

"Look at how jealous he gets," she whispers.

I turn in the direction she nods her head. Kyle is still talking to Tara, but he's glaring at Emma. Emma throws her head back and laughs, falling into my shoulder. I have to cover my mouth as I try not to laugh out loud as well.

Kyle

I playfully narrow my eyes at Emma. A week ago, she pointed out to me that I get this jealous look on my face when she and Andy fall into one of their moments. I hadn't noticed it until she said something. What she doesn't understand is where the jealousy comes from. If you can even call it jealousy at all. I'd say it's envy.

I envy the time Emma gets to spend with Andy and Mas. They've become a little family without me. In reality, I'm grateful to them both and wish I had more time to be a part of the bond that seems to be growing in my absence.

However, I won't deny the connection I do feel with Andy. He has me doing a lot of things I'd never thought I do. Like today.

I don't know what made me agree to this lunch. Maybe the hope in his eyes when he joked about his sister wanting to meet me. Next thing I knew, I told him I'd be glad to take her to lunch to talk about Mason's new puppy. The words were out of my mouth before I could think about it.

I have to admit. The opportunity to make both of my favorite guys happy won out in the end. I'd say it all over again to see that smile that covered Andy's face that day.

"You two are adorable," Tara whispers.

I turn from Andy and Emma to look down at her. Andy's sister is a female version of him. Tara's hair has more hints of red and is a lighter brown than Andy's, and her eyes are more gray than blue.

The adoring look she gives me reminds me of the way my sister would look at me when she was proud of me. I feel a little pang in my chest when I think of how Savanna will never get to meet Andy. I think she would have liked him. She definitely would have loved him as Mason's teacher.

I feel my own eyes soften. I remember Andy telling me how important his sister was to his transformation. I have so much gratitude for her being there for him.

Unable to find the words to say, I wrap an arm around her and pull her in. When we break apart she looks up at me with a curious smile on her lips. I find the words that can best sum up what I'm feeling.

"My sister was always there for me growing up. From what Andy tells me, you were the same for him. Thank you for taking care of him until I got here," I say.

"Wow, I like you." Tara grins, pulling me in for another hug.

"Enough of that," Andy teases.

Just then the waitress arrives at our table. We all order and settle into light conversation. I watch as Andy falls into his comfort zone. His confidence surfaces and he starts to shine in his own light. He even begins to aid in Emma's humor, rather than blushing from it.

"I tell you. I really enjoyed this lunch," Tara says as she wipes tears from the corners of her eyes.

"Yes, it was very entertaining to watch Andy pop the stick out his ass," Emma taunts.

"Not all of us were born tossing our asses to the wind, love," Andy retorts.

I choke on my water I just sipped. Tara falls into me giggling at the two. My stomach hurts from laughing so much.

"In my brother's defense, he doesn't have a stick up his butt. It just takes a little while for him to realize when he can be himself," Tara says.

"Is this true, Andy? Are you still questioning our loyalty?" Emma asks with a mock frown.

Andy blushes while he shakes his head. "No, no, it's not your loyalty I question. It's my ability to sit at the cool kids table that I doubt," he replies.

"You need to cut that shit out," I say. "You hold your own at the table."

"Thank you," Tara huffs. "I swear sometimes. You know, Kyle, I think you're just what he needs. Someone to call him on his shit. My brother is a great guy. He just needs to see it."

"Hey, I'm sitting here," Andy says, frowning.

"I see you," Tara replies. Her phone rings before she can dig into Andy any further. "Shoot, I need to take this and I might as well go to the bathroom."

"Oh, I'll come with. I need to go too," Emma says.

They get up and we are left at the table alone. Tara's words are still playing in my head. I slowly drag my tongue over my lips while locking eyes on Andy's. He squirms a little in his seat. The corners of my mouth turn up higher.

"When I'm done you'll be able to see a lot of things more clearly. Sometimes all it takes is unleashing all inhibitions to reveal what life truly has to offer. Once someone shows you how they see you, you free yourself to see the truth," I say now that we are the only two at the table.

"Some truths are a lot to harness once unleashed," Andy says.

I lift a brow at the dare, I like this side of Andy. I lean in toward the challenge. My eyes falling to his lips, before they return to his. I give him a wolfish grin.

"I never unleash anything I can't conquer. What's a harness to a master controller," I rumble.

"See, my favs! You two are so fucking hot. I don't know what just happen but I can tell it was something I wish I witnessed?" Emma says.

"Aye," Tara say, lifting an imaginary glass to Andy. "Grand to be you, And."

"Why me?" Andy groans and face palms, as I chuckle. "Thought you two were going to the bathroom."

"That places needs to air out a bit before it's inhabitable," Emma says waving a hand in front of her face.

We all begin to laugh for the millionth time, breaking the tension at the table that started to coil between the two of us.

Andy's eyes catch and lock with mine. We still have some unfinished business to handle. It's been a few weeks since that night at my place.

Andy lowers his lashes, looking up through them with a seductive grin that tells me there indeed is another side of him that I can't wait to explore. I have no doubts that I'm going to find nothing but heat when I unpack all that's Andy. Tara cups my cheek and kisses the other one, pulling my attention from her brother.

"You're perfect. Don't let him run from you, and don't change one thing," she says in my ear.

CHAPTER SIXTEEN

Not Our Truth

Kyle

"This isn't funny," Andy pouts.

"Yeah, it is. You see what I mean about my life. Nothing I do is private. This is some straight-up bullshit. I bet it was our waitress or some of the staff that took them," I mumble, still amused at Andy's pouting.

"The world thinks my sister is your new love interest. Look at these pictures. From those angles it really looks as if the two of you are in love," Andy says in disgust.

"True. If I weren't there, I'd totally believe what they're trying to sell. That shit is crazy." I wave the story off.

Andy continues to flip through the social media sites, looking at all the pictures that were posted from our lunch. It's a total invasion of privacy, but I'm used to it by now. Andy seems to have gone through shock, annoyance, and now he's settling on a smoldering jealousy.

I'd run over to his apartment, thinking something serious was going on when he called me freaking out. When I arrived to him shoving a tablet under my nose, relief washed through my body. I laughed hysterically once I knew he was safe. He's so far out of his depths, and it's very comical to watch. He's adorable.

I lean in to nuzzle his neck. He smells delicious, a fresh and clean scent that's light like an ocean breeze with a hint of something sweet like lavender or apple, maybe even a note of citrus. Whatever he wears, his cologne fits him just right.

I'm glad I had some free time to rush over. Mason has been taking a few mixed martial arts classes with Beau at the gym. It's been giving me some time to decompress while Beau gets to play the cool uncle.

"So what do we do about this?" Andy huffs.

"Nothing. It'll die out in a few days. Maybe a week or two. I don't answer questions about my personal life. They can ask, but I don't answer. I'm not about to start now," I reply with a shrug.

"Oh… seriously," Andy grunts, drawing the tablet closer to his face.

"What?"

"Look, this site has a few of me and Emma. It's incredible the narrative these photos give. I mean, I almost believe what they imply. Look at how we're looking at each other," Andy says, frowning as if his words taste bitter.

I scratch my chin as I look at the photo. He's right. The photo looks as intimate as the ones of myself and Tara. I just roll my eyes at it. There's always someone looking for some story to sell.

"Listen to this," Andy says indignantly. He begins to read the caption in horror. "Kyle Tyson and his assistant and longtime girlfriend, Emma Dalton, have called it quits. Emma was spotted with her new beau. We wonder if her brother, former boxing champ and Kyle Tyson's best friend, Beau Dalton, has given his approval."

I groan, letting my head fall back onto the sofa. I rub my left temple. The last thing I want to do is dwell on this. I'm sure it won't be the last time Andy will see a bunch of lies surrounding my life.

"Babe, you can't get caught up in reading all of that shit. I don't. Those gossip rags have been publishing that Emma and I have been in a relationship for years. If they did any type of research they'd know she's my adopted sister," I say, exasperated with the topic already.

"Aye, I've been meaning to ask about that. I was curious when Emma mentioned it at lunch," Andy replies, his eyes lighting up with curiosity.

My own curiosity raises. That Irish accent that slips at rare moments is sexy as fuck. It doesn't happen often enough if you ask me. Instead of prying into that, I answer his question.

"When I was sixteen, my aunt got pissed at Savanna because she caught my uncle harassing her. Savanna was nineteen, but she didn't want to leave me in that place alone. She was planning to take me and leave as soon as she had the money.

"My aunt tried to throw her out and make her leave without me. Savanna called children's services, and I was placed with Beau and Emma's family. They were so damn country." I give a short laugh. "But they were nice as shit. We all had to adjust to one another. Being newer to New York, Beau and Emma were teased in school for being country, and I was teased for living with a white family. Beau and I stuck together and have been best friends since.

"My aunt washed her hands of me after a few months. The Daltons adopted me about a year later," I explain.

Andy nods, looking down into his lap. I can see his thoughts turning in his head. I wait for what I have a feeling is coming. When he opens his mouth, I know I've almost read his mind.

"You don't have to answer if you don't want to," he starts. "Your uncle. He molested you both, didn't he? You've said... I.... I.... A few times, I've noticed the way you've said certain things."

I push out a breath, drawing a hand down my face. I think I would prefer to talk about the photos. I've known that I'd have to share this with him someday. Those years shaped so much of my life.

"Yeah, it started with me. Savanna figured it out and offered herself so he'd stop," I reply, feeling the tears burning the backs of my eyes. "My sister was a fucking superhero. She took that shit for me until the bitter end. He used it against her and me. Promising to make her watch while he made me do things if we didn't keep it a secret or do the shit he wanted. Not that my aunt would have believed us if we told her. She knew that man had a wandering eye. Again, if it wasn't her way it was the devil.

"Savanna was a whoring demon that needed to get out of her house. My aunt walked in on him pinning Savanna to the kitchen counter, and it was still all Savanna's fault. I wanted to go back and kill that son of a bitch, but Beau and Savanna convinced me that it wasn't worth it."

Andy moves to sit in my lap. I blink away images of the past, returning to the room before me. My jaw feels like it's going to snap from the rigid bite I'm holding.

"You...." Andy shakes his head as if to clear it. "You are such an amazing man. The more I learn about you, the more I feel lucky to know you. You should be so jaded by the world. Yet you give back whenever you can and you're so loving. You're gentle when you need to be, but I get the sense that you're fierce when necessary. I think I'm falling in love with your wounds as much as I'm falling for your perfection," he says.

I cup the back of his neck, drawing his lips to mine. Pushing away all the demons and tainted memories from the past, I devour every inch of his mouth. Andy groans into me, encouraging the possession I've taken of the sweet cavern that just spoke words that are a balm to my soul.

"I know I'm in love with everything about you," I breathe.

Andy pulls away with bright eyes and red cheeks. A smile takes over his face. He leans his forehead into mine. I close my eyes, absorbing all of him, his warmth, his love, the energy that makes him distinctly him.

"I love you too," he whispers.

"Consider yourself stuck with me now," I tease.

"Not complaining in the least," he replies.

I go to pull him into an embrace, but his phone rings. I twist my lips in annoyance. We're always getting interrupted. Andy rolls his eyes and sighs.

"Hello," he says into his phone.

When he moves off my lap and palms his forehead, I get the feeling we're not getting back to our moment for a while. He sits listening for a bit before he grunts and looks up at me. I lift a brow in question, but his next words answer all.

"Yes, Mom, I already saw them. I texted Tara about them earlier. She feels like quite the celebrity," Andy says dryly.

My shoulders sag. I look at my watch. I don't have much more time anyway.

"No, Ma. I'm not jealous of her dating the big sexy black guy," he says after a pause.

I bite back a laugh. Andy shoots me a death glare. I actually laugh at his next response.

"No, I'm not hating on my sister. *Hating on*? Where'd you get that from anyway? Wait, never mind don't answer that. I'm not jealous because she's not the one dating him. Ma, listen, I'll explain," he mutters.

I stand, bending to kiss him on the forehead. He looks up at me with sad, pleading eyes. We already discussed him sharing our relationship with the rest of his family. He and Tara reassured me that they would keep our privacy.

I have to go. I'll call you, I mouth.

"I love you," he covers the phone to whisper.

"Love you too." I peck his lips and turn for the door.

CHAPTER SEVENTEEN

Blitz

Andy

I wiggle my bare toes against the carpet, drumming my fingers to the beat that's taking me to another place. The music playing in the background is creating a lazy feel in the house. There's no rush to anything or anyone. Just a sense of calm and peace.

The week has rushed by, but now the weekend is here and time has taken a sweet pause. Such a good day to kick back and enjoy the company of those that mean the most to you. I've come to feel at home in Kyle's house. I think I'm here more than he is. When he's away, I spend most of my time here with Emma and Mas.

"He's licking me." Mason giggles and squeals as his new puppy wiggles in his lap, thoroughly licking his face.

"It's because he likes you."

"I like him too." He beams up at me, those brown eyes sparkling.

Blitz is still small for a pit, but I know he'll grow to be a pretty big guy. Tara made sure to get the best of the litter from a great breeder after Kyle told her what he was looking for. I think Blitz was made for Mas.

"I think your uncle picked out the perfect puppy for you. I like his name too. Blitz is so cool. How did you come up with it?"

He tilts his head, a secretive smile on his lips, seemingly assessing if he'll share. His eyes hold admiration for whatever he's thinking. He nuzzles the puppy's head, then looks up at me with a brilliant smile.

"Uncle Kyle gave him to me when my other uncles were here. Uncle Daniel was teaching me about football. Uncle Beau called him the king of the blitz," he says, lifting his little shoulders. "I liked it."

"Nice, great choice," I say and smile at him.

"You guys are the best. Not every kid knows real-life superheroes," Mas says matter-of-factly.

I'm taken back. I absorb the look of admiration on his face. Warmth spreads through me, my throat clogs. I'm speechless for a moment. Surely he's not including me in that number.

"You know superheroes?" I ask to see what's going on in his young mind.

He nods, giving that sweet smile of his. The puppy barks as if confirming Mason's reply. They are totally too cute together.

"Yeah, all of my uncles are superheroes. You guys make the world a good place, and y'all are the best at what you do," he says emphatically.

"You're a lucky kid," I say.

"Yup, I sure am. You guys are just like the Greek gods. You all have special powers. Uncle Kyle is like Zeus. He's a leader. His team follows him. When he shoots the ball it's like he's throwing thunderbolts into the net. I think Uncle Beau would be Ares," he says, tapping his bottom lip. His eyes are alit with his musings.

I've learned that Mason can sit for hours watching documentaries and YouTube videos on Greek mythology. Watching him now, I can see this is something that he has put thought into before. He'll be six this year, but sitting and listening to him articulate his thoughts has me amazed. His thoughtfulness is more conceptual than other children his age. Mason doesn't just absorb information; he knows how to adapt and apply the facts.

"He goes to battle in the ring. Although, I think Uncle Beau is a nicer version, but if someone makes him mad, all bets are off. Uncle Javi would be Apollo. He looks after the family. He loves everyone. He and Uncle Beau even fight sometimes just like Apollo and Ares would. They're funny when they do," he giggles.

I love the way his mind works. I wonder which god he would equate me to.

"Who would I be?" I ask.

"That's easy! Uncle Kyle loves having you around. He can trust you. You're funny and you're smart. At school you always fix all our problems. You would be Hermes," he says with a sage nod.

I sit completely blown away. I blink a few times as my brain tries to reconcile the fact that this is a young child. His comprehension of Greek mythology is beyond that of some adults.

Hermes had been Zeus' youngest son. Zeus did love having him around, and Hermes was a trusted problem solver. He got the description for the mythical character down to a tee.

"He's amazing. Isn't he?"

I turn to see Emma watching us with a huge smile on her lips. She was in the kitchen with the chef, checking on dinner. We're supposed to be working on Mason's surprise for Kyle, while Kyle is at an away game.

"Yes, he truly is," I reply.

"Do I get to be one of the gods?" Emma asks teasingly.

"Yup, Athena, Ares's sister," Mas gives a mischievous grin.

"I'll take it," Emma giggles. "Come on, guys. Dinner is ready. We can eat and then get back at it."

"All right! Food," I cheer and hold my hand up for a high five.

Instead of giving me five, Mas leaps from his side of the couch to wrap his arms around my neck. I'm surprised, but the warm hug is welcome. Mason still needs so much love and attention. I can see he's been getting better at school, but there are still hard days for him.

"Love you, Uncle Andy," he whispers.

My heart squeezes. This is the first time he has ever called me uncle. I embrace him and squeeze back. I'm happy to be included in that number.

"Love you too, kiddo. You're the best," I choke out.

Kyle

It's been a long day and I have a flight first thing in the morning, but I can't close my eyes without talking to my little guy. It's a part of our routine that I refuse to break. His presence has become like glue, keeping me together on my worst days.

"How is our lucky charm doing?" I ask my nephew over the phone.

"He's doing great. I think he misses you like I do," he replies.

"I miss you guys too," I say, rubbing at the tightness in my chest.

Why am I here, when my nephew needs me there? Sure, I have people that I trust helping me, but there are times when I just know in my heart my nephew needs me.

"Can we have a chill day? Just me and you?" he asks with so much hope in his voice.

"I'll clear a day just for you, promise."

"Yes!"

I shake my head at his excitement. You would think I just promised him a gallon of his favorite ice cream. I'll admit, I'm looking forward to a day of chilling out with him.

"Wait, I changed my mind," he says quickly.

The smile falls from my lips. Mentally I already had tickets purchased for the zoo, the museum, and a trip to his favorite restaurant. I frown at how quickly he changes his mind.

"Oh? You don't want to hang out with me?" I ask, my shoulder sagging from the pang of disappointment.

"No. Yes. Yeah, I do. I just wanted to know if we can ask Uncle Andy to hang out with us too," he explains.

I sit silently. I've never heard him refer to Andy as uncle. I've never told him he had to. I wonder if I'm moving too fast with Andy. This is all new to me. It's clear that Mas has become attached. Andy has effortlessly become a part of my support team.

"Uncle Ky?" Mas whispers.

"Yeah, buddy. I'm sorry. If you want to ask him, we can. I think he would like that," I say.

"All right!"

"I love you, Mas. We'll talk in the morning. Go brush your teeth and get in the bed."

"Okay, I love you too, Uncle Kyle. We'll be here waiting," he says, as if he needs to reassure me.

I hang up the phone and sit to reflect. Andy is a huge part of my life. I just didn't think all of this would happen so fast. We haven't taken our relationship to the next level, but where we are has given something special to not just me, but my nephew as well.

My lids might be growing heavy, but my heart has grown full. Sleep will come with contentment tonight. Nodding my head at my thoughts, I give myself over to my dreams.

CHAPTER EIGHTEEN

Image of Truth

Andy

"I think he's showing off for you," Emma whispers in my ear.

I turn away from the game to smile at her. The sparkle in her eyes reflects the excitement and joy I have within. Kyle is playing an amazing game. The thought of my presence being the reason behind that has me ready to explode with happiness.

"Maybe," I laugh, turning back to the game.

"I need to step out for this call," Beau announces as he stands.

Emma and I give him a quick acknowledgment with a wave. The three of us are here in the box seats Kyle insisted I watch the game from. I would have been fine with the cheaper seats I'd plan to purchase for myself.

However, I got the impression from the look on Kyle's face he wanted to know I would be sitting in the arena safely. Not wanting his mind to be distracted, I agreed being in the box would be best.

I'm not new to being in the box. My father has company season tickets. For football, basketball, and hockey games. I've been to my fair share of sporting events.

Kyle hits a three-pointer, and I come out of my seat cheering. He's been on fire tonight. That's his fourth three. He has thirteen assists, seven rebounds, and thirty-five points so far, and we're just in the third quarter.

"He's lighting it up out there," Emma says, giving me a high five.

"I know."

My chest swells with pride for my man. Kyle's always an amazing player, but tonight he's showing it all. I can't wait to have him in my arms after the game, while I tell him how amazing he is.

"Oh my God, Tyson is fine," a female voice says behind us.

"You took the thoughts right out of my head," another one purrs.

I chuckle to myself. Kyle *is* gorgeous. These two have been chirping and giggling about this player or that player all night. I've been too invested in the game up until this point to pay them much attention.

"He's definitely on my list to run into tonight at the after-party," the last one to speak continues. "I didn't wear this dress for nothing."

They both fall into a fit of cackling. I fight not to turn my head to look at them. Jealousy rises in my stomach. My jaw tightens, and my knee starts to bounce.

"You okay?" Emma asks beside me with concern in her voice.

I turn, seeing the same concern in the pinch of her brows and purse of her lips. Her eyes flicker behind us, making it clear she heard the same thing I did. I give a curt nod, not wanting to speak.

"I heard he's not the easiest one to bag. I have my eyes set on a much easier fish," the other one says.

Their voices are becoming like nails on a chalkboard. I can no longer focus on the game. Rolling my neck, I try to think rationally. Kyle wouldn't be interested in either of them. That's my man out there, not some celebrity hookup.

"I've got this. Don't worry. He'll be calling my name while I swallow those juices," she giggles to her friend.

I clinch my jeans into my fist to keep from turning. It's taking everything in me not to jump up and shout, shut the hell up. It's insane that they feel so comfortable having this conversation.

I turn around against my better judgment. The two women look back at me, and their faces light up with interest. They smile at me as if overhearing their conversation has piqued my interest in them.

"Hey," Emma calls, placing her hand over the one I have clinching my jeans.

I turn back to her, and she gives me a warm smile. The two behind us start to laugh, but I keep my gaze forward. I cringe at the next comment I hear.

"Is that his girlfriend? He's hot. Who do you think he is?"

"I don't know, but he has to be somebody to be in here," the other muses.

I am somebody. I'm Kyle Tyson's boyfriend. The reason neither of you will be going home with him.

***

I'm out of my league.

The green-eyed monster has gotten the best of me. This night has become bitter in my mouth. First the game, now there's this. This club and after-party. I don't know which feelings to settle on—anger, embarrassment, jealousy, disrespect, insecurity.

All of those feelings and more are swirling through me as I watch Kyle on the dance floor with some woman grinding all over him. She's beautiful. Her flawless skin is close to Kyle's gorgeous complexion. Her short haircut complements her high cheekbones. Her bee-stung lips are painted a gold color that sets off all her features.

Is this the norm for him? When he's away on the road, is this what he does? Does he ever leave with these women? Is Kyle bi? Does he even remember that I'm here?

"You're going to break that jaw you clench it any tighter." Beau's drawl pulls me from my thoughts.

I turn to face him, bringing my beer to my lips to take a long sip. I've been drowning my feelings for the last hour or so, if not longer. At this point, I don't know how long we've been here or how much longer I can take staying here.

"Is this the norm?" I grunt out.

"Yes and no." Beau shrugs, taking a sip of his own drink. He points a finger in Kyle's direction, then leans in to my ear. "That's his way of blending in. He'll dance with one or two different women if he feels like the guys are questioning or watching him more than usual."

"So he thinks he's being questioned tonight?" I ask, a salty tone in my voice.

"You honestly don't see the way he looks at you." Beau snorts. "I've caught him and I know he's caught himself watching you all night. If I've seen it and he knows what he's doing in his own head, then yeah. He may feel like he's being questioned."

"A part of me understands, but another part just feels… I don't know what I feel," I grind out.

"That's understandable. This is your first time encountering someone you care about that lives a double life. I can't imagine this would be easy. It annoys me and I'm not in your shoes," he says.

I suck my teeth, turning back to the dance floor. Sure enough, Kyle is looking right in our direction. Our eyes lock and his narrow on me. I turn away before he can get a read on my expression. I'm not in the mood for him to see through me right now.

"I can't stomach this," I grumble.

"I think that's what he's trying to find out. This is his world. If you're going to be a part of it, you have to understand it all," Beau says.

"Why? Why like this?"

"You've seen what happens in the media. There are times that things will appear that will make you question everything, including him. He's making you question it now so he can address it up front. It's one thing to know it happens, another to see it. I get it. I wouldn't necessarily do it this way, but I get it. This is Kyle, though. He does things his way," he replies.

"Shit, I'm not going to entertain anything you just said because it's making my fucking head hurt," I say.

Beau chuckles, turning to signal for another drink. I turn back to the dance floor like a glutton for punishment. My brain feels like it's going to short-circuit. The picture before me reads just as real as the images of Kyle with my sister. I try to root myself in the memory of how those pictures gave a false perception.

Just as now, this is a misrepresentation of the man I love and have feelings for. I can't get lost in the images. I have to remember our truth, the real truth.

"Fuck," I hiss.

All of that pep talk goes out the window when the beautiful woman turns, lifting up on her toes, and whispers in Kyle's ear. He leans back in to hers to reply, a smile dancing on his lips. I close my eyes and turn away. Beau snorts, reaching to pat me on the shoulder.

"The man is invested, fully. Don't hurt him. If this isn't for you, it's time to walk," he says, lifting his drink to his lips. He pauses and continues over the rim of his glass. "While he'll let you."

A shiver runs through me as his ominous words roll over me. I have noticed a change in Kyle. Over the last few weeks, he's been a bit more possessive. I haven't minded it at all. It makes me feel wanted and special when he does something as simple as walk up behind me and cage me in at the kitchen island while I talk to Emma or Beau.

Still, this is too much. I can't think straight. I need out of this club to clear my head and see this rationally. I down the rest of my beer and place the empty bottle on the bar we've been standing by.

"I'm leaving," I say.

"We should let him know first," Beau says.

I nod noncommittedly. I'd much rather leave and deal with this in the morning. I also know that that's not going to fly with

Kyle. He likes to be open about our feelings and handle things head-on. While any other time I love that about him, I'm just plain pissed off tonight. Last thing I want is to talk about this. Beau signals for Emma's attention, and she ends her animated conversation to come join us.

"What's up?" she says.

"Andy's ready to go. I think it might be best," Beau replies.

Emma twists her lips at me, but she doesn't say anything right away. I look away, not wanting to hear whatever she's planning to say. I just want to leave.

"Fine," Emma huffs. "The one party I'm actually enjoying. You know we're not allowed to leave you, right?"

I turn to look at her and note the glare Beau is sending her way. I knit my brows, wondering what the heck she's talking about. Beau grabs her by the elbow and nods for me to follow them.

The song changed not too long ago, ending Kyle and his pretty little partner's dance. My eyes land on him in the direction Beau is leading us in. He's standing close to some of his teammates. A smile is on his gorgeous lips as he laughs at something being said around him.

When he sees us coming, he turns to say something to the group, before stepping away from them for a little distance. Beau releases Emma, stepping into Kyle for one of those hand-clasping half hugs. I'm reluctant to move in for the same gesture when Kyle turns for me.

I swallow my feelings and shift to clasp his hand. He tugs me in for the half hug, and I have to fight everything in me not to lean into him and melt against him. I go to pull away, but he tightens his hold, dipping his head to my ear.

"What's wrong?"

"Nothing," I reply, stepping back.

"We're heading out," Beau informs him as Kyle moves to kiss Emma's cheek and hug her.

Kyle's eyes swing to me as if I'm the one that just spoke. In one glance, it's as if he strips me bare. Nothing remains hidden from his watchful gaze. His nostrils flare as he reads me. I turn away, pretending to look around the club, taking it all in.

"All right," Kyle says. "Give me a second. We'll all go."

My head whips back in his direction, but he has already closed the distance between us and his friends to give his excuses for the night. My jaw tightens. I just wanted to go home. He doesn't have to end his night for me.

He was having a great time after all. The thought sounds snarky even in my own head. I'm beyond caring at this point.

"You leaving already?" I hear a female voice say. "I thought we were going to get to have that dance."

I have a sour taste rolling in my mouth. I don't even want to look to see who the voice is coming from. I've never experienced these feelings in my life. The frown on my face and the clutching and unclutching of my fists make it evident that I'm not hiding my feelings well.

"Sorry, sweetheart. I have to go take care of home," I overhear Kyle say.

"Yo, your little dude all right?" another male voice asks.

"Yeah, he's good. I just need to be out. He has a whole day planned for us tomorrow. I'm tired thinking about it." Kyle chuckles.

"That's what's up. You have to bring him by the gym again. That kid is smart. I liked talking to him." Someone else laughs.

"Word. That kid's an old soul. I swear he's been here before," another person adds humorously.

"Yeah, he has. But I'll see y'all in practice. Stay out of trouble," Kyle says, turning to our little group.

His eyes train on me the moment he faces us. He places a hand on Emma's back as we all start out. While he's not touching me, his steps are in line with mine. He remains close enough to shield me if need be, just like he and Beau are doing with Emma.

I should take comfort in that, but my brain has too many thoughts of all the things I'm pissed and confused about. Everyone except for Emma remains quiet as we make our way to the valet to retrieve Kyle's car. She is rambling about some guys she met in the club. Meanwhile, I can feel the tension rolling off of Kyle as we wait.

When the car arrives, I jump in the back seat before anyone else gets in the car. I hear Kyle grumble something about my fast action, but it's not clear enough for me to understand. Beau chuckles but slides in beside me.

"Andy, are you okay?" Emma asks, from the front seat. "I mean, I know everything was a lot to take in, but this was a tame night."

"Emma," Beau and Kyle snap in unison.

I sink into my seat, folding my arms over my chest as I stew. The rest of the ride is dead quiet. Yet the silence is deafening.

I don't switch my seat when Beau and Emma climb out at Emma's place. Instead, I keep my eyes closed and my head pressed against the cool window as if I'm sleeping. Yes, totally childish, but between the alcohol and my emotional state, I feel it's the best move.

The next time the car comes to a stop, I open my eyes, expecting to be in front of my own apartment building. I must have fallen asleep at some point. When I blink a few times to adjust my eyes, we are outside of Kyle's house. I bite back my irritation and push the door open to climb out.

I just make it out of the car when Kyle slams the door behind me and backs me against it. My head tips back to look up at him. He lowers his face within inches of mine, his eyes blazing with emotion.

Nothing is said. We just breathe until we are breathing each other in, completely in sync. My tongue darts out to touch my lips, causing a smile to spread on Kyle's. He leans closer. I close my eyes, thinking he's going to kiss me.

The contact never comes. I lift my lids to find him still staring at me. My frustration returns, and I get ready to express it. Kyle shakes his head.

"No," he says firmly. "You questioned me tonight. You questioned us. You questioned yourself. Let me ask you something, Andy. Do you understand what you mean to me?"

I roll my lips, searching for the right words to say. He's still so close, I can't think. His cologne has my mind muddled. That charge between us has my body on high alert.

"Yeah, I didn't think you did," he replies to his own question. "I think it's time I fix our first problem."

He moves in, pinning me to the car with his hips. I feel his bulge through his jeans. His fingers lace into the short strands at my nape.

"Not once did that girl feel that. Her ass was all over me, but that... all of it belongs to you," he bites out just before crushing his mouth to mine.

I groan into his mouth, my arms going around his neck as if a puppet master guided them there. The kiss is scorching hot. Kyle guides my head just as he wants it. His hips roll into me, causing a need deep in my belly. I question if I've ever known desire before this. The want I have threatens to claw its way out from the inside of me.

"Kyle," I breathe, when his lips make their way to my neck.

He sucks the skin into his mouth and rolls it against his tongue. My fingers crawl their way down his neck to his back. My eyes roll up to the sky. I can taste the night air with each gasp I pull, in search of a cleansing breath to free me of the inferno building in my lungs. The fire is spreading to my veins.

Just when I think I'm going to burst into flames, he releases my flesh. Before my senses can return, he scoops me into his arms as if I weigh no more than a child. My cheeks flame as a surprised sound pushes past my lips. My arms go around his neck. Kyle kisses my cheek, his steps starting for the house.

"Our first problem isn't you knowing that I want you. It's you understanding that I *can* want you. You don't see you, baby. I'm going to show you what I see," he says without breaking a stride.

I press my face to the side of his. It takes so much for me not to fall apart in his arms. My past tries to tell me I don't deserve this, that I don't belong in his hold like this.

I would never forgive myself for damaging his career. Yet his breathing doesn't change a bit. I'm stock-still in his hold nonetheless.

"Alexa, dim bedroom lights," he booms when the lights come on automatically as we enter his room.

I've held my breath nearly the entire way to his bedroom where he places me on my feet. He crowds my space, pecking my lips once, twice, a third time before biting my bottom lip. The lust on his face flips my stomach in the most delectable way.

"Don't move," he commands.

I nod. He moves to the side of the bed, removing his watch to place on the bedside table. He then reaches for a remote, and a sultry, sexy song begins to fill the room.

If I'm not mistaken it's Tank, "F**in Wit Me."

I watch him while he moves to one of the accent chairs across the room. Grabbing the heavy-looking gray chair, he walks it over to me. He sets it down in front of me.

I stand and stare, not moving an inch. First, he unbuttons his navy button-down to reveal the tank underneath. Shrugging the shirt off, he allows it to fall to the floor. Next, he tugs the tank from his jean and yanks it over his head. My eyes follow the movements, watching the fluid motion of his muscles playing beneath his skin. My belly becomes taut with a need that's so gripping, it's physically manifesting itself in the form of a deep ache.

Goose bumps rush across my skin, my breathing has increased, and my cock strains against my pants to the point of pain. Beads of sweat roll down the sides of my face and back. The hairs on my body stand at attention. My scalp feels like it's tingling.

When he's down to only his jeans, he moves to me. His fingers brush from my hairline down to my jaw, following a lone drop of sweat. His eyes are focused on mine. I feel like I'm trapped in a web of his making. His other hand reaches for mine.

Gently he turns me so my back is to him. It's then that I realize he has positioned us in front of an oversized floor-length mirror. My heart knocks against my chest. There's enough light for me to see myself and Kyle fully. Nothing will be hidden to either of us.

My immediate response is to close my eyes, but Kyle's hand cups my chin, tipping my head back. He leans over me to place a chaste kiss on my lips. It's tender yet quick.

"You are a beautiful man on the inside and out. There isn't a part of you I don't love or want. You need to see what I see. You need to love what I love," he says softly. "Look, watch, learn to love."

His tongue flicks out over my lips. It's like having a key slid into a forbidden lock. Something clicks inside of me. I want to give back to him the feelings he continues to pour into me.

He pulls away, guiding my face back to the view in the mirror. I watch our reflections staring back at us. Kyle takes the zipper of the lightweight jacket I have on and tugs it down. He then grasps the shoulders of the fabric, peeling it from my body. I let it fall to the floor, not taking my eyes from us. He ducks down to kiss my neck, causing me to tilt my head to give him better access.

His arm snakes around my body, splaying his hand against my stomach. He draws my back to his front, pressing into me from behind. The hand splaying across my belly reaches for the hem of my T-shirt. In one swift motion he has it up and over my head. My first instinct is to cover myself, but I don't.

I keep my eyes fixed on his in the mirror before us. I try to see me the way he does. I take in my torso that's more defined than it's ever been. At least, it is now that I'm looking. I flex my chest, and it sinks in that I'm looking at me, really looking at me.

It's not a superficial thing. I believe I'm far from vain. I don't think my weight ever defined me. No matter my size I've been told how attractive I am. No, it's bigger than all of that.

It's... I stopped looking after my surgery and the scars. I continued the work so that I wouldn't get sick again, but I stopped looking. The scars were a painful reminder of how close I came to almost losing my life, not once but twice.

My past lovers only amplified the hurt and pain of seeing the scars. It all caused me to ignore the man in the mirror. In this moment, I'm staring at my will to fight. It's my evidence of being a fighter.

Kyle's dark hand glides across my skin as I flex once again. The sight mesmerizes me. The contrast is beautiful. Like my scars, the differences tell a story. They're a part of who we are; they make up the whole.

"You see how perfect you are?" he breathes, pinching my left nipple. "Keep looking."

I do. I watch his hand take the slow trip down the center of my body. His fingers run through the trail of hair that disappears into my waistband. When he connects with my belt, he releases it and frees the button of my jeans. My eyes lock in on the V that disappears into my jeans.

My eyes mist. When did all this definition start to show? It's been so long since I've allowed myself to look at my nude body. The long scar that runs through that V would be the main reason I'm unaware of its existence.

Kyle licks the shell of my ear, sending a shiver rocking through me, pulling me from my thoughts slightly.

"Are you seeing it yet?" he whispers.

His hand slips over the center of the V into my pants, grasping a tight hold of my hard length. I moan so loud it jars me a little. Kyle chuckles darkly, his hand beginning to stroke me.

He releases his hold on me, leaving me bereft. Squatting behind me, he hooks his fingers in my jeans and boxer briefs to peel them slowly down my legs. I'm now content with watching him in the mirror. He removes my left shoe, then moves to the right. Tapping my leg in a silent command for me to step out of my pants and underwear, he pulls them free from my body and tosses them away.

I suck in a breath when he licks a slow trail from my ankle up my scarred calf to beneath my buttcheek. I turn to look down at him. His hand whips out to slaps my ass, his head shaking at me.

"Mirror, gorgeous," he orders.

I turn back for the mirror to see the man standing before Kyle. It's me. Yes, I see my scars, but they don't seem as long, large, and ugly as they once did. Over time they may have gotten smaller and healed more than I've given attention to. I also think it has a lot to do with my mental state.

I'd go as far as saying the man I see is attractive. Better yet, I feel attractive—perhaps sexy. Battle scars can be sexy—these are mine. The feeling is driven home, as I watch Kyle's brown skin glide over mine between my legs, over my thigh and back again. He nips my ass, and my cock jumps.

As if it calls for his attention, he slides his hand back through my legs and wraps his hand around my length. All the while he takes his time kissing and nipping my ass. His tongue peeks out to trace patterns across my skin.

"Bend over. Keep your eyes on the mirror. I want you to see that sexy-ass face when you're turned on," he says. "Grab the backs of them thighs for me."

I follow his orders, bending over with my eyes on me. My palms wrap around the backs of my thighs and hold on. I groan when he licks from my hip to the center of my crack, opening me with his long fingers.

I'm so lost in the erotic image before me it takes a while before I realize he's not just eating my ass in the most skilled way I've ever had the pleasure of. He's spelling words into my opening. My brows crease, and I try to focus through the loud moans I'm releasing into the room.

I bite down on my lip. He pulls back, blowing into me, but goes back to eating and spelling. My knees go weak when I make out his name being tongued into my body.

"Oh fuck," I cry out.

I'm so close to the edge. My breath catches from the slow strokes of my penis. His teasing tongue places my sanity in question. My belly quivers, and my face twists in ecstasy.

My eyes become so bright and open. I look as if I've reached a level of pleasure that's unbearable, but it's a beautiful sight, even to me. I'm instantly filled with overwhelming emotions.

I love this man beyond what he'll ever comprehend. I don't think I have ever looked at myself like this. I begin to sob silently.

Kyle

I nearly cry with him. I see the moment the shift happens in his face. We're not nearly done, but we've reached the first step tonight. He's seeing himself. However, I have a lot more to show him about the man I see before me.

I lift to my full height and pull him to stand, turning him into my embrace. He cups the back of my head, drawing me into a kiss. I smile when I feel some of the inhibition gone.

I dip, grasping behind his thighs before straightening and bringing him onto my waist. Andy deepens the kiss, taking me by surprise. I welcome it, though. I like seeing him bloom from his broken shell.

I back up until I feel the chair at the backs of my thighs. Lowering into the seat, I bring him down with me. My hands travel up his body to his back. I put this song on repeat for a reason. I have more lessons for my Andy.

Well, I thought I had lessons for Andy. He slides from my lap to his knees. His hands make quick work of my belt and free me from my jeans. We both work to push them down my thighs, but Andy doesn't let that stop him from wrapping his lips around my tip at the same time.

I groan and clench my jaw as he sucks lightly and rolls his tongue around the crown. Like a warning of what's to come. I lift out of the chair when he dives in, taking half of me into his mouth.

Shit, I'm at the back of his throat, but he doesn't allow that to stop him. When he bobs down on me the third time, he takes it all. My toes curl and my eyes roll.

"Fuck, baby," I grunt.

"Mmm," he hums around me.

I hiss when his hands wrap around me and he works the fuck out of my dick in his mouth. My fingers grip his hair as he bounces his head up and down. My thickness seems to be an encouraging challenge to him. Even as my thoughts tangle into a mess, I can't help thinking that I doubt that he would've been as aggressive or confident as this a day ago.

"Damn, Andy," I croon. "Keep sucking the fuck out that shit."

He groans a reply but doesn't stop. My hips meet his efforts. I can't stop the thrusts, not while trying to hold back coming down his throat. Andy gives me his all—slurring, drooling, moaning, neck rolling—a sloppy toppy at its best.

When I'm getting too close, I gently cup his jaw and pull him free. My length pops from his mouth with a wet sound. I bring his face to mine, giving him a hungry kiss. When I break our lips apart, I pull him to stand and spin his back to me.

I have him bent over again, before he can take a breath. I spread his cheeks, massaging around the hole I'm about to make mine. Tara told me not to let her brother run from me. Andy's time to walk away from me is up; we're in this together. I've known that since the day he told me he loves me. He'll know it tonight.

I swirl my tongue around his puckered hole, eating his ass once again. My mouth is already watering to have him, so it's nothing to spit in his hole, before I massage the moisture into his soft skin. I push the tip of one thumb into him, pulling a moan from his lips. I smile, bring two of my fingers to my mouth to suck them. Once they're nice and wet, I play with his opening, readying him for me. I can hear my own breathing increase.

I need to put us both out of our misery. It's time for that lesson I planned to put on his ass. Reaching down for my pants, I pull a condom and a pack of lube from the pocket. Andy looks over his shoulder, lifting a brow.

I grin, biting into the lube packet first, with a shrug of my shoulders. I'd planned to steal some time away with him tonight as soon as I got a chance. He didn't know that, but I did. Patience is key with me. I always deliver.

I knew the shit I planned to put him through tonight. I was always going to make it up to him. I had only hoped I wouldn't get the reaction I got. He's going to have to learn to school that shit. He failed horribly tonight. Being in my life can be complicated. It's one thing to say he understands that, another to actually show he understands.

Once I've emptied the lube onto his waiting entrance, I roll the condom on, while his eyes eat me up. Andy is a very nice size, long with a bit of girth, but I think I'm a bit thicker. That doesn't seem to bother him at all. He's not the least bit shy about ogling me either.

I slide down in the chair a bit. Wrapping my arm around his waist, I pull him into my lap. I'm already hard as a rock. My tongue flicks out to lick his back as I line him up with my length. He wiggles back into me. Grasping his hips, I slide into him a bit.

"Kyle," he calls out.

"You okay, baby?" I ask, lifting him back up before I guide him down again.

"Yes, I need more," he breathes.

I nod to myself, watching him slide down onto me. He falls back into my chest when I'm fully seated. I nip at his ear, giving him time to relax around me. When he starts to rise, just as I expected he's timid in his movements again.

I reach to pinch his chin between my fingers. I tap his lips with my forefinger to grab his attention, leaning into his ear. His movement halts.

"Listen to the song. Let it get in you. Watch the mirror. Use your eyes and ears to move your body. Move with me, not against me. I promise it will be better for us both," I tell him.

He nods. I guide his hips as they start to move. It takes a few strokes before he catches the rhythm with my guidance. He's still stiff with apprehension, though.

"Let go. Stop thinking. It's just me and you. Do what you feel," I whisper to him. "Stop being afraid."

"Fuck, Kyle," he moans when I roll my hips up into him.

He reaches back to grasp the back of my head as he rides me. Our eyes lock in the mirror. It seems my words are what he needs. I watch the last of the broken shell fall away. Andy comes to life right before my eyes. Like a phoenix rising from the ashes.

Andy

"Yeah, that's it," he croons heavily.

I'm in awe of the beauty the two of us make in the mirror. Kyle said exactly what I needed to hear. I need to stop being afraid. He's here with me. He hasn't run from my scars or my insecurities. He's helped me through them step by step.

I reach behind me as I watch our reflection. I see nothing but lust and love in his eyes. Not the look of disgust I've seen with others. I don't have to be afraid because it's clear that I'm desired. I let go.

I move my body in ways I never have. The moans and groans coming from Kyle spur me on. It's like the sound of the music and the feel of his skin against mine possess me. I sit up and roll and rock my hips to match his.

"Yes, Andy, yes," he growls. "Fuck yeah, baby."

He pounds up into me, pulling cries from my lips. He feels so damn good. His fingers dig into my waist, his nails biting into my flesh. I place a hand on the arm of the chair, bracing myself. With my free hand, I start to jerk my cock.

"Oh yes, yes, you're fucking me so good," I manage to groan.

"Do you see it? Do you see how sexy you are? Do you see how amazing you are?" he grinds out.

"Yes, I see it. Yes," I say.

I do. I see how much I've changed emotionally, physically, and mentally. I've changed so much in just the short time we've been together. In the past, I wouldn't have taken my pleasure like this. I would've taken the scraps offered and would've been happy.

"That's it. Get into it. Put your feet on my thighs," he coaxes.

I lose my pace for a second as I process the instruction. Throwing caution to the wind, I lift one foot, then the other as he steadies me. I plant the pads of my feet on his thighs. Once I'm securely in place he drills into me.

"Oh... ah... oh, yeah. Yes," I breathe out.

My head falls back, and a loud curse rips from my lips. Kyle isn't shy about owning my body just as he likes. I turn my face to his, and he captures my lips. I return the kiss with everything I am. I'm proud to use my body, this scarred body, to please him.

I'm offering pleasure as much as it's being given. I tear my lips from his to watch this position in the mirror. Kyle's right hand wraps around my throat, squeezing lightly. This is all too powerful to be contained. I feel so empowered.

A roar rolls up from my belly, and I release it into the room. It's the most freeing sound I've ever made. His other hand reaches to pump my cock. My fingers are gripping the chair behind his back. It's all I can do to hold on and not fall over. A second roar rolls through me, and I come right along with it, feeling the release in my toes.

Kyle gets to his feet in one fluid motion. He turns us quickly. I'm now facedown in the chair. I brace myself as he rocks into me. I bite my lip and breathe through my nose. The sound of his pelvis to my ass claps through the room, blending with the music and my own husky moans.

"This is what I've wanted all fucking night. You and only you. Never, ever question that," he says through clenched teeth.

I look back over my shoulder, unable to do more than answer with my eyes. Kyle sucks his lower lip into his mouth. Seeing his pleasure written on his face takes me to new heights. I reach between our legs and knead his balls.

"Oh shit, I'm coming," he growls. "Damn, I'm about to come so hard."

He releases his own roar this time. His forehead drops to my sweaty shoulder. His soaked chest heaves against my back. Our breathing and the music become the final soundtrack. I close my eyes, but the images of us in the mirror are burned into my brain.

Those are images I can trust. They're real. They show us. They're just for us and our interpretation of who we are. As long as I have those, I can handle anything.

CHAPTER NINETEEN

Thoughtful

Kyle

Andy has been pretty silent since our lovemaking. After we caught our breath we showered and climbed into my bed for the night. We'd already planned for him to stay the night before the scene at the club.

Mason's being spoiled by Beau's mom for the weekend. She treats him just like a grandchild. She probably spent the evening baking him cookies.

Tonight, I wanted to be able to focus on the two of us. I exhale a deep breath, my fingers tracing patterns up and down his back.

"What are you frying?" I finally ask.

"Huh?"

"You haven't fallen asleep. Why are you so quiet?" I mutter.

"I'm just thinking," he says against my chest.

"Exactly, I can smell you frying your brain cells."

He gives a low laugh, snuggling closer to my chest. My lids droop for a second as I relish in his heat. I should just be content with this comfort, but I want to know what's on his mind.

"I'm not frying brain cells. I'm just thinking," he says lazily.

"About?"

A few beats of silence pass. I know he's going to answer from the tension in his body. I just wait him out, lifting my other hand to run through his hair. He grasps my palm, turning to kiss it. We both relax with the gesture. Sagging into the bed a little more, I place the hand he just kissed on his thigh thrown across me.

"I've spent my entire life afraid to be seen in one way or another. Always hiding. You walk into my life, and you see all of me without so much as trying," he says.

"That's not true. I see you because I am looking. I want to see you. I think in some ways you want to be seen, so you allow me in. Being afraid doesn't mean that we don't still want. It's that want that shines through and draws the thing we want to us," I reply.

The room falls silent. I continue to trace his skin, my thoughts moving at the same lazy pace as my fingers. My mind travels to overhearing one of the groupies at the club. She noticed Andy and asked who he was, checking to see if he was in the right paygrade for her to pounce.

Andy doesn't think that people see him but they do. He's gorgeous and pulls the attention of everyone around him. You have to look deeper to see the things I see, but that's what makes me love him more. I see all of him.

"What do you want? What's shining through you?" His voice breaks into my thoughts.

I remain silent, taking in his words. My jaw tightens as I think over my life.

"I think I'm the opposite of you. I'm not looking to have anything revealed. I've been seen all my life. I've been the center of attention that I've never wanted more often than not. All eyes are always on me." I pause, twisting my lips in thought.

"Nah, I'm not looking to be found in my shell. I'm looking to be left alone in my shell. I want to be me. Just Kyle, but I only want to share that with those I choose. I want to choose. That's what I want. I want to have a right to share, and if I don't want to, I want to be able to say that and be left alone."

"We're quite a pair," Andy replies, turning his face up to mine.

"It works," I answer.

"Yeah, I think it does." He leans in to kiss me.

I stare into his eyes when he pulls away, searching his face. I cup his jaw, running my thumb over his lower lip. There's one more thing I need to make clear tonight.

"A part of keeping what I want to myself is going to the club and—"

"Don't." He cuts me off. "You don't have to explain. I get it. I was just in my feelings tonight. I'm sorry. I understand. I'll handle it better next time."

My lips curl up in a broad smile.

"Next time?" I cock a brow at him.

"I always learn to adapt. I know I can handle this. I want you, so I'll adapt this time as well," he replies.

"Let's see if you can adapt to this." I chuckle, rolling until he's on his back.

For the first time in a long time, I feel like life is going just as I want it. Things are finally starting to fall into place. I just might be okay after all.

CHAPTER TWENTY

A Loving Family

Andy

I've taken this long to bring Kyle around my family because they're all crazy. Tara is the closest one to being sane, and that's only when she's not around the rest of the family. We're a close-knit family. We're loving and supportive, but you never know what you'll hear come out of one of their mouths.

I don't know how they'll manage to embarrass me tonight. I just know one of them will, but I wouldn't trade a single one of them for the world. The fact that I can trust them with something so important to me is enough to endure whatever they throw my way.

"Why do you look so nervous?" Kyle asks, holding a sleeping Mason on his hip.

The poor kid passed out during the drive here. I wish I could have relaxed enough to sleep during the long drive. I didn't sleep last night as it is. I kept playing in my head all the ways this night could go south.

"They're crazy. I told you this," I say, trying not to pout like a child.

"It can't be that bad." He squints at me.

I purse my lips. "Hopefully you won't understand half of what they say," I reply.

Kyle's laugh rumbles through the air. My parents retrained their Northern Irish accents although they will dial it back when around others. Mitch, being the oldest, tends to fall back on our parents' speech habits. John, Tara, and I don't slip up nearly as much, but it is known to happen, especially when we're all together.

I mutter to myself about the disaster this will be. Just as we enter the house and clear the foyer into the family room, Kyle places a hand on the small of my back and kisses my temple. The gesture is met by a loud welcoming cheer from my family as they come into view.

"Hey! Andy," my brothers shout in unison.

I roll my eyes and laugh at them. Sure, that never gets old. Mitch rushes me, lifting me into a bear hug. My other brother, John, pulls me into a headlock, messing my hair.

"Well, who do we have here?" Mitch booms.

I push John off to find Mason awake with his eyes bouncing between me and my brothers. My heart warms to see his little face calculating whether I'm in danger, as if he plans to help or come to my rescue. Mitch holds up his hand for a high five.

"Put it there, kid," my oldest brother says to Mason. "The name is Mitch."

Mason's eyes flicker to me to see if I'll give the approval. I give him a reassuring wink. His face lights up.

"My name is Mason," he replies, giving Mitch a high five.

"Nice to meet you, big guy. You like sports?"

"Yeah, I can play basketball like Uncle Kyle, but I like playing kickball and baseball with Uncle Andy too," Mason says enthusiastically.

"Jeez, kid. If my little brother is the one teaching you baseball you're in trouble," Mitch teases.

"Aye, he would teach you kickball and not soccer," John says, trying not to laugh.

Mitch stifles a laugh at the same time. Kyle stiffens next to me, not understanding the joke. I frown at my brothers and reach to rub my head.

"Oh shit, did you see that?" John bursts into laughter.

"Sure did, I did." Mitch doubles over, choking on his own laugh.

My brothers are like bulls in a china shop. They say what they feel and mean what they say. If it hurts that's your problem. When it comes to me, they'll kick my ass and tell me to get over it. Yet they'll sit with me to make sure that I indeed get over it. It's weird, I know, but I love them for it.

"Stop torturing my babe in front of his company," my mother says as she and my father join us. "The lad has turned red in front of his beau, he has. Cut it out."

"All we did was point out he's not too keen on football," Mitch says through his laughter.

My frown deepens as my mother's cheeks redden and her eyes sprinkle with mirth while she tries to suppress her own laughter. My dad doesn't even try. He lets it roar, holding his stomach.

"I'm sorry, lad. I'm sorry," my father says as he tries to compose himself.

"So, our dear brother here was actually awesome at football in grade school. He was on a team and one of the star players, he was," Mitch starts.

"Aye, the kid had talent," my father says proudly.

"He was also a little shit that broke my bike and tried to hide it. I wanted to get back at him. He was just about to score the winning goal," Mitch continues.

"I really should have battered your arse for this," my dad says to Mitch, with tears of mirth now rolling out of his eyes.

"It was too funny to," my mother blurts out, her words taking on that musical sound of hers.

Mitch shrugs. "He deserved it. Always breaking my stuff."

"See what you have to understand is Andy likes to take things apart and put them back together. He was always taking our shit apart and then running off when he couldn't put it back together," John explains.

"Watch ya mouth in front of the wee lad," my mother chides, popping John in the back of the head.

"Ouch," John hisses, rubbing the back of his head. "I want to see how long you all keep your gubs clean."

"Stook," my dad mumbles, always good for calling one of us an idiot.

"Anyway, Andy is about to score the winning goal. The ball is headed right for him. I jump up from the grass on the sidelines and start screaming at the top of my lungs." Mitch starts to laugh so hard he can't continue.

"'Andy, Andy. Oh my God, Andy. Look out.' He's screaming out," John tries to finish.

"The poor thing. He starts to look around for the danger. He couldn't have been more than eight or nine. He was so confused," my mother giggles.

"Meanwhile, the ball is still sailing towards him," Mitch starts again.

"Can we not?" I groan.

"Oh no. They have to finish," Kyle says.

"He turns around just in time for the ball to cobber him in the noodle. I mean, it bounces off his face like two times. He wasn't hurt or anything, but the look of confusion on his face. Priceless. His team lost and he was pissed. He wouldn't talk to me for weeks. I only felt bad after he started flinching whenever the ball looked like it was coming for his bake," Mitch finishes.

"He's lucky it didn't break his nose. Absolutely should have beat ya arse," my father adds.

"It's funnier if you see the videotape," Tara says as she joins us out of nowhere. "And as much as we may seem like jerks for laughing at him. We found out about a year ago that as good as he was at the game, he hated it. He played because Mitch and John did, and he thought Da wanted him to. The flinching was BS. He used it to get out of playing."

I blush as my sister outs me. Kyle's mouth falls open in shock before he joins my brothers in laughter. He's holding his own stomach. Well, if this is the least of the embarrassment for the night, I guess I can handle it. At least it's out of the way.

"Do ya know how many years I felt guilty over that?" Mitch says, but his eyes tell me he's over it.

"You didn't feel too bad," I grumble.

"Absolutely didn't," my mother huffs. "I did batter ya for taunting him with footballs after that. Forgive my lot. They're a bunch of muppets."

"I can't speak for these three, but I'm no one's fool, Ma." Mitch winks.

"I think I love your family," Kyle moves to say in my ear.

"You can have them," I mumble.

"Come on. Let your Uncle Mitch and Uncle John show ya how to play some real football," Mitch says to Mason.

"Damn right." John nods.

"Assholes," I mutter to myself.

"I heard that, prick. Just for that yer playing after dinner," Mitch calls over his shoulder as he tosses a squealing Mason in the air.

"I tell one more of ya to watch ya gub, I'll be doin' a number on ya," Mom snaps, her Irish accent showing through.

This time I don't think Kyle fully catches what she says. The Northern Irish tend to speak faster. When it's just us around, most would be lost in the speed and the slang of it all. When we visit our family in Belfast, I find myself lost at times.

"See, now you've pissed her off," Tara hisses at Mitch as she follows my brothers to play with Mason.

"The name is Oscar. We do have manners, we do," my father says with a smile, holding his hand out to Kyle.

My father is down-to-earth. Having money has never changed him. He still works hard side by side with his workers every day. Same as before he came into his first million, he has a beer every night as soon as he walks into the house. He's loyal to his friends and protective of his family.

"It's all right, sir. I feel like I know you all already," Kyle replies taking his hand.

"Aye, my lad hasn't smiled so much since he was a wee babe," my mother says, waving Kyle in for a hug. "Family ya be. I'm Honoria."

My mother is much the same as my father. She's fierce about her children and can't stand to see one of us hurting. The only reason she wasn't there for my intervention with my sister and father was because she'd made herself sick with worry. She cursed me out good for stressing her out when I got myself together.

"Nice to meet you, Honoria," Kyle says, bending to give my mother a hug.

I think her tight embrace surprises him. She holds him for a few beats, squeezes him the way she does her children. I know and understand that hug. It's tighter than you'd expect from someone so tiny but comforting just the same. It's her way of showing unconditional love.

I smile with pride, my heart swelling with love. That hug is the Connor stamp of approval. Kyle has just received the official family welcome.

Kyle

Andy is right. His family is crazy. I love them. I haven't laughed so hard in years and the way they've taken to Mason—treating him just like family—it is more than I expected.

Andy is a totally different person around his family. He's so much more sure of himself and assertive. Listening to the banter between him and his brothers has revealed so much about him.

John is like a big kid. He and Mason just ran out to get gummy bears for their ice cream once they found out they have the preference of the combination in common. Tara has been bugging Andy about modeling for one of her upcoming shows or something.

I just came out back to the grill on the deck to grab another burger. It's the first time Andy has given me space. It's like he's been shielding me all night. I chuckle mentally at the fact that he thinks he needs to protect me from his family.

"I give him a hard time, but I love that kid," Mitch says as he walks up beside me.

"I can tell," I say around a bite of burger.

"My question to ya is are ya hiding ya relationship because of the shit Andy has told us? Or are ya doing it because he's fucked-up?"

I turn to glare at him, tossing my burger back on the plate. Mitch is about six feet tall, just a bit taller than Andy. I have to look down at him. He narrows his eyes, glaring back at me. All good feelings go out the window. I toss the plate down on the nearby table when he squares up with me.

"First, you don't know me like that, to be up in my face. Back up. Second, there's nothing fucked-up about Andy. I have no reason to hide him," I say through clenched teeth and a tight jaw. "I choose to keep my personal life to myself. That has nothing to do with Andy or how I feel about him."

"How do ya feel about him?" he asks, moving farther into my space.

"That's also none of your business. But since you're the brother of the man I love, I'll keep it hundred with you. Andy and Mason are the most important people in my life. I'd lie down my life for them and you best believe I'll lay out anyone that tried to hurt either of them," I say, looking down at him pointedly.

"Hey, what the hell?" Andy rushes out the back sliding doors of the house, pushing Mitch back.

Mitch smiles, nodding his head, but I don't return it. I'm still ready to whip his ass for calling Andy fucked-up and getting in my face. I flex my fists at my sides. My entire body is coiled to fight.

"Neil Patterson," Mitch says and nods.

My brows furrow. I know the name. I just don't know how or why Mitch is bringing it up. I rub my chin, trying to calm myself.

"Who? What the fuck are ya talking about?" Andy snarls, the Irish lilt I've been hearing his family use appearing. "I warned ya ass I'd beat the fuck out of ya if ya tried this shit."

My head whips back. I look Andy over, and he looks just as ready for a fight as I am. His fists are tight at his sides; his chest is heaving. That accent, though. Yeah, I like that too. Here for it all day. Something to think about later.

"His husband works for me. Neil comes to the office parties and always brags about knowing you as a kid and how you used to protect him and beat the other kids up for messing with him. Says you were a stand-up kid. You protect what's yours," Mitch explains. "I needed to make sure that's still true."

"Are ya fucking kidding me?" Andy growls.

Mitch turns to Andy and glares. They have a stare down as Andy glares back. They look like two pits sizing each other up for a fight.

"Aye, I know I taught ya how to kick ass," Mitch snaps. "But if he wants my baby brother, he better have ya fucking back. Now shut ya bake. He's a good guy and he loves ya. That's all I needed to know. I'm grand."

"Is that you?" Andy bites out.

"Aye, I'm done," Mitch grumbles. "I told ya. I'm grand."

"Asshole," Andy snaps.

Mitch shrugs, turning to me he tips an imaginary hat. I relax and nod back. No hard feelings. I was the same way with Savanna.

"So were you about to fight your brother for me?" I say with a grin.

"Shut up," Andy mutters, the corners of his mouth twitching up.

"Andy's a scrapper. Noted." I chuckle.

"Don't forget it," he tosses back and winks.

"Don't plan to, babe."

CHAPTER TWENTY-ONE

Bitter-Ex

Kyle

"To our new interests, good times, and some fun." Javier lifts his glass to give our customary toast.

"Salud," we say as one.

This party is the first time in months my crew has all been in one place at the same time. With the seven of us all playing one professional sport or another, it's hard to link up. Beau is the only one of us who's retired. Although, I hope someday he'll get back in the ring.

As I look around Javier's office at my friends, I count myself lucky. These guys have accepted me as I am. When I need support, they're always there. Each knows if they need me, I'll do the same.

We're dressed to impress tonight, each one of us in a black tux. I have to say, I'm in some damn good-looking company. Darwin likes to call us his den of dimes, seven perfect tens. At first glance, most would probably think that, but there's a lot of pain, struggles, and scars in this room.

"It's good to see you all in one place," Javier says, speaking my own thoughts.

"It has been too long." Jordan nods.

"Tell me about it," Chris agrees. "I feel like I've been doing nothing but running. It's good to have a down moment with family. Kyle, how's Mas? I want to spend some time with you guys after the playoffs."

"He's good. He's happy and healthy. That's what's most important to me," I reply.

"The kid is a beast. I think he may end up in the ring," Beau says proudly.

Ray groans. "You're letting him in the gym with this guy. You know you're going to be up at the school every week for him kicking someone's ass."

"Exactly what I was thinking," Chris snorts. "Beau probably didn't even bother to teach him not to go around knocking kids out."

"Bite me," Beau grunts. "He knows better. The kid has talent and he's still young."

"Nah, I think he likes baseball," I say with some disappointment.

"All right, the niño has taste," Javier croons.

"Whatever." I laugh.

"Doesn't he have a birthday coming?" Daniel asks.

"Sure does." I nod.

"Emma is going nuts on the party." Beau shakes his head. "Has my mama helping her."

"Oh, this is going to be one for the books," Javier says, with mirth in his voice.

"Wait, so we just going to skip over Kyle walking in here with Bae? You don't walk in here with someone as fine as that and just think we're going to skate right over it like it didn't happen," Daniel says.

"Okay, it's not just me," Jordan chortles.

I grin. I was surprised when Andy said he's never been to Club Refuge. Darwin is known for parading pretty boys around the club. That is unless you're one of his *boys*. Darwin has a group of us he looks out for and treats like sons. From listening to Andy, I can see he's a part of that group.

"What do you want to know?"

That gets everyone's attention. I never open up so easily. Fine, I'll admit it. I kind of do want to show Andy off. It's odd. That's so unlike me, but my closet friends are in attendance and I want them to know Andy.

Tonight, Javier is throwing a black-and-white affair. I thought it would be cool to bring Andy. It'll be sort of a celebration.

Mas has made it through kindergarten without me breaking him or scarring him for life, I made the playoffs without killing any of my teammates, and Andy was offered a position as vice principal at his school. This seemed like something fun to kick back and look at all that we've accomplished.

Daniel gives a long low whistle. "This must be serious," he says.

"Must be," Chris adds. "You look good, happy."

"I am."

"Good. Does Mas like him?" Jordan asks.

"Yeah, he was his kindergarten teacher," I reply.

"Wait, I thought you said he met him at your barbecue," Chris directs at Javier.

I should have known this was a topic behind my back. My smile broadens. I'm not hurt. They are always looking out for me. Andy and Beau already get along great. Andy knows Javier and Ray from the barbecue. However, there's still Jordan, Daniel, and Chris. They were all out of town when Andy and I ran into each other at Javier's. The seven of us are like brothers. Just like the Connors gave me their stamp of approval, I want my family to have a chance to meet Andy and do the same.

"We already knew each other. We just got to know each other better after," I answer.

"How's Michael taking all of this? Smug-ass prick. I never liked his ass," Jordan says.

A series of agreeing grumbles fills the room. I'm more than aware that a lot of my friends didn't like Michael. It's not like this is the first time I'm hearing Jordan say it.

"Honestly, I don't give a fuck. I'm happy. I haven't spoken to Michael in months," I say.

"Wait, you do know he's here tonight?" Ray says, his brows drawn.

"No."

"How?" Javier snarls at the same time.

"You're asking me," Ray scoffs.

"Is he in white or black?" Javier snaps.

"White," Ray replies.

"Son of a bitch. Whoever brought him loses their membership tonight!" Javier says angrily.

I'm already heading for the door. I don't trust Michael, and to use someone to get an invite says he's up to no good. I'm surprised his entitled ass didn't show up in black and claim his invitation must have gotten lost in the mail.

I step out of Javier's office and can feel my brothers at my back. I'm sure we make quite the sight, storming up the hallway dressed in tuxes and frowns. Rage is boiling inside of me.

When we make it to the main room where the party is happening, I scan the room for Andy. With everyone in either a white or black tux, I don't find him right away.

Andy and I are sporting matching navy-blue silk ties. I gave him a pair of diamond cufflinks that match mine as a gift before we left the house. The look on his face was worth it. I almost changed my mind about coming out, but he looked so excited to meet my friends.

"Over there." Beau points.

I'm ready to lose my shit when I see Andy standing next to Michael. Andy has an innocent smile on his face, while Michael looks like a wolf in sheep's clothing. Michael's eyes lock on mine, and that smug grin turns into a megawatt smile.

I cut the room in half with my long strides. I don't know what Michael is up to, but I don't like it. The one time I dated someone during one of our breaks Michael cost the guy his job. He still claims to have had nothing to do with it, but I know that's bullshit.

I'm not having it this time. I go to war for those I love. Something Michael is about to be reminded of.

Andy

I'm having such a great time. Tonight has been amazing. First, Kyle's gift. I mean, I was so surprised when he gave me the cufflinks. They're covered in diamonds and make out his initials. He's wearing a matching pair, with my initials. So thoughtful and sweet.

The next highlight of the night so far was walking in on Kyle's arm. He looks amazing in his black tux and navy-blue tie. I love a man in a suit, and Kyle is wearing the hell out of his tailored tux. I felt so proud when we entered the party and all heads began to turn in our direction. I know I haven't been able to keep my eyes off him.

Everyone has been so welcoming, and Kyle was more than affectionate before he disappeared. Having so much of his attention in public almost caused me to revert to my shy shell, although after a few glasses of champagne I relaxed.

"It's been a while since I've been to one of the games," Simon, the friendly artist, says.

He came over to introduce himself as Javier's date for the evening. We've been talking for the past fifteen minutes, while I wait for Kyle. According to Kyle, he and his friends have a ritual of having a drink together and catching up quickly at these events.

"I'm excited for the playoffs," I reply.

"You and Kyle look pretty cozy. You two make a stunning couple," a newcomer says, interrupting our conversation.

My cheeks heat, but I give a warm smile. This guy is older and distinguished-looking. He's quite handsome with his dark eyes and blond hair. He's graying at the left temple, but it's attractive on him. He seems friendly, although his smile suggests he has a secret.

"Thank you," I reply.

"You're welcome. It's nice to see him smiling. I know he went through a hard time last year," he says smoothly.

"Yes." I nod, but say no more.

I'm not sure who this man is. I know Kyle said his friends that would be here are like brothers to him. However, Kyle went to drink with those brothers.

"Do you know—"

"How is his nephew?" Simon's words are cut off. "He's such an adorable little boy. Savanna was a lovely young woman. I was so sad that Kyle and Mason lost her."

I watch Simon shift, his face looking uncomfortable. I'm unsure of what has him so unsettled. Although, being cut off is kind of rude.

I hesitate for a moment before giving an answer about Mas. However, this guy has to know Kyle if he's asking after Mas and knew Kyle's sister. His interest seems genuine.

"He's doing great, actually. Thrilled about graduating kindergarten and excited for his coming birthday," I say.

Something crosses this guy's face, causing me to pause. I realize I still don't know his name. I'm starting to feel a little uneasy, but I don't let it show.

"I'm sorry. I'm Andy."

"Nice to meet you, Andy," he says with a wolfish grin, but I can see his attention has been drawn across the room.

I turn slightly to see what has his focus. My breath nearly catches in my throat. The sight of Kyle and six other drop-dead-gorgeous men storming toward us is a sight I will never forget. I note they are all in black tuxedos. As I look closer, I realize I know a few of them.

Beau and Javier are right on Kyle's heels. Followed by a tall light brown guy with a full beard and broad shoulders. It clicks in my head. He's Daniel Hunt, the NFL player. I note the tall blond with piercing blue eyes next, Jordan Sokolov. I'd know that face anywhere; he's a hockey player and known as a playboy. I've met Ray Vincent before, but that's Chris Lionel beside him. They're both players in the NBA like Kyle.

They are moving across the room quickly, each one of them wearing pissed expressions on their gorgeous faces. My face scrunches in confusion. My hairs begin to rise in alarm. Kyle looks to be the most upset. I step into his side as soon as he reaches me. When I take in that his concentration is trained on the newcomer that never gave his name, my brows draw in. I turn back to what seems to be the source of all the tension.

"I'm Michael. Michael Fairchild," the newcomer says, while staring directly at Kyle.

I stiffen. I've never seen pictures of the man, but I know the name. I try not to curl into myself. I knew he had to be handsome to hold his own next to someone as sexy as Kyle. However, this is beyond what I imagined.

"You're playing with fire," Kyle says in a warning tone.

"Is that anyway to greet your former lover?" Michael says slyly.

"Best word in that sentence was former," Beau drawls.

"What are you up to, Michael?" Kyle says with a deadly calm.

"No, no." Javier waves his hand. "This is not the question I want to know. How are you here? Who invited you?"

"I have friends everywhere," Michael replies, looking at me this time.

He places his hands into his pockets and rocks back on his heels. The look on his face begins to reveal him for the snake he is. At any moment, he's about to strike.

"Let me be clear. Stay away from me and mine. Whatever game you're thinking about playing… dead it. Don't come for me, 'cause I haven't sent for you," Kyle seethes.

"Where's all the hostility coming from?" Michael asks, showing those perfect white teeth.

Kyle steps forward, getting into his face. I can feel the anger coming off him. It's so palpable I can taste it. Michael just continues to smile as if he's unbothered.

"You come to my club uninvited. Knowing I've revoked your membership. A membership I revoked after you threatened me and my friend and you want to know why *I'm* hostile," Javier hisses.

Kyle's head whips in Javier's direction, shock painted across his face. Javier's features are so tight with anger I think he's going to explode. Javier is such a laid-back, mild-mannered guy. I never thought I'd see him like this.

"Wait… he threatened you?" Kyle asks.

"I didn't want to involve you. Our friend here has overstepped his reach. Walk away, Fairchild. This will not end well for you. These are my brothers," Javier says, gesturing in a circle with his finger to encompass the men around him. "I am their keeper, as they are mine. You don't run a place like this with clean hands and a shallow reach. You still want to tango with me?"

"I think you've done outstayed your welcome," Beau drawls.

Michael throws his hands in the air. That smug smile still in place. I want to punch it right off. Kyle has told me a few stories that make me wonder why he ever bothered with him.

"No worries, fellas. I thought we were all friends. I see that has changed. Besides, I only came to scope out the competition." He pauses, allowing his eyes to turn to me. "I see you've done well finding a placeholder, Kyle. Gorgeous, very gorgeous. Maybe we'll keep him around when you're done having fun."

Kyle lunges for Michael, but Beau and Javier restrain him. Beau leans in to his ear to whisper something to calm him. I move to Kyle's side, placing a hand on his chest. It seems to soothe his anger. He wraps an arm around my waist, pulling me into him.

I can feel the eyes boring into the back of my head. I turn to look over my shoulder, and sure enough, Michael has a death glare aimed in my direction. He looks as if he might spit fire. It's the first time that stupid smile of his has completely fallen from his face. When Kyle's lips brush my temple, I see the flames of rage that blaze in Michael's eyes.

"We're done. Stop the phone calls, stop showing up unannounced, don't come to another one of my games," Kyle growls.

Michael moves to get in Kyle's face, but Chris and Ray block his stride. Michael tries to glare past them as if he's going to keep coming. Ray steps up in his face.

"You don't want this smoke," Ray says. "You just turn that ass around and walk away. You have no business here."

"I made you what you are, Kyle. You were a scared little boy before me. Don't ever forget that," Michael snarls.

"What?" Kyle scoffs. "Yeah, you're tripping. Do yourself a favor and stop with the recreational snorting. That coke is frying your brain."

Michael's face turns red. His jaw works as his glare moves around our small group. You can hear a pin drop in the rest of the room. I turn to see we have the attention of everyone, guests, staff. Heck, it feels like the decorations and lighting are leaning in and focusing on us.

"Your petty threats are like shit on the bottom of my shoe. I'll pay to have it washed away. I don't think any of you know who you're dealing with. We're not done," Michael bites out one last time before he turns and storms out.

He's words send a shiver through me. Like last words spoken before a wrath is unleashed. I don't think they should be taken lightly at all.

"Piece of trash," Javier mutters.

"You are going to tell me everything," Kyle says, pointing a finger at Javier.

"Sí, I already know this," Javier says on a frustrated breath.

CHAPTER TWENTY-TWO

A Little Favor

Andy

I'll admit. I've been in my feelings since meeting Michael in person. He left me unsettled for a number of reasons. When someone like that feels they own you, they never want to let go. I could see the possessiveness in his eyes, which has led me here to Mitch's security office.

I'm standing before a stony-faced Mitch. My brother isn't happy. As I flip through the pages in the file he's handed me, I can see why. I feel like someone has poured salt down my throat. I roll my tongue around in my mouth, trying to get rid of the nasty taste that's there.

"How do you know this guy, Andy?" Mitch says.

"He knows a friend of mine," I murmur, not looking up from the pages.

"This bastard is bad news," he says tightly.

"Yeah, I can see that."

"Do ya? I mean, he's an entitled prick, a real ratten chancer. The Fairchild's have done a lot of good for a lot of people in their past, but I think that family did a disservice to everyone adopting that fucker. He has a chip on his shoulder and feels the world owes him something.

"That file is jammers with shit that's way fucked-up. I don't like him, and I don't like the type of power he has. People like that never use it for any good. He's a chancer, he is. Dodgy as can be. I want ya to stay far away from him," Mitch warns.

"I'm not the one pursuing him. I think I may have caught his attention, though," I say, tossing the file back on Mitch's desk. "Thanks for doing this for me."

"Ya ask me to look into someone, I'm going to do it. I just don't like the drobes yer feeding me," he replies and shrugs.

You can take the detective off the force but never the detective out of the man. Mitch was all over digging into Michael Fairchild when I asked him to. I'm not so sure I should have now.

"I know it's killing you," I tease. "Thanks anyway."

"Ya take the piss out of me now, but I want to see ya laughing when this muppet shows his ass. Ya do know I'll feed a body to the wolves for ya?" he says, lifting a brow at me.

I grin at my big brother. I know he would. I'm just not asking him to. I wanted to know what I'm dealing with. I didn't come to Mitch to take care of my bullies for me.

"Aye, I know."

"Listen. This guy has a history of destroying careers for something as simple as disagreeing with him in a courtroom. The list of ex-boyfriends that have been blackballed and/or ruined after breaking up with him is insane. I'm still looking into a few things that don't look right. His ass should be disbarred for some of the shit in that file. If yer in some shit with him, ya tell me now. I'll run interference. Ya know it's what I do," Mitch offers.

"I won't be needing your expertise at the moment. I'll let you and the boys know if it comes to that," I reply.

"No, this one ya keep close. That motherfucker." He points to the file. "I'm serious about making him disappear. That's the only way to handle his kind."

"Aye, I hear ya," I mutter and frown, my own accent surfacing stronger. I ponder my brother's words and how on-target they are. I feel my own frustration rising. I start to think aloud. "But he's had a hard life. I think I just need to handle this right."

"What is this all about, And? Talk to me," Mitch says with concern lacing his voice.

"It's fine, Mitch. I just wanted to know a little more about him," I try to reassure him.

He shakes his head.

"No. You take that with ya and read it closely. Ya don't handle a guy like that. He handles you. Ya watch ya back. Deep pockets and a family that spoils just because they can makes a man like that dangerous. Dodgy as fuck he is. He was in the clink twice before he was eighteen, Andy. They sealed that shit away like it never happened."

"I'm not even going to ask how you got your hands on those sealed records, but yeah. I hear you," I say, pushing a hand through the front of my hair.

"I sure as fuck hope ya do. I don't want ya doin' a number on Ma. Ya make sure this isn't a problem," Mitch warns.

"Yeah, thanks," I reply, snatching the file and making my way out of his office.

CHAPTER TWENTY-THREE

Sweeter Things

Kyle

It's been a few weeks since the incident at Club Refuge. I'd been ignoring Michael's calls and his showing up to random games. For the most part he has been keeping his distance. Seeing him standing next to Andy was just a tipping point for me. If I would have known he was tripping and threatening my friends, I would have approached him sooner.

I refuse to let him and his bullshit come between me and Andy. Even though it seems like it has. There's been a little tension between us since the party. I haven't had the time to see where Andy's head is at. It's the playoffs. I hardly have a moment to myself.

We may have gotten ourselves together during the season, but tensions always run high during the playoffs. This is when all hell breaks loose and the team starts to fall to pieces. The outside world will blame me, not knowing all the inner workings of a team and a locker room. Some games, I'm exhausted just from snapping at my team to get over their shit for the forty-eight minutes we have to lay it all on the line.

It's like all of the bad shit that's been building up comes to a head right during the time we've worked so hard to get to all year. I've wanted to punch a teammate or two in the face for making dumb-ass choices that affect our team—not just their personal lives. It's one of the reasons I like to keep my personal life separate. We have enough weight on us, our bodies, and our team.

Although, what I don't want is to have conflict in my relationship on my mind. I plan to deal with that here and now while we have a short break in the series. Our next opponent hasn't been decided yet. We nearly swept our last one, which afforded us a small breather.

"Watch your step," I say as I lead a blindfolded Andy forward.

I try not to laugh at the way he's reaching out trying to feel his way. I wanted to do something that said Andy. Something I know he would do all alone and be completely content with.

"Where are we going?" he asks for the millionth time.

"Just keep moving. We're almost there. A few more steps," I respond.

I stop us in the center of the room. I called in a few favors for this one. Tara and Emma were a big help in getting it all set up for me. I'm a bit nervous. I've never done anything like this for anyone.

"Okay, stop right here," I say when we get to the center of the room.

From here he'll be able to take it all in. I look around and reassure myself that everything is in place. I wipe a hand across my forehead, biting my lip. Flexing my fingers, I suck up my nerves and reach to remove the blindfold I placed on Andy when we left my house.

When I release the fabric and it falls away, Andy slowly turns his head, taking in the room. He turns in a circle before facing me. His blue-gray eyes are soft, and a smile graces his full lips. Grabbing the front of my shirt, he tugs me to him.

"I don't know how you do it every time. This is amazing," he says against my lips.

"You like?"

Andy pulls away slightly, looking up at me like I've lost my mind. He waves his hands around, with wide eyes. His mouth opens and closes, and a hand locks into the front of his hair as he gathers himself and his thoughts.

"Are you kidding me? A dinner in the middle of a library. I can smell the pages and the leather binds of the older books, mixed with the aroma of something delicious. Where are we?"

"It's an old mansion of a friend of a friend's. It's been in their family for generations, and the library has thousands of books. Mostly rare and first editions," I explain.

"This is amazing. I've always wanted a library like this. I'd be lost in here for hours," he muses, his eyes lighting up with the thought.

"Noted, no building a library for you to hide from me in and definitely not a workshop for those antiques," I tease. "I'd never see you again."

Andy's arms go around my neck.

"You say that as if we'll be living together," he says quietly.

"I've been thinking about it. I'm just not sure. Mason's so young. I don't think he'll understand. I promised my sister—"

"Relax, Kyle. I know. He always comes first. We're just talking. I'm not trying to pack my things and move in," he cuts me off teasingly.

I blow out a breath, swaying us where we stand. I've been thinking about this a lot. I want to take our relationship to the next level, but I don't know how this will affect Mason. I worry every day if I'm making the right choices concerning him.

Should I start to bring him on the road with me and provide a tutor? I'm his only parent. Is it really okay for me to always be away? Am I spoiling him too much because of my guilt? The list goes on and on.

My sister always used to say let a child be a child. To expose my nephew to the truth is also asking him to hide it as well. That's adult shit. I want him to be a kid. Sure, coming out to the world would solve that, but then I'm handing my nephew a cruel world that will force him to defend me.

He's already a young black male in a world that's designed to see your skin first and everything else about you last. He has enough on his plate.

"Come back," Andy whispers.

When my eyes focus on him, I can see his searching my face. The concern I see there helps me to breathe again. That soothing feeling fills me, and I allow it to take over.

"You're an amazing uncle. Mason is the luckiest little boy in the world. We don't have to rush into anything you don't feel is right for him. I'm here no matter what. Whatever you need from me. If you want me to step up and help out more next school year, I can," Andy offers.

"Michael and I would sleep in separate rooms sometimes when Mason was over," I blurt out without thinking.

The air shifts around us. Andy drops his arms from around my neck and looks away from me. I want to kick myself for opening my mouth. Yet at the same time, we need to address this. I need to know what's been going through his head.

"Let's sit and eat. Then we can talk," I say.

Andy moves to the table set in the center of the room. It's like he can't get away from me fast enough. He's in his seat before I get a chance to pull his chair. So much for me trying to cater to him tonight.

Boy, how a single sentence can change an entire night.

I lift the lids from both plates and set them aside. Watching his reaction, I go to take my own seat across from him. At least he can't hide his smile when he sees his favorite dish—his mother's shepherd's pie. Tara got her to make it for me.

Without a word, Andy tucks into his food. I do the same, giving myself time to find the right words to address this without it ruining the entire night completely. Andy's moan pulls me from my thoughts. I look up into his blue-grays to see the sincere smile there.

"This is Ma's. I would know it anywhere," he says.

"I see why you're always bragging about it. This is good," I reply.

"She's gifted. Best shepherd's pie in the world," Andy croons. "This will be worth the ten-mile run in the morning."

"I thought we'd spend the morning in. I don't fly out until tomorrow night," I say, gauging his response.

"Thought Mason would be at the house," he says cautiously.

"He and Emma are staying the night at the house. We're staying the night here."

"Oh," he says. A thousand other unsaid words can be heard in the single utterance.

I place my fork down and sit back in my seat. I look deep, prodding for the root of the problem. The things Andy won't say aloud. When I see the latch I need to pop to release my Andy, I inhale.

Once again, I'm going to step out of my comfort zone for this man. I'm going to give him a piece of me that no one else has. More wounds that I've suppressed in order to survive.

"I've told you before. He was my first real relationship. I stuck with it because it was what I knew. I met him at nineteen. He chased me down for almost a year. I was in awe that he wanted someone as young as me, someone from the hood just barely making it out because of some luck, talent, and determination. Michael offered me things I hadn't allowed anyone else to—attention, what I thought was love." I pause, staring at my palms.

As I run my right thumb over the lines of my left palm. I take a moment to think before lifting my eyes back to Andy's.

"He played off the things he could see we had in common, things I shielded others from seeing. His own abuse. I... I felt understood," I scoff.

I stop, opening my mouth to let a breath escape as I draw a hand down my face. Frustration with my younger self has my knee bouncing under the table.

"I was young and dumb. I didn't see that it was all a way to control me and the relationship. My friends tried to warn me. I thought I was mature and could hold my own. My maturity was both a gift and curse in that relationship. I knew what I wanted for my career. I was determined in having that. It's what got in the way of Michael fully controlling me.

"He's a master manipulator. If he wants something he does whatever he has to get it. Lie, cheat, steal…. When I bought my house, I had no intension of him moving in. I came home from training camp and he had it fully furnished and had moved his stuff in." I snort, shaking my head.

"We fought about it. Even broke up over it. It was about two months later when I got into another relationship. It wasn't anything serious, but Michael manipulated the situation, causing a breakup, and I believe he cost Martin his job." I finish my words, making a sour face.

"Who's to say he won't try that with us? I could lose you. I saw the look in his face. He's not just giving up. What makes you so sure you won't go back? That he won't suck you back in," Andy says, pushing his plate away.

"I'm not going back into that. Losing my sister was the worst thing that's ever happened to me—and I've been through some shit. She was there for me all of my life, and then the times she needed me, I couldn't do shit.

"I had to sit there and watch her die. Nothing hurts as much as failing the one person that means everything to you. The person that believed in you. Yeah, I have some great friends, but my sister… she went through the dirt with me. She knew me when I felt like I'd always be filthy. When I felt like no one could ever love me. And… and I couldn't do shit to take her pain and suffering like she did for me."

I have to pause. The tears have started to flow. I've never shared with anyone how I felt about the last two and a half years of my life. I've buried it all to be there for my sister when she needed and then to be there for nephew and my team. I haven't stopped for a single moment to deal with my own feelings and hurts.

"Kyle—"

"Let me finish. I couldn't give her what she needed, and she died. That was the time Michael was supposed to forget himself and think about me. When someone loves you, that's what they do. When he left and made everything about him. I felt like I was watching that shit from outside of my body, but at the same time, I told myself not to stop him. If he could go then, he was toxic to begin with.

"It clicked that I was in a relationship with a narcissist. It will always be about him. I've failed one person I love in my life. I don't plan to ever repeat that. If I let Michael come between us, I'll be failing everyone I love," I say, wiping the tears from my eyes.

"I don't like him. He's a snake, and I get a bad vibe from him," Andy mutters.

Something else weighs his words down. However, I visibly see when the shutters slam down. I don't catch it fast enough, but I immediately assume it could have been fear.

"I'm not going to let him come at you. I've got this," I reassure him.

"You're underestimating me. I'm sure he is too. I'm not a punk. I know who he is now. I'll be ready next time," he replies, folding his arms over his chest.

I bite my lip, tilting my head to the side as I stare at Andy. Yeah, I've underestimated him a time or two. Yet I'm learning. Andy is a lot more than meets the eyes.

Andy

I feel guilty. Kyle opened himself up to tell me how he felt while losing his sister and breaking up with Michael after. That should have taken this date over the top, but I'm hiding my own secret.

I haven't told Kyle about everything Mitch found out for me. I'm not sure how much of it Kyle already knows. I can't see him knowing half of what I know and still allowing Michael anywhere near Mason. A shiver runs through me every time I think of that file.

My biggest problem now is that I don't know how to tell Kyle what I did—or if I even want to. Trust is a big thing for Kyle. I should just come out and tell him, but I still can't get over that look on Michael's face. Like I'm easy prey. After what I now know, that look is burned in my mind.

"What are you thinking about?" Kyle asks while running his hand through my hair.

After dinner Kyle sat watching me as I got lost in the library. Eventually, I found something I wanted to read. I settled on *A Tale of Two Cities*. We moved to the perfect little reading alcove I hadn't noticed until Kyle pointed it out.

A cute cozy spot tucked beneath the stairs. Almost like a window seat but wider. Wide enough for Kyle to sit and still have room for me to lie on my back with my head in his lap. A window provides a view of the grounds behind the house leading to the gorgeous maze of a garden—Kyle promised we'd walk it in the morning.

"I can just imagine this spot being built for someone that was ill or unable to get about. On warm summer days this was where they could sit and read while basking in the rays of the sun," I murmur. "Or on a rainy day, they spent their day reading and getting lost in a world far away."

I speak my thoughts from before my mind wondered to my guilt. It's the first thing I can think of to say as the internal war within continues. I lean the book against my chest, looking up over my head at him.

He's staring back at me, watching closely just as he always does. My curiosity is piqued. I once attributed his watchfulness as him being in tune or intuitive. Now, as I hold my breath trying to keep my secret locked away from his talent for pulling at the truth, I see something else.

It's deep in those dark brown eyes. Almost like the fear of not knowing or not seeing. It tugs my heartstring, pulling me up from his lap as I catch it.

"You watch everyone so closely. You see everything. I never thought about it before," I muse aloud.

Kyle turns his gaze away from mine. This time I can feel that he's trying to hide. I sit the book down on a nearby table. Like he always does to get my attention, I reach to place my fingers beneath his chin and turn his head to me.

Neither of us says a word. I dig deep just as he does, looking to see what goes unnoticed by others. My eyes narrow in, and almost instantly his words slam into me.

"She was there for me all of my life, and then the times she needed me, I couldn't do shit."

I don't know why those words rush me, but I know they hold the key to what I'm missing. I drop my own eyes, searching my feelings and thinking of the knowledge I have of Kyle. I close my eyes slowly when it starts to add up.

"You didn't know she took the abuse for you. You didn't see it," I say on a shallow breath.

"No." His word comes out broken.

"You were a kid. Kyle—"

"Don't."

I open my eyes and see the torture written all over his face. The ache I feel runs so deep. I understand him on so many levels now. His need to protect, the need to be a team player, but not the center of attention, his need to always have a choice. It all clicks into place like a lock and key.

"She did what she thought would protect yo—"

"I should have seen it. I was so busy thinking that I'd finally become invisible. It was almost a year before he told me why he stopped coming into my room. It was his way of punishing us both. Shaming her in front of me and tearing me to pieces. There's nothing in this world that will ever make that right," he says tightly.

"I... Okay. One of the things that used to make me feel so pissed off was when people would tell me they understood what I was going through or when they'd tell me how to feel. I won't do that. I can want to understand how you feel, but that doesn't mean I will. I can never be in your feelings. So...." I stop talking.

There's nothing else I can say. I don't even want to imagine what that all must have been like for him. I don't think I would have survived sanity. I'm just as protective of my siblings as they are of me. Not being able to keep something terrible from happening to them would have broken me in two.

"After that... I knew. I knew every single time he touched her. I could see it in her eyes. When I started to get big enough to challenge him, I did all I could to protect her. He'd just wait until I wasn't around, and she would try to hide it from me.

"I offered him me, just like she did. I wasn't small enough for him anymore. He couldn't get his kicks off of placing that same fear in me. He told my aunt I was gay. No matter how hard I denied it, she wouldn't listen. She took me to the church to have me baptized for the second time and made me tell the pastor my *impure thoughts*," he tells me.

"Wow." My own hands are trembling with rage.

"I was thirteen. Already angry and confused. That shit just made me hate everyone. When kids would pick fights with me, I'd beat the shit out of them. I didn't have to take shit from anyone outside of that house after all I went through. Savanna and I would beat up bullies together. It was our way to feel like we had some control, I guess," he says, his eyes distant as if lost in the memories.

"We don't have to talk about this," I say.

"Nah, it's out there now…. He stole our innocence. We never got to be kids after we lost our mother. We were turned into the villains when we were the victims. My aunt blamed Savanna. Love was such a confusing thing for me for so long. I had my aunt and uncle claiming everything they did, they did out of love." He goes quiet after his last words.

I toe off my shoes and pull my knees to my chest. I shift until my back meets the wall behind me. Waving him to me, I let my legs slide down a bit and make room between my thighs.

"Come here," I say.

He looks at me for a beat before moving toward me. I reach for his arm, causing him to turn his back to me, settling in between my legs. I wrap my arms and legs around him and bury my face into his neck.

"This is what love feels like. If you ever need a reminder, you let me know. I'll show you anytime you need," I whisper into his skin.

His hands cover mine, and he nods slowly. I don't know how much time passes as I nuzzle his neck and pour my love into him. I hold on for dear life. As if letting go would be releasing him into harm's way.

"Thanks," he says into the silence a while later.

"I love you," I say back.

"I think I might love you more," he says reflectively.

"Not a chance."

If only you knew, I'd die for you.

CHAPTER TWENTY-FOUR

Best Uncle Ever

Kyle

"Today we have Kyle Tyson with us. Kyle is a dynamic player. I personally love watching him on the court. Welcome, Kyle," the interviewer says as he sits across from me.

I try not to show my annoyance as this interview runs late, keeping me from my plans for the evening with Mas. He has texted me so much through Emma's phone that I told her to bring him down to the studio, thinking I'd be finished by now. They should be arriving any minute.

"Thanks for having me, Derrick," I say, forcing a smile to my face.

"Man, I'm so glad to have you here. I tell you, watching your team crash and burn during the playoffs last year was painful. You guys started the season off rough with those critical injuries, but I was rooting for you. You pulled that team together and carried them to the playoffs, but things just fell apart in the second round," Derrick says.

"I mean, we play as a team. We all worked hard last year to get as far as we went. We learned some lessons in that second round. Things I think we can avoid this year," I reply.

"You know, that's one of the things I admire about you as a player. You don't take credit on or off the court. Your team is a part of the process. It would be so easy for you to claim stardom. Yet you don't. Do you think that has an impact on how your team performs?"

"I think my team is my family. It's my job to always do what's in our best interest. Whether that's passing the ball, sitting a game out when I know I'm off, being there for a teammate in need. That's what makes us a powerhouse. Knowing we have each other's back," I reply.

"I'm glad you say that. I wasn't expecting you to perform the same last year or this year after your loss. I'm sorry about your sister, by the way. Actually, you've played three seasons since, barely taking a breather. Can you say that your team was a part of you returning to the court so soon, seemingly without missing a beat?"

I shift in my seat, not hiding the frown that forms on my lips. I told them not to go there. I'm already stewing because my agent talked me into this interview.

I've had to take on more of a leadership role this season, but we're taking care of business. Just as I thought, the media has been up my ass, but I've been playing my position. They get what I give them. Not that they don't still try to put out there what they want just to give the people something.

"I'm feeling optimistic this year. The few trades we've had has brought the synergy back to the team. I have a good feeling about the playoffs," I say, totally dodging his question.

Actually, I think we can take it all this year. I'd rather focus on that. This first series is one we should sail through.

"Yes, you had some big trades. I'd say it left you with the brunt of the work on the team. You're handling it all extremely well, though. Especially now that you've become the sole leader on the team and for all intents and purposes you're now a single father. How are you managing to juggle all of that? Let me tell you, the pictures from Sky Zone were adorable," he says with a big-ass fake smile.

I feel my own face tighten. My nostrils flare. I turn to look over at my agent and scowl. Furious doesn't begin to name how I felt when pictures of me and Mas at Sky Zone appeared on the internet. That's my personal time with my nephew as I spent some of the break with him. I think what upset me most about the story is the fact that it added that Mason lost his mom and how I had to step in to be his guardian.

My agent received endless calls for a feature on my story. The sports networks were drooling for the opportunity. I'm just not that guy. I'm not about to do a forty-minute mini documentary on my and my nephew's deepest pain to push the emotional buttons of the fans. They're just not going to use us so they can fill seats in the arena and drive ratings for games.

"Thanks," I reply sternly as I turn back to Derrick. "I'm doing what's best in each situation."

The interviewer laughs. "Wow, you're always so closed off about your personal life. I, for one, enjoy seeing other sides of you. It adds to my respect for you on the court."

"Here's the thing, though. My life is not for anyone's enjoyment. It's not a game—"

"Uncle Kyle!" My words are cut off by Mason's squeal.

My head jerks in his direction, and I groan internally. He's rushing toward me faster than Emma can catch him. At seven, he's not worried about the cameras and people around. This should have been over by now. If they hadn't rearranged the lineup, this wouldn't be happening.

Mason reaches me before anyone can stop him, and he hops right into my lap, wrapping his arms around me. I instinctively embrace him back. His tight hug melts my anger. I kiss the top of his head, and he pulls away to beam up at me.

"Are you ready? I have a surprise for you. I've been waiting *all day*." He drags out the last two words exasperatedly.

I can't help laughing at him.

"Buddy, I'm in the middle of work. I need a few more minutes," I explain.

"Aw, man," he whines.

"Hey, Mason. We were just talking about you. How are you, little buddy?" This slick-ass reporter purrs.

Mason turns around to face him, settling in my lap to reply to him. I can see the innocence in his face showing on the monitors around us. His eyes light up when he takes in his surroundings.

"I'm great," he sings out. Then his voice lowers to a secret whisper. "I came to get my Uncle Kyle. I have a surprise for him. Aunt Emma and Uncle Andy have been helping me plan it for a long time."

It takes everything in me not to stiffen at the mention of Andy's name. I place a hand on Mason's forehead, tipping his head back to place another kiss on top his head. Lifting him from my lap, I place him on his feet.

"We're going to go soon. Let me finish up. Emma," I call for her to come closer to get Mason.

"Okay. Bye," Mason says, waving at the interviewer.

"Bye," Derrick chuckles, before returning his attention to me. "Precious kid."

"Thank you. At the end of the day he's the reason I work as hard as I do. But, hey, you heard the little guy. He has a surprise for me. I don't want to disappoint him. Hope we give the fans a great playoffs to watch. I know the guys are ready and I'm ready, so it's go time. Thank you for having me," I say, bringing the interview to a close.

"You guys have started off strong. I'm sure your sister would be proud of you," Derrick says slyly.

"She'd want me to keep my promise and be on time for my playdate." I flash a smile, showing all my teeth as I stand.

Derrick rushes to close the segment as I start to walk off set. I'm pulling my mic off heading right for my agent. I'm going to ream his ass. I was very specific about them not mentioning my sister or nephew.

"Kyle, I'm all over it, man," Mark groans, rubbing his temples. "I'm seriously sorry. I got this. You take the little guy and get out of here."

"You ready, Uncle Kyle?" Mason asks, almost jumping out of his skin.

I bite back my words and turn on a smile for my nephew. The sparkle in his eyes soothes my soul. It reminds me I have too much to be happy about.

It was good to finally get time with him during the off-season. He has been doing so well in school. He's crushing the first grade. I'm so proud of him and all the awards and good grades he has brought home this year.

He's happy and safe. That's what matters. I brush off the interview and scoop my little man up. I tickle his stomach as I glare at Mark over his shoulder.

We'll talk, I mouth to my agent.

He gives me a defeated nod. I'm not stupid enough to think this wasn't a well-planned ambush. The interview had been running on time until Mark and I mentioned my nephew coming to meet up with me. Someone had to have overheard. Mason just innocently fell into their scheme.

"You said you had a good practice when I texted you. Do you think you guys are going to win this time?" Mason asks, wrapping an arm around my neck.

"I think we have a great chance this year," I reply, walking toward the exit while taking in his pensive face.

"I think Blitz will bring you luck this time. He was too small last year to do you any good. This time will be different," he says confidently, nodding his head to himself with a beaming smile on his face.

My brows dip. This kid is up to something in that little brain. I wonder if I'll be getting him another dog this time around. Blitz, our blue pit, adores Mason as much as Mason adores him. I thought the kid would be crushed when his lucky charm for me didn't work out last season.

"Luck is always great to have, but hard work and talent come into play as well. Me and the guys have to show up so we can benefit from Blitz's magic," I tell him.

"You got this, Uncle Kyle. No one works as hard as you do. Believe in yourself. You can do anything, and you have me, Blitz, Uncle Andy, Uncle Beau, and Aunt Emma. Happy people win, and you make us happy, so we're here to make you happy too," he replies like the wisest little kid in the world.

"What's this surprise about?" I ask.

"We have to go to it so you can see it," he giggles while I strap him up in the booster seat.

"Well, let's get out of here," I say.

Andy

I've always known that Mason was a special child, but I've watched him spend over a year planning this for Kyle—I have no words. I think this is just what Kyle needs. He's still so unsure of himself when it comes to Mason. He doesn't give himself enough credit for how well Mason is developing.

Emma outdid herself on this one. If Kyle thought she went over-the-top on Mason's last birthday party, he will be floored by this. Mason's focus on the details for this is mind-blowing.

I can't wait for them to arrive.

"They're here," Beau calls.

"This is just so adorable," Mrs. Dalton gushes. She pulls Beau into a hug. "I'm so proud of your brother. And that little one is an angel."

"I'm so glad I could help and be a part of this," I say.

"Oh, darlin', you did such a good job. Emma has done nothing but rave about all you've done. This place looks amazing," Mrs. Dalton coos.

"Thanks, Mrs. Dalton," I reply.

"You stop that. I told you to call me Daphne," she says. "I can't wait until my Beau here finds someone like you."

"Mama," Beau says dryly.

"What? You have to live again at some point," she huffs.

"I don't see you dating," he mumbles.

"Actually… I do have a date this weekend," she says, waving him off.

"What? Who—"

"Keep your eyes closed, Uncle Kyle." Mason's small excited voice rings as they enter the house where we're awaiting them, cutting Beau's words off.

Beau curses low as Mason and Emma lead Kyle into the living room. I'm holding my breath, while feeling a rush running through my veins. I can only imagine how excited Mason must be. From the beaming smile on his tiny face, he's ready to burst.

"Okay, you can open them now!" Mason squeals, causing Blitz to bark.

I've never seen Kyle look more gorgeous than in this moment. The look of awe and vulnerability in his face is breathtaking. His mouth falls open, he stumbles back a few steps, his head turns to take it all in. I can see the moment his eyes mist over. It's too perfect a moment for anyone to speak.

This is perfect. You so deserve it, babe.

Kyle

I don't know what to say. I can't believe my eyes. I have no idea how they did this. I have no words for what I feel. I place my hand on Mason's shoulder and pull him closer.

"This was all his idea. He wanted to do this for you," Emma says beside me.

"Do you like it?" Mason whispers, his voice sounding nervous.

I kneel beside him, partly to get eye level with him and partly too overwhelmed to stand on my own two feet. I place my forehead to his and envelop him in the biggest hug I have to give. My sister left me with one of the greatest parts of her.

"I love it," I choke out.

"They're all digital frames. Uncle Andy and Aunt Emma helped me to find all the pictures, and Uncle Andy loaded them to the frames. Uncle Beau put them on the walls. He said we can take them down without messing up the walls," Mason says proudly.

"This is awesome," I reply, still not able to express how I truly feel.

"Come on. Let me show you." He wiggles free to tug me with him.

We move to the first living room wall that has different-sized digital frames flashing on it. My jaw works beneath my skin as I try to hold back the tears. The first few frames have pictures of me and Savanna.

We're at my high school graduation, the day I bought my first car, my draft day, the day Mason was born and I held him for the first time. All of the images flood my mind with memories. Good times in my life.

"You have to remember all of the happy," Mason says, turning his face up to look at me. "You're a winner, Uncle Kyle. This is the right lucky charm this time. Our family and all our good stuff. See, that's us with Uncle Mitch and Uncle John."

I follow his finger to the picture he's pointing to. It dawns on me that I've brought so many new people into Mason's life and they treat him like one of their own. I never have to worry about who's going to look after him. They're usually fighting over him.

"These all looks amazing. Where'd you come up with this idea?" I ask.

"Remember when Mommy wasn't feeling well and you helped me make her the picture book?" he answers.

My brow furrows as I think back. I do remember it, but that seems like so long ago.

"Yeah, I remember."

"Mommy said it was what she needed. It was her book of love. No matter where she was she would remember how happy her family always made her, and it would make her happy and brave to get through anything, anywhere," he explains. "Mommy would want to do this for you. She would want you to be happy and brave when you go to play. It's your time, Uncle Kyle. Look at how big your family is now. You have all the love in the world."

I shove my fist in my mouth to bite back the sob that wants to tear through me. Beau and Andy come to my sides to wrap their arms around my shoulders and waist. I feel like they're holding me up. Mason wraps his small body around my leg.

"I'm so proud of you, Uncle Kyle. I want to be just like you when I grow up. You're the best uncle ever," Mason says, taking my knees right out from under me.

My arms go around him as I fall to the floor. I do something I haven't done since the day my sister passed. It just feels right. It's the only way I know how to let out what I feel.

Andy

I'm stunned. The room has stopped. No one has moved since the first note left his mouth. I've never heard Kyle sing before. I have goose bumps, chills, and every hair on my body is standing up.

He is crooning out "A Change is Gonna Come" in such a soulful way each note is running through me straight to my core. Mason has his arms bound around Kyle's neck while Kyle rocks back and forth singing. I feel like I'm intruding on something that's not meant to be seen by anyone else.

Emma is to my left with her arms wrapped around her middle as she sways to the words that are pouring from somewhere deep inside of Kyle. Beau has his head bent, with his mother tucked under his arm. Daphne has a hand raised in the air as her head shakes and tears roll down her cheeks.

I read so much into the lyrics. Kyle's harder days have ended and it's time for change. This will be his new beginning. He starts to sing his own lyrics to the song.

"My change has come. Oh… little one… you've help me stop running. It's been too long… so long for me… but you open my eyes for me… I know…."

He falls silent, still rocking Mason. I don't realize I'm trying to rub my chills away until Emma reaches to grasp my hand. I squeeze her fingers tightly.

Kyle lifts his head almost on cue. He looks over Mason's head at me, capturing my gaze and holding it. The intensity in his eyes sends a tremor through me. He bites his lip as he sends a heated look of promise my way.

Thank you. I love you, he mouths.

I feel my entire face go up in flames. He's lips turn up at the sight of my blush. Almost two years and he still has this effect on me.

"You know, you could have just said thank you," Beau deadpans, breaking up the thick atmosphere.

Everyone bursts into laughter. Kyle flips him the finger behind Mason's back. Beau shrugs, pulling a face that says, *what?*

"I'll remember that the next time you ask me to sing for one of your little friends," Kyle tosses back.

"When was the last time that happened?" Beau waves him off.

"It needs to happen soon," Daphne mumbles.

"Oh boy. See what you started?" Beau rolls his eyes. "Wait, we need to talk about this date."

"My daddy has been long gone, son. I don't need to talk you about a thing," she says.

"Wait, what?" Kyle's head whips in Daphne's direction.

"Exactly," Beau replies.

"Come on, Mas. It's getting crowded in here. Grandma has ice cream," Daphne sings and saunters off.

Emma and I look at each other, trying to hold in our laughter. I roll my lips, but the shake of Emma's shoulders makes me release my laughter. That woman is feisty. Her date is in for a surprise.

I turn to look at Kyle, and he winks at me. That promise of things to come highlighted in his eyes again. I give my own sly smile and wink back. I'm totally game.

CHAPTER TWENTY-FIVE

Blindsided

Kyle

We've breezed through the first round and the conference semifinals, two teams so far. None of them made it easy for us, but I've been on fire like never before. I feel unstoppable. I've been averaging thirty points and better.

Every time I think of Mason sitting in front of the TV cheering me on, thinking of me as his hero, I push harder. I've dug so deep with each game I've been surprising myself. I can't wait to start the next series. I know we can bring this one home once we move to the next level. The conference finals will be ours once we get there.

Tonight we're all celebrating. The complex is 75 percent of the way complete, Andy received a raise at work, and there may be an opening for the principal position at his school sooner than he thought.

Beau, Emma, and Tara came out to celebrate with us since Mas wanted to spend the weekend with Daphne. I think she bribed him with cookies and her famous chili. He had his things packed and set by the door this morning, ready to go.

"Man, I haven't had this much fun in a long time." Beau laughs as we make our way out of the bar and grill we just dined at.

"I know. Andy and Tara are always good for a laugh," Emma tries to say innocently.

"Us? You were the one causing all of the trouble this time," Tara tosses back.

"Me," Emma mock gasps, placing a hand to her chest.

"Always the troublemaker." I pull Emma into a headlock, causing her to laugh.

"I don't know—"

Emma stops midsentence as flashing lights bombard us. There are cameras flashing all around us. I'm confused at first. They're all calling out questions at the same time.

"Kyle, Kyle, over here. Is it true? Are you dating Andy Connor?" I hear shouted over everyone else.

I freeze. What do I say to that? Who even asked the question? I don't know what would prompt them to ask it in the first place.

"We have pictures of you two on what looks like a date. Would you like to confirm?" someone else shouts.

"Bullshit, prove it," I say without thinking.

I know there aren't any pictures because we never go anywhere in public as a couple. We go out with groups of friends, we take Mason places together occasionally, but Emma is always with us and we never act like a couple. Fury rises from this invasion of my privacy.

"Here, I have the photos," one guys responds.

I go to look, but Emma places a hand on my arm, stepping forward instead to take the device from his hand. I watch her face as she takes in the image. The guy is so helpful, he swipes right for her to see more. Emma purses her lips and nearly tosses the device back at him.

"I have to agree with Kyle. These are bullshit," Emma scoffs.

Andy is off to the left staring down at his phone with a confused look on his face. I move to hold my hand out for the device, wanting to see for myself. Emma goes to Andy's side, huddling over his phone, while she starts to murmur something to him. Tara and Beau crowd my sides.

"You guys need to do better research. You'll find the originals to those were posted almost two years ago. When I first started dating Emma." Andy's voice booms firmly over the crowd.

I try not to look stunned as the words leave his mouth. Looking out of the corner of my eye, I see Emma standing beside him with her hand on his chest and a smile on her lips. The cameras are still all in my face, causing me not to lift my head. I turn my eyes back to the device in my hands.

Emma.

I groan internally. She shouldn't be dragging herself into this. She's known me long enough to know better. I can't believe Andy is going along with this.

The pictures are from my first meeting with Tara. The lunch when we met to talk about getting Mason a puppy. These are the same pictures that painted Tara and I as a couple, but they seem to be altered or taken from a different angle or something.

"Oh my God," Tara giggles. "Babe, these are the pictures from our first date."

She looks up at me lovingly, throwing me for a loop just like her brother. Tara pulls out her phone and holds it up. I start to laugh inside. It's a running joke in the Connor home that Tara is out to steal me from Andy. She keeps that photo as her screensaver. At the moment, it's about to be a prop in what these three have decided to pull.

"I have the real photo here." She lights the screen up and holds it up. "I mean, it's from so long ago. You can still find the originals online. This is just someone sending you all on a wild goose chase."

"Emma, we thought you and Kyle were together. How did you end up with Andy?" someone calls out.

"You also thought Kyle was with Andy just a few seconds ago. I mean, y'all are never very well-informed. I've told you a million times Kyle is like a brother to me, literally. We've never been romantically involved. Could my family and I enjoy the rest of our night?" Emma turns up that Southern charm, her words sounding sugary sweet.

"The rumor has it that you guys live together," someone else pushes. "Kyle, are you sure this isn't true?"

I flip the bird and start pushing my way through. I'm not explaining a single fucking thing to these people. I appreciate what these three just did, but it was too much of a response to something that doesn't deserve life. Emma should know better. I never answer those types of questions. We shouldn't have started now.

Andy

Kyle has been in a funky mood since we arrived at his place. With Mason staying the night at Daphne's, we had planned for me to stay over. This isn't the kind of night I had in mind.

When Kyle isn't pacing and grumbling to himself, he's slamming or throwing something at the wall. I've never seen him this pissed off. I've just been waiting for him to cool down.

"It's Michael. I know it is." His words shoot ice through my veins.

I thought the same thing. That snake has been way too quiet. I never expected him to just run away with his tail tucked between his legs. This totally reeks of the foul types of shit that man would do.

I've never had such a feeling of loathing for anyone in my life. I can just see my fingers clutching his neck as I squeeze the life out of those cold eyes. I shake that thought off. I'm not the monster he is.

"Why now?" I ask.

"Because his ass has been sitting and watching. Mas mentioned you in that live interview. I've been playing well in the playoffs. He's been looking for the right time to disrupt our lives. I'm sure hearing Mason say your name sent him into boiling bunnies land," Kyle says.

"How can you be so sure he heard that?"

"Because his bitch ass sent me a text from a number I didn't have blocked," he grumbles.

"When?"

"The next day," Kyle grunts, flopping down on the couch beside me.

I let his words sink in. We've been going strong for almost two years. I'm not going to stand by and watch this monster come and destroy our relationship.

I never told Kyle about all the things I found out about Michael. Given how angry he is now, I don't think it's the best time to. He leans his head back against the couch, and I reach to brush a hand over his hair.

His hand shoots out to catch mine, bring it to his lips. With a gentle tug he pulls me toward him. I go willingly. His hand grasps my thigh, pulling me to straddle his hips.

Kyle cups the back of my neck, drawing me in. I meet his lips, and he captures mine. I go to deepen the kiss, but he pulls away.

"Are we good?"

"Yeah, why wouldn't we be?" I reply.

"I reacted earlier. I wasn't thinking about my words or your feelings," he says cautiously.

"You and I both know I'm not that sensitive about stuff like that anymore. I understand."

"You and Emma really didn't have to do what you guys did, Tara either. I would have preferred if you didn't. It's better not to give them anything at all," he says, pulling a face.

"Sorry, I think we were trying to defuse the situation. When Emma whispered to me what to do, I sort of just reacted like you did.

"I totally understand what you mean, though. I was just shocked. The pictures weren't doctored. They were taken from a different angle. Someone else took them. It's the exact same moments." I reveal what I've been thinking all night.

"Yeah, I noticed that too. They look more professional than the originals as well," he points out.

"You caught that too?"

"Yup," he says, popping the p at the end of his word. "He's been planning for a while."

I cup his face, placing my forehead to his.

"Let him," I breathe. "He can plan whatever he wants. We're not going to let that ruin any more of our night."

I lean in and nip his lower lip. He groans, catching my lip with his teeth and pulling. I let my hands glide to his silky waves.

"You sure you want to start this?" he breathes against my chin. "You're asking for trouble."

"I know what I want," I purr back, reaching for the hem of my shirt and tugging it over my head.

His eyes devour me, making me feel like the most desirable man in the world. Knowing Kyle, he's only deciding where he wants to start. He lifts a finger under my jaw and drags it down my neck, to my collarbone, down to my belly button where he pauses, tilting his head.

"Are you feeling adventurous tonight?" he says.

I bite my lip and nod.

"Get up," he commands.

It's such a sharp order, I move before I process the words. I'm standing before him as he lifts to his feet, looming over me. His brown eyes glow with something I've never seen before. My heart rate picks up. I'm turned on by the dark look.

"Do you trust me?"

"Yes," I answer without question.

Kyle leads me to his bedroom by the hand. I've come to anticipate these moments each and every time. He has a way of making me insane with want. Maybe it's the time we spend apart, or it could just be the fact that he oozes sex appeal. It's in his every move. Even now, his back muscles move so fluidly beneath his shirt. He owns each step he takes.

His body would be the perfect sonata if his motions had their own music. It would be a composition I would want to hear on repeat. My belly tightens with expectations of the music we'll make together tonight.

When we enter the bedroom, he stops at the foot of the bed, turning to me. He releases my belt, completing the task of underdressing me. I'm so hard I spring free as soon as he peels my jeans down my hips.

He steps back, and his gaze swipe over me. I fight not to cross my arms over my chest. I'm still working on that reaction. It doesn't hurt that Kyle makes me feel as if I'm in the perfect body. He loves the skin I'm in, flaws and all.

He tilts his head toward the bed, prompting me to get onto it. I follow his unspoken directions, climbing to the center. I sit and watch as he peels his clothes from that flawless body. His skin is so smooth and unblemished, as if he were airbrushed. Only markings are a few skillfully done tats on his arms. He's painfully gorgeous.

When he's completely nude, he turns to me in a stance that demands attention. His thick cock is pointing straight at me. I can't help staring down at it. He doesn't make a move. I look up into those eyes, and I start to shake.

Silently, he climbs onto the bed, moving like a panther about to pounce on its prey. His intense gaze on me, his fluid and graceful movements—it's all enough to knock the wind from my lungs. I marvel at his overwhelming presence.

This man is all mine.

I move back on the bed as he makes the slow crawl up my body. Just when I think he's going to move to kiss me, he detours. He reaches for the drawer of one of the bedside tables. He pulls something out and turns back to face me.

The sly smile that takes over his lips proves very telling. I bite my own lip ready and willing. He hasn't taken me to a single wrong place yet.

Although, my brows do knit when he shifts, lifting his hands. A black silk tie comes into my view just before he deftly ties it around my eyes, cutting off my vision. Everything changes instantly. I become hyperaware of his cologne as he looms over me. I can almost taste the lush flavor of the brandy he downed earlier when we first arrived home.

"Relax. Just feel me," he coaxes.

His warm breath fans my ear as his voice vibrates through me. I hadn't noticed that I was tense. I allow myself to loosen up, settling back on the bed. I can feel him shift back away from me.

His hand is at my ankle, lifting my leg. A few seconds later I feel his tongue at the heel of my foot. He drags it to the center of the pad of my foot, where he starts a slow circling pattern. A breath escapes my lips, when the sensation shoots to my groin.

He chuckles darkly, continuing his trail until he sucks my big toe into his mouth. I squirm on the bed beneath him. When he pops the digit from his mouth, I hear the sound over my own panting breaths.

"You taste so good, baby. Do you know that?" His voice fills the room heavy with lust.

"No," I reply breathlessly.

He places a few featherlight kisses against my ankle. The feeling zings through me, humming through every cell. I lift a hand to my hair, tugging at the front.

"You like that?" he croons at me, pleasure forming in his words.

"Yes."

His tongue taking over is his response. I feel the wet path he makes from my ankle to my inner thigh. His own groans of gratification caress my ears. I swallow hard, tangling my fingers in the sheets beneath me, arching my back off the bed. When his warm lips kiss at my balls, I widen my legs only to have him slide beneath my thighs, tossing both of my legs over his shoulders.

I feel it in the bottom of my stomach when he licks his way up the center of my sack. He continues up the underside of my cock, until he reaches the tip. My nostrils flare. I throw my head back into the pillow. He teases the crown, swirling his tongue around it.

I wait with bated breath for him to take it all in. Yet he doesn't. I feel the bed shift beneath his weight once again. I turn my head in the direction I feel him move in. I want to call out to him, but I opt to be patient. After all, he asked if I trust him. This is deeper for him. He needs this reassurance.

I sense him moving back toward me on the bed. He shifts around a bit before something cool begins to drip down onto the skin of my torso. My stomach caves in retreat. Seconds after the dripping stops, his warm hands are on me.

His palms glide over my stomach, warming and smoothing the moistness into my skin. The scent of coconut wafts up to my nose. One hand slides up to my right nipple, pinching it with just the right amount of pressure. Not too soft, but just rough enough to bring a bite to it.

I squirm, wanting and needing more. I feel his lips and tongue join the party. He's taking a trip across my scar. It's his way of reassuring me that it doesn't bother him; he takes me for who I am.

I'm on sensory overload, even without my sight. Or it could be because I'm not able to see a thing. His hands continue to massage and roam my midsection. I feel when his long fingers claw their way to my sides. I lift up from the bed as he drags his fingers up and over my rib cage.

His teeth move over the skin on my chin, catching the light stubble. When his lips cover mine, I breathe him in. The taste of coconut fills my mouth. His cologne and the coconut make a heady mix that consumes me.

He sips from my lips as I try to give as good as I'm getting. I lift my head, flicking my tongue out, searching for his face to taste more of the coconut flavor. He allows me to try to clean his face, before backing away once again. My tongue tingles from scraping his five-o'clock shadow. I note the swollen feel of my thoroughly kissed lips.

My eyes roll behind my lids and the fabric of the blindfold. His slow torturous kisses moving down my body are driving me insane. I've been gripping the bedspread so tightly my fingers ache. His big body moves fluidly to settle between my legs again, one of my limbs resting back over his shoulder.

This time when the cool dripping greets my cock, I groan so loud it echoes throughout the room. It's such an erotic sound, even to my own ears. What I hear next is Kyle's firm hand wrapping around my length and pumping over the slick oil, followed by a tortured sound from my own lips.

"Fuck," I hiss.

The slick, wet sucking sound of his hand caressing me from slow to quick, then back to slow motion again, is enough to drive me straight to the edge.

"Kyle," I pant out.

Just as I do, he lifts my other leg over his other shoulder and takes me into his mouth. I bite my lip and nearly come all the way off the bed. I fall back, but my hips have a mind of their own as they start to pump into his mouth.

"Mmm," he hums around me.

His head is bobbing and rolling as he throws himself into my pleasure. Releasing the covers, I reach to grasp the back of his head. My fingers lock into place. I love the feel of his waves beneath my palms. One more layer of sensation in the midst of so many others that have contributed to my pleasure.

"I'm not going to last," I rasp out. "I'm so fucking close."

He grunts around my length. His saliva drips down over my balls into my crack. It sounds as sloppy as it feels. The slurping and sucking sends me over. He takes me to the back of his throat just as I start to squirt my hot seed.

"*Fuck!*" I roar into the room.

I'm limp against the bed as he sucks at me until I'm dry. When I do pop free from his mouth, I feel him shift, moving to the left again. I then sense him crawling up my body. I think he's going to release the blindfold, but he doesn't. Instead, I hear the same sound from when he pumped my cock with the oil. Only, a new scent is tickling my senses. I don't place it right away, too spent to think.

It's when I feel his tip on my lips and I flick out my tongue that the smell registers with my brain. The taste of strawberry and coconut bursts against my taste buds. My lips curl into a smile. I love strawberries, one more way Kyle proves he knows me so well.

I open wide to take him in. Kyle slips past my lips slowly, teasingly, before he backs away. I lift on my elbows, trying to follow. The bite of his fingers in my hair becomes a guide as he thrusts into my waiting mouth on this pass. I hum, totally turned on by his natural scent and taste that are now mixed with the fruity flavors.

I relax my throat to take more of him. Kyle rides my face like only he can. I hear him grunting and hissing above me. I can just imagine the sight of him. His head thrown back, his lips parted, I bet he looks glorious hovering above me with an iron lock on my hair. The thought just turns me on more.

I grasp on to his ass to really get into it, allowing him to be my support. I bob and suck, moving my head from side to side as best I can while savoring his flavor.

"Shit," he hisses out. "So good, baby."

My chest swells when I hear the heaviness in his voice. It's so tight with desire, deep and husky. I swear it feels like it scrapes across my skin. It eggs me on, pushing me to work him more with increased vigor.

I'm rewarded for my efforts when the sweet, salty warmth of his semen coats my mouth. My hum of satisfaction vibrates through my chest. I love the popping sound of him pulling from my mouth. It's like a prize for a job well done.

Again, I think that he's going to release the blindfold. Instead, he buries his face in my neck and begins to suck. The warmth of his mouth does nothing to help the flames that are consuming me.

"Come here," he says into my ear.

I follow his lead as he turns my back to his front. I plant my hands on the mattress. He nudges my legs apart with his own thick thighs. I arch like a cat in front of him when I feel that now familiar slick dripping. His palms start to roam my back.

His warm lips join in to caress my skin, moving from my shoulder down the center of my back. Wrapping his hands around my pulsing arousal, he strokes me slowly. I grow harder against his heated palm. My body is like molding clay for his pleasure.

"Nice, I like that. Give yourself to me," he croons.

"Take it. Take it all," I breathe back.

"I will," he says with promise.

His breath strokes my bare ass seconds before I feel his wet tongue circling my pucker. I don't know if I can handle the torturous skills of his mouth tonight. Not like this. Thankfully, he graces me with a reprieve.

It's not much. Cool moisture greets my opening. His slick erection bumps up against my butt, dragging across the cheek. His gentle nudge sends anticipation rocketing through my entire being. The heat from his hand on the small of my back is welcoming, like a guiding force. He pushes his hips into mine, opening me for his anticipated penetration.

We groan in unison. His slow movements giving me enough time to adjust. My head drops between my shoulders, my mind reeling. The way he rolls his body into me starts to stir something within. He clutches my hips as he increases his pace. The sound of his pelvis slapping against my ass takes over the room.

"Yes," I groan.

He slaps my ass, not breaking his stride. I reach to stroke myself as I take him. Kyle hovers over me licking a path up my spine. My teeth sink into my lip as I push back against him. Sweat is pouring from my face onto the bed. I can hear it hitting the sheets. Kyle's sweat is starting to drop onto my back, rolling against my already slick skin.

His hand locks into my hair, tugging my head back, bending me in an awkward position. In this moment, I wish I could see him. I certainly feel him. I sense his body bent over mine. He captures my lips, kissing me passionately. My toes dig into the bed. My hand is stroking in slower motions now.

"I love you," he breathes into my mouth. "Nothing will come between us. With you is where my love lives."

"I love you too," I pant out. "I don't doubt you, and I know where my heart belongs."

The blindfold loosens, and the fabric slips away. I blink up into dark brown eyes that have a wide gamut of emotions running through them. We stare at each other. His hand glides down my torso to take over my stroking.

"Finish with me," he says in that sexy commanding way of his.

I lean in to kiss him. Our lips meet, and sparks fly. It's all charged up to this moment—our bodies moving as one, our tongues dancing against each other. We both explode like a timed cosmic shower.

When I inhale in awe, he exhales. It's as if I'm taking him into my soul. I feel like he's just given me a part of him. When his arms wrap securely around me, his body guiding us both to our sides, I feel like something has changed.

We're one. No one can break us. I am him and he is me. We are our love.

CHAPTER TWENTY-SIX

Happy Birthday

Andy

"Hello," I say sleepily into the phone.

"Hey, sleepyhead. Wake up." Kyle's voice rumbles through the line.

"What time is it?" I yawn.

"About two in the morning," he replies, humor in his voice.

I sit up bolt straight in bed, squinting at the clock. I'm disoriented. Something must be wrong if he's calling at this time. I clear my thoughts, scratching my head.

"Is something wrong? Did your teammates place girls in your room again?" I ask.

Hearing the sound of his laughter on the other end, my sleepy brain allows me to relax. He's in a good mood. His voice starts to wake me a bit more, sending a warmth spreading in my belly.

"Happy birthday, baby," he croons into the phone.

He starts to sing to me, bringing me fully to life. It's my birthday. We've both been bummed that he wouldn't be here. He has a game tonight in Atlanta.

"Thank you," I say when his singing comes to an end.

"You're an old man now," he teases.

"Don't remind me," I say.

"You know you're bugging, right? Thirty-one and you're still sexy as fuck. I need you to do something for me. I need you to get up and go to the garage. Can you do that for me?" he says smoothly.

I look down at my pajamas. I'll need to change. I'm already climbing out of bed before I answer.

"I'll need a few minutes," I reply.

"All right, call me when you're on the way," he says and ends the call.

I'm stumbling around in the dark feeling curious. Rushing into the bathroom, I brush my teeth. When I get back into the bedroom, I change into jeans and a T-shirt. I slide my feet into a pair of flip-flops and head for the door.

On the way to the elevator, I call Kyle back. I don't wait long for him to answer. He picks up on the first ring.

"Are you on the way?" he asks as a greeting.

"Yeah, I'm stepping into the elevator now. Reception may get choppy," I reply.

"Don't... up... when... get to the gar...." The line goes in and out.

I twist my lips in frustration, watching the numbers count down to the garage floor. When the elevator dings, I go to step out. My steps halt midway out of the doors. I drop the phone from my ear and stand in shock with my mouth hanging open.

Kyle is here, standing with a huge smile on his lips. He looks so good in a gray T-shirt, a pair of gray jeans, and black sneakers. He's in that sexy stance that oozes confidence and sensuality. I feel like I'm staring at the front cover of a hot magazine.

He crooks a finger at me to come to him, snapping my brain into action. I rush forward and wrap my arms around him. I've been missing him. He has been under so much stress with the playoffs and those pictures steering up all kinds of drama. I've wanted nothing more than to be there for him.

"What are you doing here?"

"You didn't really think I'd miss my baby's birthday, did you?" he says into my neck.

"But how? The team isn't going to freak out?"

"Mark is covering my ass," he replies. "I chartered a flight. I'll fly right back after I give you your birthday present."

I place my hands on the sides of his face to bring it down to mine. He takes my lips and kisses me senseless. I melt into him, savoring this moment. Kyle groans, pulling away reluctantly.

"Happy birthday," he purrs, turning me slightly.

My eyes about pop from my head. I was so focused on him, I didn't see the Maserati SUV parked behind him with a huge blue bow on it. I lift my head up to look him in the eyes. He's watching me, his lips turned up.

He brushes his thumb over my swollen lips. His gorgeous orbs have a hint of lust building in them. I lean in to place a kiss on his lush mouth.

"This is insane, babe," I say.

"It's the one you were looking at," he replies, rubbing a hand up and down my arms. "I wanted you to have it. Something good for your birthday."

I look between the SUV and him, then back at the SUV. It's the gray color I wanted and all. I can't believe he did this. I've never had anyone do something like this for me outside of my family.

"Yeah, but—"

He pinches my jaw, turning my face up to him. His lips crush mine, taking the words right from my mouth. My toes curl in my flip-flops.

"You're welcome," he says against my lips.

"Thank you," I whisper back.

"Let's go upstairs. I have something else I want to give you." He wiggles his brows.

"Let me park the car in a spot," I say.

He shakes his head.

"I have Javier's security with me tonight. One of the guys will handle it. Come on. I want to get as much time with you as I can, before I have to go."

I lift to kiss his lips again.

"I love you. Thank you," I say.

CHAPTER TWENTY-SEVEN

Family?

Kyle

Just as I thought, that story hasn't died down. It won't because Michael doesn't want it to. He's somewhere fanning the flames. It's his way to distract me, to throw my happiness off-balance.

It has backfired. At least it did until now. Before today, I used all the bullshit to drive me forward. We've blown through game one and two without me batting an eye.

However, today, right now, I'm just trying to keep it together. My sister has been gone for almost two and a half years. Where the fuck was my aunt then? She showed interest in raising Mas for a nanosecond before he was forgotten. Why the hell she thinks someone needs her now is beyond me.

"I don't like what's been going on in the news. I think Mason would be better off with me," she says with her nose turned up.

I snort. She must have bumped her damn head. I'm doing my best to show her respect because she's my mother's sister, but it's a tight rope that's about to snap.

"That's not going to happen," I scoff.

"You know this ain't right. You raising that little boy. You're not married. You don't have a mother figure around him. For all I know, those rumors are true. Don't think I forgot about your past. I thought you allowed the Lord to deal with that, but it's clear you're backsliding." She purses her lips at me.

Lips black from smoking weed and cigarettes. It's funny how people pick and choose which sins they want to ignore for their own pleasure. She probably has a joint in her bag now or one rolled up at home. Not to mention, a nice bottle of vodka to go along with it.

I clap my hands together loudly, trying to rein in my temper. I can see Mas and Emma in the backyard from my place in the living room.

"See what you're not going to do is come up in my house talking all that bullshit. You sleep with the devil every night, but you want to come in here talking shit and try to remove my nephew from the safety of my home. Let me ask you a question. Where were you when I needed help getting him to school and someone to watch him on the weekend while I had to work?"

I'm pissed. My voice rises with each sentence as I clap my way through every single word. If she wasn't my aunt, I would have picked her up by her collar and dragged her ass out of my damn house.

"You better watch your tone with me. That boy needs stability. You just said so yourself. You just let me take things from here. You can send the checks to the house, and I'll handle the rest," she says with a straight-as-fuck face.

My mouth falls open. I'm appalled and disgusted. I should have figured.

"Well, ain't that a bitch," I say to myself. "You're here for money? Don't I pay y'all enough to stay the fuck away from me?"

"I don't know what you're talking about. You don't give me a dime," she snaps.

"Yeah, act blind like you always do. You really think Rodney is working for that money he's throwing around?" I snort again and shake my head. "You're a real saint, all right."

"Rodney works hard for his family. I don't know what you're talking about. You always tried to act like we were treating you so badly. You and that ungrateful sister of yours," she huffs.

"I swear to God. Don't you ever mention my sister and that piece of shit in the same breath again. Ungrateful, my ass," I snarl.

"Don't you take the Lord's name in vain," she chides me.

"God help you," I boom. "Get out of my house before it takes Jesus himself to hold me back from telling you all the things I've been wanting to say since I was a kid. Don't come here anymore. Don't reach out to me either."

"We'll see about all this. I've already talked to a lawyer. I'm coming for my sister's grandbaby. He said we have an excellent shot at getting him. I was on the fence, because I'm too old to be raising any more of you ungrateful, raggedy brats, but I see what's going on here. You've turned yourself over to the enemy. Talking to me any old type of way."

I close my eyes and started to count back from ten. I never should have lost my temper and I shouldn't have cursed her out, but I can't believe the nerve of her. The fact that she believes the things she says proves purely insane to me. The woman wouldn't know the truth if it kissed her on the mouth.

"So heavenly minded, you're no earthly good," I mutter.

"What did you say?" She stands narrowing her eyes at me like she plans to whip me like she used to.

"I said look into your own house before you start throwing stones. You come for my nephew, and I will let all of your skeletons out of that closet. I bet the congregation would love to know all about the once-a-month deacon. Showing up when he wants to because he's too busy with his other life," I seethe.

"You heathenness *faggot*! You'd probably catch fire if you tried to step in a church. I'm not scared of you and your threats. Your sister was a slut. She tempted Rodney into her clutches. He saw the error in his ways and got right with the Lord," she hurls back at me.

I see red. Any restraint I had left flies out the window. I move to stand in front of her and duck to get into her face.

"Was I a slut too? At eight years old, did I tempt him too? Did I ask him to teach me to suck his dick? I'm just asking for a friend, auntie," I hiss.

She has the nerve to look like someone slapped her. Her eyes water and tears spill over. She raises a trembling hand to her lips, her head moving from side to side.

"No," she whispers. "You're a liar. You're both liars."

"Man." I back away and suck my teeth. "I always hoped that once I told you, you would see the light. You would believe me because I'm your family. Your nephew."

"You don't do things like this to your family," she yells at me.

"Family? Family? Get a dictionary and look that word up. Then get your bible and read it instead of using it for a coaster.

That sand hat doesn't become you. It's time to pull your head out," I toss back at her.

"Please leave" comes the voice of someone I consider true family.

I turn to see Emma standing with tears in her eyes. I look around for Mason, but he's still outside happily playing on the swing I made for him in the backyard. I feel my body relax.

"Go," I say, not turning to face my aunt again.

"I'm going to pray on this. If the Lord sees fit, I'm going to go with the attorney and file for custody," she says just above a whisper.

"Make sure you're hearing God this time. Don't ignore him like you did when he was showing you something was wrong in your home all those years ago," I reply.

"Fuck you, Kyle." My head whips in my aunt's direction.

She glares back at me. I let a smile take over my face, tipping an imaginary hat to her.

"I think your husband did plenty of that, so that would be a no thank you, Aunt Bethany. Goodbye."

CHAPTER TWENTY-EIGHT

Broken

Andy

"I'm so sorry. I'm so, so sorry. I only did what Savanna asked me to do," Emma says hysterically.

"Slow down," I say. "What's going on? Where's Mason?"

"Mom came and got him. I didn't know what else to do. Beau's out of town and h… he won't come out. He hasn't come out since I gave it to him," she says, shaking her hands out in front of her.

"Calm down. What did you give him?"

"It's a letter. Savanna asked me to give him the letter if their aunt ever appeared asking for Mason. She was here yesterday. I brought it over this morning. Oh God, Andy. That scream." She looks at me with haunted eyes, a shiver visibly rolling through her. "I've never heard anything like that in my life. Please, just see if he's okay in there."

"I will. Maybe you should go check on Mas and your mom. I'm messaging the car service," I say soothingly. "I'll text you as soon as I can. Okay?"

"Oh, okay. Yeah, I can do that. Yeah." She nods jerkily, moving for her purse. "I'm sorry."

"Stop apologizing."

"Okay, sorry. I mean, sorry," she says, her face twisting in frustration with herself.

I give her a small smile and pull her into a hug. When her car arrives, I walk her out of the house. When I close and lock the door behind her, I lean up against it and close my eyes. When we spoke last night and Kyle told me about his aunt's visit, I was speechless. I'm afraid of what I'll find hiding in that room.

I push off the door and head for the bedroom. He has a flight to catch in the morning and a game to play tomorrow night. Whatever is going on, I want to help him through it so he can focus on what he's worked so hard for. I never want to hear him sound the way he did last night again.

I'm relieved when I try the knob on the door. It turns and the door pops open. Pushing my way into the room I look around. I don't see Kyle in the sitting area, so I keep moving into the room. His bed is neatly made and his duffel bag is packed sitting at the foot, but there's still no sign of him.

I train my eyes on the bathroom door that's closed. I pick up in the sound of the shower running. I release a breath. Perhaps that's why he wasn't responding to Emma. My thoughts go wild. I push aside the whispers of the negative outcomes that could greet me.

When I push the bathroom door open, steam billows into my face. I step inside and close the door behind me. My brows draw in when I take in the sight before me. I can see a figure through the completely steamed-up shower glass, but it's not nearly as tall as Kyle is.

As I get close enough, I pull the door open to look inside. My heart aches when I take it all in. Kyle is sitting on the shower floor, his arms resting over his knees, his fist clenching and unclenching. His jaw is tight with tension, and his eyes are bloodshot red. I know instantly that his face is wet from more than the shower raining down on him.

"Kyle—"

He shakes his head, then gestures behind me. As I turn, my eyes find a few crumpled pages sitting on the bathroom vanity. I move to it, lifting the pages to smooth them out.

I read them once, but my brain twists against the words. I go back to the beginning. Surely, I'm reading this all wrong. I turn, leaning my butt against the sink for support.

If you're reading this Aunt Bethany has come for Mason. Don't let anything that woman says cause you to walk away from my son. I picked you for a reason. Not only are you smart and talented, you're a fierce protector. My baby needs your protection.

Let me first say this. I didn't teach you to be tough so that you could hide who you are. I taught you to be tough so you could be who you are without hiding. This world has to learn to accept good people for being good people. Turning a blind eye to evil doers isn't right.

What happened to us wasn't right, but it didn't make us the evil doers. It didn't make us the bad people. My son isn't a bad person because of who his father is.

You asked me so many times who Mason's father was and I never told you for a reason. You have always been destined for greatness. I never wanted anything to get in the way of that. I know you and that damn Beau would have gone right to jail if I told you the truth then.

I'm only about to tell you now because my baby needs you. You can't afford to be the wrath that avenges me. You do the right thing by my son, little brother. You stay out of jail for Mas.

I moved in with you because that bastard started showing up at my apartment a few months before. He threatened to tell the world about how I seduced him and broke up his happy marriage. Can you believe that shit?

When I didn't cave and ask you for money for him, he.... This is hard for me to say even in this letter. I tried to forget that night. I moved in with you the next day. I thought I would never have to think of it again. Then Mas came along. He is the best thing that has ever happened to me, to us.

I want my son to grow up to be just like you, Kyle. Strong, loving, and a protector. I know what you tried to do for me. I see the way you are with your teammates. You're everything a real man is supposed to be. Who you love has nothing to do with that.

But I want you to listen. Michael is not for you. You're thickheaded, so I kept my mouth shut for the most part. That man is toxic. He doesn't love you, he wants to own you. Much like that monster. Don't settle for one monster over another. Leave him.

I've never been ashamed of you. I don't think you know that. Never! I'm so proud of you. Teach my son what love sounds and feels like. If you do, when the time is right, he'll know what it looks like for him.

Don't let our hurt place my son in that house of horrors. Don't let Aunt Bethany play to your weakness. You're a good man. You're the best and Mason deserves only the best.

I love you, K.

I blink back the tears that threaten to spill. I drop the letter on the counter as if it has burst into flames. I vow to be the one that rights some things on Kyle's behalf. I tuck those thoughts to the side, turning back for my man in the shower. Stepping out of my shoes, I walk inside, close the door, and sit in front of him.

"She come here on that bullshit. Trying to make me feel bad. 'You need to set good examples, Kyle.' 'He needs to be in an environment of strong black men, Kyle.' 'What do you know about raising a child?' 'You can't be teaching him all that confused mess you grow up thinking.' She spent a good hour poking at old wounds, trying to find the right spot," he murmurs. "I'm not a little kid anymore. I wasn't letting it go down like that."

"Good for you. I'm sure Savanna is smiling down on you," I say.

"He wanted her to ask me for money," he says bitterly. "You know what the fucked-up part is?"

I shake my head, unable to speak.

"I was already giving him money. It was one of the first things Michael did for me. He drew up some papers, and we opened a bank account just for my so-called uncle. I give that bastard money every month to stay out of our lives, and he...."

I grab a hold of the front of his shirt, pulling him to me. He comes without a fight, moving between my legs and curling against my chest. I embrace him in the silence.

"It was the first trap Michael set for me. I thought he was superman for handling that for me. I agreed to our first date." He gives a dry laugh. "Why now? Why is she pulling this shit now? After all I've been through. I'm not going to lose my nephew, and I'm not going to allow anyone else to ruin our happiness. I'm tired. It has to end."

"It will," I reply, kissing his forehead.

"Yeah, it will. I see what he's doing. He's pushing all the right buttons to expose me. He knew she would start asking questions and come for Mas. I won't be forced out. I told my aunt all that shit in anger, but... I'm not going to feed into this shit. That letter only reminded me of how strong I am. How strong I've had to be. It revealed me."

"Then I think your sister did exactly what she aimed to. She set you free," I say against his skin.

"Yeah. She did."

CHAPTER TWENTY-NINE

Pressure

Kyle

This is it. We win tonight or go home. I've allowed my personal life to follow me onto the court. We started the conference finals up three, and now we're tied. Everyone is blaming me. I see it in their faces. The commentators make no bones about it. Kyle Tyson is throwing the series.

The locker room has been thick with tension. You could slice into it. It's not about the game anymore.

"Tyson, we could get you some pussy and get your game right," they taunt.

"If you stop letting that white boy plunge you in the ass, you'd be able to move it on the court," someone else said.

It has gone far beyond that. I could fight them all. I could tell them to suck my dick and go play without me, but that's not the man I am. The man my sister saw me as.

Which is why tonight, I've left my everything on the floor. Fuck not being seen, everyone sees me anyway. Just like Andy. He thought no one could see him, but I proved him wrong. Now it's my turn.

I refuse to hide behind my team to keep from having to say... I'm here. This is my choice to play like I own this court. To play like the star player I was born to be. Stars don't hide; they shine. If shining means a closer look, let them look. I'm proud of who I am.

"Take the shot, Tyson. *Take the shot*," my coach bellows from the sidelines.

It's a three-pointer for the game. The clock is running out, and this is the moment that will define my future. A breeze brushes my fingertips as the ball releases from my hands. The arena goes completely silent. It's like everything is in slow motion.

I can't take my eyes off the ball. My lips are parted, my hands are still in the air in the same pose from when I released the shot. The whooshing sound unfreezes everything. The crowd roars with excitement, my team rushes me.

Nothing but net. I just sank an impossible three-pointer. We're headed to the next round. I close my eyes and thank God. Tonight, this was all Him on this court. I pushed myself to limits I've never gone before. The whole time hearing in my head that I had this.

"Yeah, baby. I knew we could do it," Rashad croons.

I should tell him to kiss my ass. He didn't do shit. On top of that he's been riding me the hardest about the rumors about my sexuality. Taunting me, dropping his towel and watching to see if my eyes follow him. His ass should grow a dick before he tries to walk around like a peacock.

I let it roll off my back. This is too big a moment to allow any of that bull to get to me. I took a stand tonight. I may be the only one who knows and understands that, but I'm all that needs to know. I value the freedom in the decision I made to win.

I smile when I see Chris headed my way. He reaches out a hand for me to clasp and pulls me into a hug. He didn't make this easy for me tonight at all.

"If I'm going to lose to anyone, I'm glad it's you," he says in my ear. "You stay strong and take it all, you got this. Remember you have a family that has your back. I'll be on your couch for the next round cheering you on with your pretty-ass bae."

"Don't get punched in your mouth." I chuckle at his teasing.

I'm not worried about Chris. His man would cut him, and he knows it. It's just good-natured ribbing, unlike the locker room trash talking.

"Nah, you know it's all love. I'm happy for you, man," he says, before patting my shoulder and releasing me.

"You coming to the house in the morning?"

"No doubt." Chris nods, moving out of the way for others that are clamoring to get to me.

I smile for the cameras and make my way through a few interviews before I get off the court. I'm on a high all the way to the locker room. I don't let the press get to me as I shower and get ready to head home.

I'm slinging my bag over my shoulder when my agent, Mark, comes into view. My smile falters a bit. I know that forced smile on his face. Something is up.

"What's up?" I dip my head and ask when I reach him.

"Not here. Let's go," he rushes out.

My brows draw in confusion, but I don't argue. Mark's quick pace has my hackles up. His legs aren't half as long as mine, but I'm putting in effort to keep up with him.

I'm surprised when Mark leads us to my car and stands at the passenger side waiting to get in. I unlock the door and we both climb inside. I shift to toss my bag in the back, then focus on Mark.

"Drive. We want to get away from here before the vultures swoop in," he says.

I start the car and pull out of the garage, my thoughts running a mile a minute. I know we had a few deals in the works, but tonight should have only sealed them.

"What do you know about a sex tape involving you?" Mark starts.

I have to slam on the breaks to keep from running into the car in front of me as my foot slips on the accelerator. I get caught at the light, and my head whips in his direction. I stare at him with shock written all over my face.

"What the hell are you talking about?"

Mark pulls a hand down the front of his jaw. He looks stressed and just as confused as I feel. His green eyes trying to see through me for the truth. No way in hell I would ever consent to a sex tape.

"Dude, I get this crazy call after you won the game. Apparently someone's claiming to have a tape of you and some dude. They said they can corroborate the stories about you and Andy Connor as well as other relationships—"

"You can stop right there with all that bullshit. There's no tape," I say.

"Are you absolutely sure?"

"Man, there's no tape," I say firmly.

"Listen, man. It's okay if you're gay. I hadn't said anything before, but I've been getting calls since those pictures surfaced—"

"Pictures that meant nothing. The same pictures that are taken from a different angle showing a different scenario. What's your point?" I cut him off.

"What I'm trying to say is... you have offers from companies that would love to back a gay NBA player. You can make this work in your favor. Let's get ahead of this. I don't know what's going on, but it seems like someone's out to expose you. Let's beat them at their own game," Mark replies.

"First of all, I'm not playing anyone's game. I've told you over and over my life is not for anyone's entertainment. Stop trying to make money off some shit you heard," I fume.

A horn blares behind me, causing me to turn back to the road. I grind my teeth, ready to hit the roof. This is some crazy bullshit. I've seen this happen a million times. Someone cries red and players toss out money to hush a situation so it doesn't get back to their wives.

I'm not having this shit. I've never placed myself in a position to have any intimate moments recorded. I'm not feeding into this.

"What do they want?" I bite out.

"That's the thing. I thought they would want money or something. When I ask how we could get our hands on the video or keep it from surfacing, they hung up. I don't know what you want me to do with this. I thought we could jump ahead of it. I know the locker room has been strained with the rumors. If you didn't play your ass off tonight, the team was ready to talk trades to avoid the controversy—"

"Wait. What?"

"The team—"

"No, fuck them. They don't have a team without me. They hung up?"

"Yeah, it was weird," Mark replies.

I freeze.

Michael.

This is him. I know it is. Now, my question is did he record me without my knowledge, or is he just bluffing? All of this chaos—the rumors from out of thin air, the pictures, a sex tape—it started after that text. I know he's behind the gasoline that keeps getting thrown on the flames.

"Don't do a damn thing, Mark. I'll take care of this," I say.

"You sure? We can strategize," he responds.

"I'm sure."

Andy

The TV suddenly cuts off. I turn to find the source, only to find Javier holding the remote with his hazel gaze now trained on me. It registers that the room is now completely silent. I look around, and everyone's staring in my direction.

We're all at Kyle's house to watch the playoff game he just put his whole heart into tonight. The plan was for everyone to hang around to support him either way. I know it had to be hard for them to watch two of their good friends rivaling each other for the win. Chris played hard, but Kyle just took things to another level.

Darwin, Beau, Javier, Daniel, and Jordan are all here, as well as my two brothers. I somehow get the feeling that everyone knows what's going on except for me and my siblings. John looks amused, and Mitch looks like his about to go on defense. Yet the two are watching me for a response to the shift in the atmosphere. I'm just as clueless as the two of them.

"We're all his family. We know something is going on. Yes, he played amazing tonight, but we all know he hasn't been himself. What isn't he telling us?" Javier starts.

"There's a lot going on, but it's not my place to tell you what," I reply.

"Does this have anything to do with that wanker ya had me look into? That slimy-as-fuck prick," Mitch asks, narrowing his gaze at me.

"Mitch," I warn.

"Has he been causing trouble?" my brother presses. "Has he come around?"

"No," I huff.

"Are ya sure? Does he know about the car Kyle just bought ya?"

I pause. I still haven't told Mitch my connection to Michael. Him bringing up the car suggests he may have dug some more after I told him to drop it.

"What would make you ask that?" I ask cautiously.

"Because his name came up on my radar again the other day," Mitch says, his gaze homing in on me.

"Wait, who are we talking about here? And you better not say who I think," Beau says.

"Michael Fairchild," Mitch responds.

"Mitch, shut ya fucking gub," I snap.

"No, please do continue," Darwin says. "I've been waiting for that one to reappear. Never known him to turn away from anything he felt was his."

"Hold on." Mitch leans forward. "Ya were involved with that prick?"

"If yer going to run ya lips ya should at least pay attention to the whole shebang," I grumble, rolling my eyes. My ears feel hot as my frustration mounts and my blood begins to boil. "He and Kyle were involved."

"I can see that. It makes perfect sense. He has a type," Mitch muses.

"What's that supposed to mean?" Javier asks.

"All of the others were young and on their way to stardom. Black or Latino usually. From the inner city, just becoming exposed to wealth. Makes it easier for him to control their worlds and what they get accustomed to," my brother says. "That and the funny flower. That stook has a thing for the white stuff."

"Yeah, we all know that. He tried to get Kyle into that shit, but he wasn't having it," Daniel grumbles, making a sour face.

I feel the blood drain from my face. This is something I didn't know. Michael has a number of DUIs that were swept up under the rug. I remember Kyle telling him to stay away from the coke at the party during their confrontation, but I had no idea he had tried to introduce Kyle to that shit.

"All of the others? Why does that sound so seedy? What are we missing?" Beau says, leaning in toward Mitch.

"That fucker has ruined the lives of several young lads. Kyle is the only one flying it. The rest have met with something real stink right after cutting ties with that dirty tooth," Mitch says.

"Wait," Jordan says, his blue eyes dancing with dark mirth. "I know this is serious, but the way you put things. I just want to clarify. Michael gets his guys hooked on cocaine. That's something I sort of figured. But you're also saying that Kyle is the only one that's done well for himself after dating Michael. What the fuck happened to the rest of them?"

"Aye, ya got me, ya do," Mitch replies. "Two lost their noodle and were committed to the funny house. He drove them mad as a box of frogs, he did.

"He has kicked and booted a few. They had hospital records longer than my arm while dating that piece of shit. Broken arms, ribs, let's not forget the overdose. Wouldn't have found that one odd if his nose wasn't broken, after the consumption.

"I think one got cut to the bone, he did, fed up for sure, he was. Beat the shit out of Fairchild and ended up in jail. Most of the charges were bullshit, had nothing to do with the assault. That poor kid was on his way to the big leagues. A football player. Three others have been missing since ending their relationships with ya friend," Mitch explains, his eyes darkening with each word, displaying his distaste.

"He's no friend of mine," Beau says in disgust.

"You think he was connected to all of that stuff?" Jordan asks, his blond brows wrinkled. "I mean, there was always something in his eyes."

"I have proof. My boys are the best. Mr. Fairchild is so far from being a saint. He lights the fire in hell every night, he does," Mitch replies.

"I have no doubt," Darwin says with a troubled look on his face. "I've known Michael for years. I warned Kyle he wasn't for him."

The room falls silent. I can barely pull my thoughts together. I knew most of these things. I've read the file over and over. However, hearing them out loud makes them all the more real. I feel sick to my stomach. Kyle is so lucky he didn't fall into any of that monster's traps.

"What does he have to do with the way Kyle has been playing?" Jordan asks.

"Nothing," I mutter.

"Bullshit," Beau challenges.

I inhale deeply and release it roughly. I've come to know all of the men in this room. When it comes to their friendship, their brotherhood, they will stop at nothing to make sure the other is okay. I'm up against a brick wall here.

I look around the room. All eyes are again on me, waiting for answers. Answers to a topic I've been rolling around in my head since finding a broken Kyle in that shower.

"It'll be fine. I'm handling it," I say.

John grunts in his seat. We already talked about a little plan I have. I want to address a least one of Kyle's problems. He does so much for me. It's the least I can do.

"Oh nah, you don't get to say shit like that and think we're going to ignore it. You don't have to give us details. In this family, we never need details. You just tell us what needs handling, we're there," Daniel says.

I look around the room, thinking over the offer. Maybe I'll take them up on it. I just don't know how without providing details and reason.

"It's not just Michael. There are a number of reasons for him being so distracted, but we think Michael is the one behind those pictures that surfaced," I relent.

"Sounds like good old Michael." Javier snorts.

"You should know Kyle is the baby out of all of us. We're protective of him. You do know we're here to help?" Daniel says.

I feel a pang in my chest. I know they're only trying to be to Kyle what my brothers and sister are to me. I love and admire them for it. I just don't think it's my place to disclose the things going on in Kyle's life.

"I get that. But you're going to have to get the story from him," I say, with a shrug.

"You know it's going to be like pulling teeth to get him to tell us what's going on," Beau mumbles, falling back into his seat.

"Again, I don't need the story. Just who." Jordan's piercing eyes cloud over.

"Same here," Javier adds.

"Listen, I never told Kyle that I dug into Michael's past. I want to be the one to tell him that. I just need the right time to do so. There hasn't been one yet." I turn to look my brother in the eyes. "I'd appreciate if you all would keep it to yourselves."

"I have a question. Why were you digging into Michael?" Beau asks, his sharp eyes homing in on me.

"I needed to know what I was dealing with," I answer protectively, keeping my face impassive.

"I knew I liked you," Daniel croons, laughter lacing his words.

"Well, here he comes. I'd like some answers," Darwin says. "That hasn't been Kyle out there. It's his time for greatness. I won't have anyone messing with my boy."

CHAPTER THIRTY

Heckle

Kyle

A weight had been lifted off my shoulders when I shared with my friends what has been going on in my life. I was grateful for the ambush after the game that night. I thought I'd be able to breathe easier after that.

Boy, was I wrong.

I'm trying to hold it together until I get to my room. Just my luck my room would be the one that got fucked-up. Coach is trying to straighten it out for me. He knows I'm hanging on by a thread.

I'm standing here with my hood pulled up just trying to take my next breath. I've been off to the side waiting like a ticking time bomb. Somehow, I woke in the twilight zone today. I just need to sit down and collect my thoughts.

I went from being served custody papers to having to jump in the car to get to the airport. I still had the papers clenched in my fist when I boarded the plane. I think I'm still in shock. I don't understand for the life of me why my aunt is doing this. She's not the most maternal woman in the world.

I don't want to believe she's doing it for the money. There was something else going on in her body language when she came by the house. Now, as I look back on the visit, certain things are sticking out at me.

"You all right, Tyson?" one of the rookie players walks up to ask me.

I close my eyes and try to nod. The gesture alone takes everything in me. There have been times when I've been filled with so much rage it feels like my head is about to explode right off my shoulders. That's exactly how I feel as I stand here letting reality set in.

"You need anything, man?" he asks nervously.

I know he means well, but someone needs to come get him so he can leave me the fuck alone. Yes, I need something, but no one here can help me with it. My nephew is my life. I need my aunt to fuck off and leave us to live in peace. I'm not giving up custody of Mason. That shit will happen over my dead body or someone else's.

"I'm good, man," I manage to bite out.

I'm not good. Isn't it already bad enough that those pictures have been the topic of every conversation that has my name in it? Every single time I turn the TV on, there's a debate about them. Are they real? Is it true? Should it matter? Is this what's affecting my game?

Hell, if everyone feels like my game is suffering because of all this media blowup, why not stop? Leave me and my personal life alone so I can play in peace. That would only make sense.

It's a fucking shit show. None of it has anything to do with the game itself. They just want to have something to talk about, and they've been handed me on a platter.

It doesn't matter that they have the other photos of me and Tara or of Andy and Emma. They just keep going and going. Now, this fucking sex tape has been adding to the mix. Not that one person has actually seen it. There's just talk of it being seen.

I had my doubts at first. I thought maybe, just maybe Michael caught me slipping. He would be the only person that could have such a tape. I never slept with Martin during the brief time we dated.

Javier is not with that shit. You're not allowed to even have a phone or recording device on you when you enter Club Refuge. If you're into that type of thing, there are consent forms and an entire process. Then, and only then, will Javier be the one to provide the recording setup and monitoring.

I know my friend isn't behind this one. Besides, Michael would be the only one that would have been able to have access to those vulnerable moments at Refuge. I was a voyeur at the club until I got involved with him.

"Y... you should keep your head up, Tyson. You're one of the best. I hate to see you like this," the rookie continues to push.

I look him in the eyes, narrowing mine at him. His eyes are still bright, his face fresh and new. He hasn't had a taste of what this league will make of him.

What does he know about what I'm going through? He doesn't know this world eats their young. He'll learn, if he makes it another year or two. He's just food, par for the course. His mama is helping him juggle all of this and still keep his head above water.

At this point, I don't give two fucks about this shit. My real world is crumbling. I could get hurt tonight, and I would be discarded by this league. Forgotten and returned to where I come from, replaced by this fresh-faced rookie standing before me as they make him the next star.

With Mas, he needs me as much as I need him. No matter my flaws or shortcomings, that kid counts on me. I'm the one who has held him through his tears and reassured him that he'll be okay. I'm the one who provides for him and protects him. It's my job, the only one that matters to me. I can't breathe just thinking about losing him.

All my emotions turn into rage. Not having time to process this is fucking with my head, and I need to be left alone. Why can't this kid see that?

"See me like what?" I hiss. "Do you even know what the fuck you're talking about?"

"I just... I just. I wanted...," he stammers out.

He stumbles back with wide eyes. I try to rein in my temper. He hasn't done anything to me. He was just trying to help. I know some of the younger players come in looking up to the rest of us who have been here.

I purse my lips and release a harsh breath from my nose, getting ready to apologize. However, the Universe has other plans. It's set on me detonating. Rashad saunters over with that dumb-ass grin on his face. This guy needs to think about his life.

He does the bare minimum on the court but is the first to brag or jump into the limelight. He always has an opinion on things that have nothing to do with him, and if he can sniff out some drama to be in the middle of, he's there.

To be honest, he's been the one keeping the tension going on the locker room. A lot of the other guys moved on. They have their own homes to worry about. For the most part, no one cares what I do in mine.

Rashad has been the one to make it a problem for the team. Amplifying it to make it an issue that it's not. Goading the simple-minded players into following his lead. All so he can get a few laughs or a little attention on his dumb ass.

I'm not in the mood for that shit today. I've let a lot roll off my back, but I will fuck him up and not bat two lashes about it. I should have put the brakes to his ass a long time ago.

"Rook, why you over here with Princess? You trying to get into that special room they getting for him? Let me find out you want to get on the next sex tape," he says with that dumb-ass grin.

"Nobody has time for you and your shit. Keep it moving, son. For real," I grind out.

"What's the matter? You been acting shitty since you got on the plane." Rashad frowns at me, looking me up and down.

I scoff to myself. Why can't everyone take a clue and leave me alone? I'm vibrating with anger. It's clear I need to be left to myself.

"Yo, I asked you to keep it moving," I reply.

He sucks his teeth and waves me off. "What happened? That white boy stopped calling your ass? All this attention too much for him? Or is that tape of you sucking his little d—"

I black out. One minute, I'm trying to count to ten. The next my fist is flying. I punch him so hard I rock his ass to sleep.

Everyone has their limits.

CHAPTER THIRTY-ONE

Poison

Andy

I haven't stopped smiling all day. Kyle and I had an interesting weekend. We spent some time with Mason and made a little visit to Club Refuge. That was a learning experience for me. One I'm not soon to forget.

Between thinking of all of the fun we had racing go-carts around Kyle's property and the flowers Kyle had delivered to my apartment this morning, my face aches from my lips being turned up all day. I look down at my desk, and my smile grows a bit more. I smooth my hands over the letter.

"You did it," I say to myself.

My cell phone rings, drawing my attention. This day just keeps getting better. K.T. lights up my screen. He couldn't have called at a better time. I'm bursting at the seams to tell him my good news.

"Hello," I answer the phone, looking up at my closed office door.

"What are you up to? You have a minute for me?"

"Always have time for you. What's up?" I reply.

"Just wanted to hear your voice. You sound happy. How has your day been?" he says smoothly.

Something is off, but I don't pry. Kyle opens up when he's ready, never before. I look down at the letter on my desk. Maybe some good news will cheer him up.

"It's official. I got the offer for the principal position. It will go into effect next year," I say excitedly, but in a hushed tone.

I'm not sure who might be roaming around outside my office. The announcement won't be made until after I accept and sign the contract. Until then only the school board and the committee know.

I'd been nervous about getting the offer. All the rumors about my relationship with Kyle have rocked the boat a bit. I know my father has a lot of sway with a few board members, but this truly could have gone either way. It's no secret that a few members are close-minded, and one even has a lesbian daughter she refuses to acknowledge.

I've taken a page from Kyle's book and chosen to ignore all prying into the subject. Most of the staff knows I go the extra mile to help my students and their families. Most believe that I've just been helping Kyle out with Mas, when Emma can't be there. All just a part of me being a nice a guy.

"That's what's up," Kyle says with genuine excitement. "I wish I were there to take you out to celebrate."

"Win the finals, that would be enough for me," I say.

He releases a deep breath. My brows furrow. That melancholy mood oozes through the phone. Something is wrong. I remain quiet for a few beats, hoping he'll tell me what.

"I lost my shit," he blurts out.

"What happened?"

"My aunt filed for custody. I was served with the papers this morning on my way out. Rashad said some bullshit about that sex tape noise while we were checking in at the hotel, and I snapped," he grumbles.

"Ah fuck," I huff, pushing a hand into my hair. "Are you okay?"

He sucks his teeth. "Man, his bitch ass ain't seeing me."

"That's not what I mean. After the shit he's been saying to you, I don't blame you. It was only a matter of time before you kicked his ass. I'm talking about the custody crap. How are you holding up?"

"Something isn't sitting well with me. I still don't get why she's doing this now. My aunt is selfish as fuck. At first, I was willing to believe it was about the money, but nah. That's not it. I already give her husband plenty of that. I know for a fact he takes care of her to keep her out of his hair," he muses aloud.

His voice trails off as if he's thinking his own words over.

There is no way he can lose Mason. It would destroy them both. I won't stand by and watch it happen.

"I can have Mitch look into things for you if you like," I offer.

"I was kind of thinking of asking you to do that," he says hopefully.

"It's done. I'll call him as soon as we hang up."

"Let me know the cost. I'll wire the money," he says.

"Are ya langered? Ya must have been drinking or ya crack ya noodle during that fight. Aye, hit your head, you did," I snap. "Yer family."

Kyle's laughter fills the phone. I pull it away from my ear and frown at the device. He's lost it.

"I love when you talk like that. You don't realize it. You and your sister do it when you're pissed off. Mitch and John I'm used to by now, but it's so sexy and cute when you do it," he says.

I roll my eyes and blow out a breath. He did piss me off a little. Kyle should know how much my family loves him and Mas.

"Mitch would never take your money. Mason is like a nephew to him. We're all going to do whatever we can to help you with this. Don't let this worry you. Play your game tonight. No worrying about anything else."

"Thanks," he murmurs.

"I mean it, baby. Don't get in your head about this. Everything is going to work out. I know it looks like the sky is falling in the midst of it all, but we'll make it through this. I'll be here every step of the way," I promise.

"I love you," he replies.

"I love you more." I smile into the phone.

"You wish," he says sexily. "After I win this championship, we're getting out of here for a while. I need to just fall off the map and breathe. You know?"

"Yup, just opened up my laptop. Anywhere you have in mind?"

"Somewhere with a beach. I want to take Mas somewhere he's never been. Someplace on his list," he says thoughtfully.

"Greece it is." I laugh.

"Yeah, I was thinking the same thing. That kid is something else. I swear he makes me question my life daily," he says with amusement in his voice.

"I'll take care of it. You're not to worry about a thing," I say. "He'll love it."

"I owe you. Call Emma, she can help. She should probably come along to help with Mas. Hey, I have to go. Love you," he rushes into the phone and cuts the call.

I call my brother but get his voicemail. I frown and hang up without leaving a message. He never checks his personal messages anyway. I get ready to call Emma when a knock sounds on my office door. I close my laptop and stand.

"Come in," I call out.

Leslie pokes her head into the door. She's one of the third-grade teachers. For the most part, she's been keeping to herself this year. I know she has a little girl at home and she's newly divorced.

I give her a welcoming smile since she seems to be a ball of nervous energy. I want my teachers to always feel like they can approach me. I have an open-door policy.

"Hey, Leslie. What can I do for you?" I ask.

"I was hoping I could talk to you," she says softly.

"Sure, come on in." I wave her into the office.

"Thanks," she replies, looking over her shoulder before she steps inside.

My forehead wrinkles. I've never seen her behave like this. I wave her to sit in the seat across from my desk, before reclaiming my own.

"I think I'm going to puke," she says when she flops down into the seat.

"Excuse me," I say.

"I came in here to do something really stupid, but you've never been anything but nice to me," she says, dropping her face into her hands. "This is so crazy."

"O… kay. First, I think you should tell me what's going on here," I say slowly.

"I… I." She blows out a breath that causes her lips to flap, then pulls a face. "Listen, things have been crazy for me. My ex made sure I got nothing in the divorce but my little girl. I'm so tired. We make great money here, but with a little girl it's still not enough. I've been working odd jobs. I've considered joining one of those sugar daddy sites for Christ's sake—"

"Calm down. Where is all of this going?" I ask as she looks worried—wringing her hands one second and shaking them out the next.

"This guy turned up on my doorstep. He offered me so much money. I mean, a hundred grand would go a long way. You're the nicest guy ever, so at first I was reluctant, but my car broke down. The camp I need to send my daughter to this summer so I can work went up on its price. I just don't know how I'm going to make it all work," she rambles on.

"Wait, someone offered you money to do what?" I narrow my eyes.

"I was supposed to make sure people saw me come in here and then burst out of here like I have fire on my ass," she replies, biting her lip while giving me an apologetic look. "In a few days, I'm supposed to file a sexual harassment claim with the board."

"You have to be shitting me," I say incredulously.

"I'm sorry, Andy. If you fire me for this, I don't blame you." She starts to fan her face as tears begin to roll down her cheeks. "I just didn't think I could live with going through with it. You truly are a very nice guy. I was just going to turn around and leave, but I thought you should know someone is out to sabotage you. You wouldn't hurt a fly. These children love you."

"Can you tell me what this guy looks like?"

"Yeah, I'll never forget someone like him. He has the coldest dark eyes and blond hair that's graying around the left temple. I remember that because I found it so odd. I got the feeling he felt like talking to me was beneath him, but he never turned off that wolfish smile," she says and gives a shudder. "It was kind of creepy actually."

"Did he tell you his name?"

"No." She shakes her head. "He never gave me a name. When he left his number in case I decided to take his offer, the number was printed on a simple plain black card. Nothing but the number. I found that sort of weird too."

I sit and stare at her for a few minutes. Just then Mitch's name comes up on my phone. My mind is working overtime. I have a feeling when my brother looks into Kyle's aunt he's going to find one big rat behind all of this.

"Don't move," I say to Leslie, holding my finger up at her.

I answer my phone, grateful my mother insisted we learn Gaelic. I fill my brother in on everything Kyle told me and the bomb Leslie just dropped in my lap. I'm fuming by the time I'm done.

"Tell her to do what she came to do. I have a plan to throttle that rumbly fuck, I do. He picked the right one to fuck with, he did. Let's give him some rope," Mitch says and hangs up.

I look into Leslie's eyes. She stares back, fidgeting in her seat. She looks a lot like a scared mouse. That will help with what I'm about to tell her.

"Make your money, hon. Don't tell him anything you told me. Rush out and make it look good," I say tightly.

CHAPTER THIRTY-TWO

Warning

Andy

It's been one hell of a day. I'm still fuming when I leave my office for the day. To think, I was in such a great mood only hours ago. Now, I'm so mad my head could pop. I don't know how I made it through the rest of the day.

To be so conniving and deceitful. Using that woman's situation against her. I couldn't loathe Michael any more than I do in this moment.

With my messenger bag over my shoulder, I head to the empty parking lot to get into my SUV. I had to stay late to look over the summer budget and place the order for the new curriculum we're implementing next year.

Cracking my knuckles the entire way through the lot, I'm ranting in my head about Leslie. I've just placed my bag inside the car when I hear something move behind my truck, drawing my attention.

"Hey, gorgeous," Michael purrs, leaning against the back of my car.

"Get your ass off of my car," I hiss.

"Oh, so there is a bit of fire in the little schoolteacher," he says, flashing that annoying grin.

"More than a bit. Trust me, you don't want to find out how much. Get off of my car and get away from me," I fume.

"Why so hostile?" he says with a pout, his head twisting to the side. "Has Kyle been telling you bad things about me?"

I rein in my temper, remembering he's not supposed to know that he's been exposed, nor does he know that I've had my brother prying into his life. My fists are tight at my side as I look into his smug face. Not for the first time, I want to punch that smile right off of his face.

"What do you want?"

He drags a finger across the paint of my truck, pulling his hand away to look at it. He rubs his fingers together, making a distasteful face. His eyes are dead when they turn back to me.

"You should take better care of the gifts Kyle gives you," he says in disgust.

"You have to be shitting me. You're here to chastise me for dirt on my car?"

I give him an incredulous look. I realize too late that I've fallen into his trap. He was only fishing for information. His eyes light up, homing in on me, with the new detail I unknowingly coughed up.

"Nice gift. Was it for your birthday? Something to drive the little brat around in? Just a lover's reward? You look like you're a good pet," he says condescendingly.

"Again, why are you here?" I snarl.

"One of your employees paid you an interesting visit today," he says slyly.

I tighten my jaw, trying not to give him a reaction. I don't want to give Leslie away. I'm not sure if he knows she turned on him. I measure his words carefully. He sounds too smug to know the truth.

"I would be concerned about that visit if I were you," he continues.

"What are you talking about?"

I want to know his end game. I fold my arms over my chest, focusing on his body language. He is so sure of himself. I want to laugh in his face.

"Let's just say, you do something for me and I'll make sure she doesn't go telling stories to the board that just offered you that pretty little promotion," he replies.

My head whips back. I don't know how he knows about the promotion. It hasn't been announced.

"You're a complete asshole," I retort.

"That's up for debate," he says, waving me off. "Walk away. Leave Kyle. Don't give him a reason, just leave."

"You want to me to break up with him in the middle of the finals. Have you lost your mind? Ya have... this is what yer aiming for. Distracting him from winning. Trying to take everything from him. And on top of all the other shitty stuff happening to him, ya have been trying to expose him and our relationship," I say in complete revulsion.

Michael starts a slow clap, his grin turning into a full-out wolfish smile. His eyes roll over me with a look that makes my skin crawl. He licks his lips slowly.

"You're not only nice to look at, you're a smart one. I see why my Kyle likes you. But let me tell you something, sweetheart, you have no idea how far I'm willing to take this. How far I've already taken this," he says, his face turning dark. "You don't want to test me. Walk away."

"Fuck ya and the rock ya crawled out from under. Ya better go ask about me. Don't let me poormouthing fool ya. I'm not scared of ya or ya money. Threaten me again, y'all be sure to find out who yer taking a piss at, ya will," I fume.

"Oh, that's just sexy. Do you use that accent when he fucks you? Do you really think I care about your little Irish clan? I've looked into your family. Everyone thinks it's the money that gets me what I want. It's a lot more than that. I'm relentless in my pursuits. I'm willing to annihilate anyone standing in my path, anyway I can," he tossed back.

"Then ya bring all ya got," I say and spit in his direction. "Kyle and I aren't crawling into some hole to please ya."

"Feisty, I like it. You're still missing one critical point, pretty. I don't want him in a hole. I want him out. I want him standing by my side in all his glory," he says.

"Go fuck yerself," I snarl.

"Good luck with that promotion. It was nice to know you could've had it, isn't it?"

With that he turns to walk away. I'm tempted to jump in my car and run him over. The asshole isn't worth it.

Instead, I pull out my phone and text Mitch. I need to figure this out without disturbing Kyle's focus on the finals. He has enough on his plate.

CHAPTER THIRTY-THREE

Remember

Andy

"How are you feeling?" I ask as I stare at the screen on my phone.

For someone about to go play such an important game, Kyle looks so serene. His eyes are clear, and there's this peacefulness written all over his face. The finals have stretched all the way to game seven.

I've watched every game in awe of him. Still, this is the most calm I've seen him since the series started. It's a quiet determination that I admire.

"We're going to win," he states with such assurance.

"Cocky much?" I tease.

He twists his lips into a smile and shakes his head. "Nah, not at all. I just feel it in my bones. We're going to win, even if I have to drag us there," he responds.

"Well, when you do, know I'm right there cheering you on." I smile.

His eyes take on a thoughtful look. His brows pinch a bit. He nods at his own thoughts.

"And?"

"Yeah."

"When I win, I want you to know how much I appreciate you for being behind me and having my back. I love you for understanding me and helping me with Mas. I just... tonight. Remember this...." He shifts the phone, pounding his chest. "My family."

My eyes soften, and I smile. "Sure, babe. I'll remember. I love you too."

Kyle

The clock runs out, and I throw my arms out to my sides, letting a roar rip from my chest as I drop to my knees. I don't hold back my emotions as tears roll down my cheeks. I did it. I dragged this team to the championship.

Some of the team had been ready to give up three games ago, but I refused. Seven games, but this one meant everything. This was my answer to Michael, my example to my nephew, my thank-you to Andy, and my tribute to my sister.

"Yeah, Tyson, Yeah, yeah, baby," someone cheers.

My teammates crash into me, almost knocking me over. The moment is surreal. I've dreamed of this for so long. I've overcome so much to get to this point in my life.

"You did it, bro," someone says in my ear, as they hold me in a headlock and embrace me. "That's how you light up the court, B. I'm proud of you. Glad to be on your team."

My body is charged with energy, my scalp is tingling. Through my tears and silent praise, I recognize the voice as my teammate Russ. He has had my back during all of this. One of the few I've been able to count on, on and off the court.

Others are patting me on the back. I have goose bumps all over my skin. I came for this win and I got it. Now, my job here is done.

Andy

My voice is gone. I hollered so hard when the clock ran out, sealing the deal. Not that the other team had a chance to turn things around. Kyle was a true god on that court tonight. I saw him glow with focus and determination from the time he stepped out there.

"I knew he would do it," Mason says with a huge grin.

"That he did," I say hoarsely to Mas.

"All he needed was his family," he says, looking around the box.

This moment couldn't be better. I look around as well, taking in our family as they're gathered around us with smiling face. Everyone is here, my family and Kyle's. The joy I see is confirmation of Mason's words. We've cheered and sent our love down onto those hardwoods.

However, in the end, it was Kyle's heart that pulled in that victory. I just wish I could be down on the floor embracing him during his celebration. That would make this all the more memorable.

"Your boy did the thing." Chris comes over to pat me on the back.

I nod proudly.

"This calls for a huge celebration," Javier croons. "I've already planned something at the club."

"As if you need a reason to throw a celebration," Beau teases.

"What?" Javier shrugs.

Beau waves him off. I laugh, looking around again at all the people that Kyle has in his life. His friends would give the shirts off their backs for him. My family has fallen into the fold as well. Kyle is well loved.

"Everyone quiet down," Emma calls over the group as she turns up the sound on the monitors.

Kyle appears on the screen. Tears mixed with sweat on his face. He lifts his jersey to wipe the combination away. My throat clogs with my own emotions as I watch him rein it all in.

"That was an exceptional performance tonight, Kyle. How are you feeling?" the commentator asks.

"I'm feeling a whole lot of things. I can't even describe this," he responds, shaking his head and running a hand over his hair.

"You've put up an amazing fight this series. Can you attribute the heart you displayed to any one thing in particular?"

"My family," he says, pounding a fist over his heart.

My eyes close as tears threaten to overtake me. It's a simple gesture that no one else would catch, but it means the world to me. It's almost as good as being on the court with my arms around him. No, I think it's better.

I didn't understand that this was what he meant this morning. That he wanted me to remember because he planned to send me a message. Thinking back to that call now, it all makes sense. Kyle's thoughtfulness chokes me up.

I seriously didn't think I could fall more in love with you, Kyle Tyson. Boy, was I wrong.

CHAPTER THIRTY-FOUR

Get Away

Andy

"Mas wants to go to the Ideon Cave," Kyle says. "We can take him tomorrow."

As I sit in the middle of the bed, I barely follow his words. Between him rubbing oil into all of that gorgeous brown skin, the towel around his waist, and my scattered thoughts—I'm having a hard time staying focused.

This trip to Greece was supposed to be a reprieve, but I've been on edge for weeks. Once Michael threatened me, things changed. Mitch was livid and wanted to make him disappear that night. Once I calmed him down, he went back to his plan, but he did decide to take Leslie and her daughter somewhere safe. I covered for her at the school. The school year was already coming to an end anyway.

My lids close, cutting off the image of Kyle rubbing his chest. I shake my head to focus my thoughts. Taking Mason to the cave is an awesome idea.

"Oh, he is going to love that," I reply.

I open my eyes, locking them on Kyle's face. He breaks into a breathtaking smile that warms my belly. I love it when he gives that smile that reveals his teeth. It's him in all of his glory.

"Yeah, I know. The birthplace of Zeus himself. Might not be able to get him to leave." Kyle chuckles.

"That I'm sure of." I smile, looking down at my phone for the millionth time.

I've been waiting for Mitch to give me something, anything. I need to know what's going on back home. Everything seems fine, but I know what's lurking in the shadows.

When I placed the request to take a week this summer, it was granted without a problem. I trust my brother, but I'm starting to worry about what he's up to. So much is riding on him having my back. Michael is a psychopath, and I want to deal with this without involving Kyle in all of Michael's crazy.

I frown. If only I could keep my mind from running off. I need to stay in the moment.

"He's having a great time," I continue, looking up from my phone, fighting to stay focused.

"True. He's not the only one. As a kid, I never thought I'd get to come some place like this. It's so beautiful here," he replies, his eyes taking on a distant look.

"You deserve it. You worked hard."

Kyle nods. "It's bittersweet, you know what I mean? I wish my sister were here. None of this would have been possible without her pushing me when I was younger."

"Yeah, I understand. I'm sure she's smiling down on you. So proud of you and everything you've done."

"Yeah," he says softly, swallowing hard.

Sensing the need for a change in subject, I place my phone down on the bed and crawl to the edge. Reaching for his waist, I pull him closer. We've been sleeping in separate rooms while here. With all of the sightseeing and spending time with Mason, we haven't had much alone time.

"You know, you're rivaling the Greek gods in this towel," I tease.

"Is that right?" He grins.

"Yes, it is."

He leans in to take my lips. I sag into the kiss, my arms going around his neck. He breaks it much too soon, leaving me breathless and dazed.

His eyes search my face with a heated look—desire dripping from his gaze as his jaw works. Biting my lip, I stare back at him. Mischief lights his face.

Releasing my arms from around him, I sit my butt on my heels. I wait for him to share what he's thinking, eyeing him warily. I know he's plotting something in that head.

"Do you think you can keep it down? I have that gag you asked about," he says after a few beats.

My mouth drops open. Laughter bubbles up. We had a long talk about some of the kinks Kyle has preferred in the past, things that floored me.

"You do know I was joking about that?"

"Told you stop playing," he says with a wicked grin. "You know I bring it when you ask for it."

"Oh my God, you're a freak," I push out.

"I'll show you a freak," he says just before lunging for me.

I dash to the side, leaping from the bed. Kyle is right on my heels as I dart out of his room across the hall to mine. I just make it out his door and barely through mine, before he has the door closed behind us once again. Kyle pounces, knocking me to the bed.

We both chuckle low as our bodies hit the mattress with a bounce. I wiggle beneath him to turn onto my back. Reaching for his towel, I snatch it away.

He locks eyes with me, his lids lower, brows creasing. I follow his gaze as it drops to my lips, right before bouncing back to stare into my eyes. So much emotion rests in that look.

"Do you know how much I love you?" he murmurs.

"Not as much as I love you."

"Then you don't know," he says with a depth of sincerity in his voice. He leans into my ear. "Let me help you with that."

Kyle

Nipping my way to Andy's lips, I take them in a kiss that pours out all of my emotions. This trip has placed me on an internal journey. Winning the championship fulfilled my biggest dream. It also left me wondering what's next.

I realized I don't know. A ring has always been my goal. To push my way to the top. Now, I have to confess to myself that there wasn't much else on that list. Yet this man has me looking to create a new one.

"Kyle," he groans, as I bite his lower lip and tug.

"Yeah, baby. You want something?"

"Yes. You," he pants.

"I left the condoms in my room," I say, moving to get up.

Andy's fingers dig into my back. Looking down into his eyes, I watch his blue-grays search my face. He swallows.

"I'm ready to take that next step. You don't need them. We just got those results. We're both clea—"

I take his lips before he can finish. Devouring his mouth, I reach for the hem of his T-shirt. I let him up for air long enough for me to lift it over his head and toss it off the bed. My hands are at the drawstring of his sweats next.

We work together to get his pants off, nipping and sipping from each other's mouths at the same time. Andy's fingers bite into my back, pulling me down on top of him once I have him undressed. He takes me by surprise when he flips me on my back.

It's a little out of character for him but hot as fuck. My eyes remain on him as he makes his way down my body. He watches me as he cups my erection and rolls his tongue around the tip.

"Nah, baby, fair play. Bring the ass here," I say.

Andy grins around the crown now in his mouth. Shifting, he turns his body and climbs over my head. I lock my arms around his waist, bringing him down to my face.

"Mm," I hum around him as he fills my mouth.

Our moans and the sound of wet sucking fill the room. We both share in pleasuring each other. It becomes almost a battle. He swirls his tongue around me as he bobs. I swirl my tongue and hollow my cheeks. Andy does the same and deep throats me. We continue the back and forth.

Both of our hips are thrusting. I plant my feet on the mattress to thrust more. Andy moans, allowing drool to pour from his mouth, between my crack. His light natural musk is turning me on as it flavors his taste.

I feel him swell, telling me he's close. I am as well. Slapping his ass with a growl from my lips, he fills my mouth at the same time I fill his.

Popping free from the warm cavern of my mouth, Andy falls onto his side next to me. I stare at him with my chest heaving. Watching his sated glow already has me growing hard again.

My eyes shift to his bag in the corner. It's the same bag he uses to come to the house. I know he keeps lube packs in there. Standing from the bed, I go to retrieve them from the front pocket.

"Good thinking." He chuckles, breathlessly. "I forgot about those."

"You have a few condoms," I say, looking over my shoulder.

I catch him staring at my ass, and my lips turn up. He bites his lip and blushes. Shaking his head at the gold packets I found, he waves me back to the bed.

"I told you. We don't need them," he says.

I nod, dropping them back onto the bag. Sauntering back to the bed, I climb on, resting on my knees before him. Andy lifts up, wrapping his arms around my neck. His lips press to my jaw, moving under my chin to my neck.

A moan slips past my lips when he moves to the side of my neck, sucking the skin into his mouth. I palm his ass in one hand, using the knuckles of the other to glide down his spine. My eyes follow the path I'm making. The contrast of his skin to mine has my dick twitching between us.

I grow harder by the second. Andy stops sucking on my neck to look up at me. Dipping my head, I crush my lips to his swollen ones. His moans and groans make me impatient. Throwing the extra packets aside, I tear into one. Getting the lube onto my fingers, I toss the pack away.

One palm spreads his cheeks while the other one shifts to lube his pucker. Settling back on my heels, I lift him by the waist. Andy wraps his legs around me, while reaching between us to help guide me into him.

His other hand grips the back of my neck, holding on. His head falls back as I start to ease into him. We groan in unison.

"Kyle, please," he whispers.

"Please what, baby?"

"Please, I need you."

"Take what you need. I'm all yours. Don't hold back, ride it like you own it," I rasp. "Show me it's yours, And."

His head lifts, looking me in my eyes. That spark that's been appearing more and more fires up. He plants his feet into the mattress and starts to work his hips on me.

"Fuck yeah, that's what I'm talking about," I moan.

"You like that, baby?" Andy purrs. "You're going to come for me?"

"You know I am," I say.

Andy flicks his tongue over my lips, pulling a smile from me. Grabbing his rocking hips with one hand, I slap his ass with the other. The sound cracks through the room, mixing with Andy's gasps and groans. I give a few more good slaps, spurring him on.

Placing my hand on his stomach, I run it up his chest, tipping him back. Andy leans back, both of his hands grasping behind my neck as he works his hips on me. I roll up into him, catching everything he's giving.

My hand takes the trip back down his torso, until I have my palm wrapped around him, pulsing in my grasp. I start to stroke him. He shifts his head to look down his body.

My tongue peeks out of my mouth, resting between my teeth as I watch him. Those blue-gray eyes place me in a trance. Andy has been distracted lately, but I can see in this moment I have his full attention. His face twists in ecstasy, mirroring the feeling rising within me.

Sweat soaks his hair and face, and his cheeks are pink. From the tremor in his body, I know he's teetering on the edge. Biting my lip, my eyes narrow as I watch him. He's gorgeous on my dick. My nostrils flaring, my gaze shift down just in time to see him come all over my stomach.

My hands shift to his shoulder blades, bringing his chest to mine. I lock him in my embrace as I drive up into him. I'm close. His voice calling my name in my ear pushes me that much closer.

"Kyle, I love you," he whispers.

His words send a shiver rocking through me. I close my eyes, my jaw tightens, and a growl rumbles from deep within as I release. Our sweat-soaked torsos heave against each other.

I kiss his shoulder. "I love you too."

Pecking his forehead, I shift our bodies, lying on my back, pulling him to lie on top of me. Sucking in air, I gather my thoughts. That was intense. However, too soon Andy's body stiffens, telling me he's retreated into his head again.

"We should buy a place here," I say to test my theory.

Andy

I try to catch my breath, my chest heaving against Kyle's. He kisses my forehead and rolls onto his back, pulling me with him. I should be relaxed in his arms, but my thoughts start to take over again.

"Baby, did you hear what I said?" Kyle's voice pulls at my attention.

"No, sorry," I admit. "What did you say?"

"Never mind," he murmurs.

My brows crease, and my lips twist. I start to lazily rub his skin. I want to be here in the moment, I promise I do. I'm frustrated with myself and the situation.

Mitch demanded I let him take care of everything, but trying to do that is proving harder than I thought. He wanted to keep things in play without Michael catching on to us. That meant placing my career on the line with a written complaint from Leslie.

Something like this could leave lasting damage. It isn't whether the allegations are true. It's that they were made in the first place, and that will always sit in the back of people's minds—kind of like the drama going on with Kyle.

You're lucky I trust you, Mitch. God, I don't know why.

"I'm going to get some water. Do you want some?" Kyle asks.

"I'll get it," I say, needing a moment to walk off my thoughts.

Sitting up, I wipe the sweat from my forehead. My mind drafts again as I stare ahead. Being here in Crete has allowed me to think more rationally.

I let Mitch make this crazy decision to go through with Michael's scheme in a moment of blinding rage. I didn't take the time to think it through. Now, I'm paying for it because I can't think straight. I don't know what to expect. I'm also worried about Leslie and her daughter. Their whole life has been upended.

Fuck, Andy. You're making a damn mess. What if Mitch drops the ball on something?

I thought this was the right thing to do in the beginning. However, I've grown more concerned as my rage has weaned. It's the Connor hotheaded tempers that always get us in trouble. Kyle isn't going to be happy about any of this.

"You all right?" Kyle asks when I don't get out of bed.

"Uh, yeah, just need a second."

Blowing out a breath, I run my hand into the front of my hair. I need a second and a call from Mitch. I need to know what's going on back home. My brother keeps telling me he has it under control and he'll tell me when he has the details I need.

Freaking control freak.

"Are you going to talk to me or not?" Kyle asks gruffly.

"About what?" I reply, turning to look back at him.

"You've been distracted for weeks. It's only getting worse. At first, I let it go because you asked me to focus on winning the championship. Then you kept me distracted with getting Mas ready for this trip. But not distracted enough. I can see something is going on with you. Now talk," he says in that commanding tone.

I don't know how to tell him what's wrong with me without opening a huge can of worms. I don't want to ruin this vacation. When I am checked in, we have been having a great time. To see this beautiful place through the eyes of an inquisitive seven-year-old—who's fascinated with Greek mythology—has been quite the experience.

We still have a few more days left to this trip. If I tell Kyle everything now it will bring this vacation to a halt and turn our life on its head. We deserve better. We can deal with the mess when we return, or at least that's how I rationalize my silence.

"You know what? I have enough on my plate. You let me know when you want back in the relationship," Kyle says in frustration, climbing out of bed.

"Kyle, wait," I call after him.

"Nah, I'm good. Mas will be up in a bit. I'm going back to my room to shower," he says over his shoulder, not bothering to turn back to me.

Wrapping the towel around his waist that he entered the room in, he storms out the door. I get up to start after him, tossing on my sweats and T-shirt. The last thing I want is for him to be pissed off at me. This is turning out to be a total clusterfuck.

My cell phone starts to ring, but when I spin to look for it I don't see it in the room. It sounds so far away. That's when it hits me. I left it on his bed before I ran out.

Looking at the bedside clock, I see it's seven in the morning here in Greece. That means it's about midnight back home. My brow draws. I hope nothing has gone wrong with this shitstorm. I rush out of my room for Kyle's to get my phone from off his bed.

"Hey, Mitch. Is everything okay?" I hear Kyle say as I enter his room.

There is a short pause as my brother answers him.

"No, he's right here," he says into the phone, his face going from concerned to confused.

"Okay, hold on."

Kyle pulls the phone from his ear and places it on speaker, his eyes lifting to mine. I can see the concern there. We've been waiting to see what all Mitch will find out about Kyle's aunt. She's still pushing this custody thing. I can't say I haven't been keeping my brother busy. He took on all of this personally.

"Okay, you're on speaker. What's going on?" Kyle questions.

"Ya uncle was found dead last night. A bullet to the head. Body was found in an old crack house. My sources say that's not where he took his last breath. Ya aunt was confirmed to be in church at the estimated time of death, but she knows something, I see it in her eyes, I do," Mitch mutters.

My eyes close. I'll kill John if he went behind my back to do this. I wanted to go kick Rodney's ass and scare him a bit. We were holding off until I got this Michael mess squared away. After Michael's visit to my job, I just felt it would be better to wait. There's no telling if that nut job has people watching me. The last thing we need is someone bearing witness to what we had planned.

"Honestly, someone did the world a favor. Fuck him," Kyle snorts.

"Yeah, but it's a wee bit convenient for ya aunt. There's an insurance policy, and she is in need of the money," Mitch replies.

"For what?" Kyle asks. "I've been giving her husband money."

"It seems ya dear ol' uncle had a gambling problem. He's been paying out most of that money every month. Things have gotten tight. Ya aunt isn't doing too well. She has cancer, and the insurance company won't cover her treatments anymore," Mitch explains.

I push my hand into my hair and tug. This would give Kyle's aunt's motive for her sudden interest in taking Mas from him. It would also give her a reason to take Michael's help if he offered. My gut is telling me he used her hardship just as he did with Leslie. Rage starts to boil inside me.

"So you think my aunt had him killed?"

"Nope, ya didn't hear me say that. I said it would be convenient for her. Anyone that digs deep enough would come to that conclusion and think the same thing. Ya uncle's murder was sloppy. Not the type of work a highfalutin piece-of-shit lawyer would hire out," Mitch replies.

"So you think Michael has something to do with this?" Kyle nearly growls.

"I think it's his own insurance. I connected the dots. He's paying for ya aunt's lawyer. I get the feeling she may have been ready to back out of the deal just like our lass Leslie did," Mitch says.

"Leslie? Who's Leslie?" Kyle asks, his voice sounding confused as his brows come together.

"Thanks, Mitch. I appreciate you doing all of this. I'll call you back later," I rush.

"I told ya I'd take care of things. I put a huge wrench in his plans, I did," Mitch replies. "Ya don't have to worry about the school board. I pulled some strings to get the word back to Fairchild without the entire board being in on what's going on. Only the necessary players that would have our boy ready to make his next move. He hasn't a clue we're on to him. Ya owe me a beer. See ya when you get back."

The call ends and I think I may see the end of my relationship happening with it. I swear steam is blowing from Kyle's ears. The look of distrust he gives me is too much to bear. I start singing like a canary.

Kyle

Suddenly it's all making sense. The distance in Andy's eyes, his mind always off somewhere else. He's been hiding things from me. Michael has been fucking with him, and he has kept it from me.

"You needed to focus on the game, not on him trying to ruin my career. I had it handled," Andy blurts out.

I shake my head, holding up my hand.

"I'm not even trying to hear any of that. You have to be kidding me. He tried to fuck with your job? How? When? How long have you been hiding this? What else have you been keeping from me?" I snap.

He licks his lips nervously, shifting his weight to one leg and placing his hands on his hips. He looks at the floor between us as if it will provide him with answers. I cross my arms over my chest and wait impatiently.

"Mitch ran a background check on Michael for me. Mitch found out a lot of seedy shit. Things I'm sure you don't know.

"Leslie, one of my third-grade teachers, came to my office after Michael offered her money. She was to stage a scene and file a sexual harassment claim. She couldn't bring herself to do it and spilled everything. Later that day, Michael cornered me in the parking lot of the school. He demanded I walk away from you.

"Mitch and Javier have had a few of their guys watching over me since. Mitch has been working to find Michael's weakness to help me to end this all," he mutters in explanation.

"Un-fucking-real," I bite out. "You can't be serious with this."

"I'm very serious. Do you know the things that man has done? You heard what my brother said. He could be behind a murder. A few to be honest. He needs to be dealt with," he says in frustration, his eyes blazing.

"Yes, he does need to be dealt with, and what your brother said is the exact reason I don't want you involved," I snap back. "Fuck, Andy. My friends know about this and I don't! What the hell?"

"The guys know, but not because of me. Mitch felt they should," he says pleadingly.

"But I didn't need to know? He showed up at your job! You didn't think I needed to know that?"

"You can't keep handling me, Kyle. I'm a grown man, for fuck's sake. I know how to take care of myself. Yeah, I was fucked-up and insecure when we met, but I've never been this... this. I don't know. You act like I'm so fragile," he barks.

I cross the space between us and allow all the shutters to rise. The emotions and guarded feelings are in my eyes. My sorrows, my fears, my vulnerability in its entirety. For once, I unveil the truth for him to take in. I allow him to see the real me. All of me. I bare who Kyle Tyson truly is.

"No! You're not the fragile one. I am," I say as we stand face-to-face. "I love you so fucking much. I can't afford to lose you. I'd fall apart. You and Mas are my world, and someone is trying to take you both from me—"

He reaches for my arm, cutting me off.

"No one can take me—"

"No, you don't get it. I'm just barely holding on. I don't handle you, Andy. I protect you with everything I am so that *I* don't get hurt again. Because if I lose you or my nephew, I'm a dead man. There's no coming back from that. I'm just not that strong.

"It's too soon. He's aiming right for my weakness. You and Mas. I'll fight like hell for the two of you. I'm finally starting to breathe again after Savanna.

"I thought I had this, but I didn't start breathing until that letter was dropped in my lap. This is me, Andy. This is who I am. A man that loves hard and protects those he loves harder. You don't get to take that from me or deny me that. If you love me, then you have to love that about me. You have to allow me to always know you're safe. That I've done everything I could to keep you safe," I finish, breathing harshly.

"Sorry," he says, nodding and reaching to cup my face. "I want the same. To keep you safe. To keep the stress away. I know I did this wrong. I should've told you what I was doing and what was going on. I'll tell you everything I know, and we can decide together what to do next. It's a compromise. Will that work?"

I stare at him a moment, still angry that so much was going on behind my back. I place my forehead to his, closing my eyes. My arms go around him, holding him against me as close as I can get him. Breathing him in, I relent.

"Yeah, I can compromise," I concede, kissing the tip of his nose. "Your ass has a lot of making up to do."

"Yeah, figured," he says and huffs.

CHAPTER THIRTY-FIVE

Wisdom of a Babe

Kyle

It's a gorgeous day. Crete is such a beautiful island. The water here in Greece is a teal color that's so clear and inviting. It's nothing like Rockaway Beach in New York. I've never seen pink sand before. I'm in awe of this place.

Andy and Emma went to check out a restaurant for brunch and do a little shopping, while Mas and I got to spend some one-on-one time together. It's the first time it's been just the two of us since we arrived in Greece.

I took him out on the Jet Ski. We ran around in the sand for a bit and splashed in the ocean. Now, we're taking a breather, sitting side by side in the sand. We'll head back for lunch in a little while.

I look over at my nephew, observing him. He's getting so tall. My sister wasn't as tall as me, but I think Mas might get up there. I remember when he was just born. I was so amazed by him. I still am.

Whenever I look at him, I see his mother. She'd be so proud of her precious boy. I hope she can see how hard I'm trying to get this right.

"I think I want my own boat one day," he says out of nowhere.

"You'll make it happen. Whatever you want in life, I know you'll make it happen," I say.

"Yeah, I think you're right. I'm going to work hard and take care of my family just like you," he says.

I rub a hand over his head. He turns to look at me with that smile that owns my world. If I could keep him covered from the world forever, I would. I wish I could bottle his innocence and keep it in a safe place.

"You'll be a better man than me." I grin at him.

"That would be really hard, Uncle Kyle. You're amazing," he says with all seriousness.

"I think you've got this." I wink at him.

His eyes light up, but he doesn't reply. He turns to look back out at the water. I continue to watch him. Time seems to be flying.

My heart pangs as I think of his senior prom, him going off to college, the day he gets married. He'll be his own man before you know it. I want to steer him into all the right things in life.

"You still want to play piano?" I ask, remembering his request on the plane here.

His head swings back my way. His eyes are the size of saucers. I know instantly Emma will be booking him lessons as soon as we get home.

"Yeah! Can I?"

"Of course, kid," I reply.

"Thanks," he gushes.

"You're welcome."

We fall silent again, still watching the waves before us. I think back to my life at his age. I never thought I'd end up here, on this beautiful beach in Greece. I have my first championship ring, someone I love, and I want for nothing.

There were times I didn't want to live. Now I can't see myself not here in this earth to be around for Mas or Andy. I start to wonder how long Andy will be satisfied with the way we are. Once I fix things—and I plan to as soon as we get home—I wonder if the way things are will be enough.

Changes to my world mean changes to Mason's world. I don't know if he's ready for the changes I want to make to my personal life. I know one thing for sure—he's not going anywhere. All that custody shit is about to get squashed.

I come out of my musings to look over at him again. I find him looking pensive. My brows furrow. He's too young to look so weighed down.

"You look like you have the weight of the world on your shoulders," I say to my nephew, bumping his skinny arm.

He turns his head from wave watching to look up at me. He looks so perplexed, as if he's trying to form the right words to say to me. I wait him out.

"Can I ask you something?" he starts with.

"Yeah, anything, anytime," I reply.

"When is Uncle Andy going to come live with us?"

My brows draw in. He's looking up at me with the sincerest eyes. I don't know how to answer his question.

"What do you mean?"

He inhales and releases the deep breath. I can see the wheels turning in his head. He looks down, his eyes bouncing around with his thoughts. I know my nephew well enough to know he is in his feelings about what he's going to say.

"He loves you and you love him. Are you guys going to get married? When are we going to be a real family?"

"I… we—"

Holy shit.

I trip over my words until I'm simply rendered speechless. Mas holds my gaze, waiting for my reply. I purse my lips as I sort out my thoughts. Andy and I are always careful about PDA in front of Mas. I comb my brain for a time that he might have seen us revealing more than a friendship.

"You know, I'm smart, Uncle Kyle. I see things other people don't pay attention to. You guys can stop hiding from me. I know you're more than friends with Uncle Andy. It's not like you are with Aunt Emma and my other uncles.

"One of my friends at school has two moms. I think it would be cool to have two dads," he says.

"Is that something you want?"

He lifts his eyes up to the sky thoughtfully. I see the determination in his eyes when he looks back into my mine. He gives me a big smile.

"Yeah, Mommy would want it too. I want to see you happy. That's what matters, right?"

"You're a wise kid. Yeah, that's what matters," I tell him, choking back my emotions.

"Good, you should ask Uncle Andy to marry you. He's good for you. We should be a family. When I grow up, I'm going to have a family that makes me happy. You should think about doing that. You only live once, you know?" he says.

I roar with laughter. He is an old soul if I've ever seen one. I grab my nephew and tickle him. He laughs with me and it's the greatest sound in the world. I forget all the drama back at home and stay grounded in the moment. This is what I live for, the very thing I'll give my life to keep.

He's right. You only live once.

With that thought rolling around in my head, I begin to think over a few decisions I need to make. I'm ready for some change in my life. My priorities have been so out of order. I think it's time I fix that.

"So does this mean you're going to come ring shopping with me?" I ask him when our laughter dies down.

"Yeah! I can be your wingman." He beams up at me.

"My wingman? Where do you get this stuff from?" I chuckle.

"What can I say? I have the wisdom of Zeus." He grins at me.

"Yes, I believe you do."

CHAPTER THIRTY-SIX

Get This Straight

Kyle

I promised Andy I would compromise and I did. It took everything in me not to disappoint my nephew by ending our vacation to come back home. Mitch has been working a plan that doesn't land my ass in jail. My first instincts were to come back home and beat the shit out of Michael, but Andy reminded me of my sister's words.

However, Mitch has been taking his sweet time, and I'm getting impatient. That's why when he called tonight and asked us to meet him at Beau's gym, I was eager to get down here and hear him out. What I wasn't expecting to find was all of my friends.

"So what's this all about?" I ask.

"Fairchild is making a play for the gym," Mitch answers. "Created some shady paperwork, a deed and all."

My jaw clenches. I'm tired of this. I thought I was coming here to find out we were getting ready to put this to an end once and for all.

Instead, I'm hearing that Michael is coming for the one thing that means everything to Beau, Emma, and myself. Their father left it to the three of us. I hadn't been in their family for more than a heartbeat, and he added me to his will. Michael knows what this place means to the three of us.

"What the fuck? So what now?" I bark.

"We wait." Mitch shrugs.

"What?"

"He's coming to us. His arrogant ass wants to put on a show. A little birdie happened to let him know we'd all be here tonight," John explains. In the moment, he looks just like Andy as anticipation lights his eyes.

I'm going to break my foot off in Michael's ass. On everything I love, he is going to learn I'm not playing with him. It's one thing to try to fuck with my life. It's another to jeopardize the lives of the people I care about.

"Don't look so stressed out." Mitch smiles. "I promised ya I'd take care of this. I've got ya."

"I'm far from stressed. I'm livid. I want this over," I say tightly.

This is all about earning my attention. The more I ignore Michael the more bullshit he has pulled. He doesn't love me. This isn't about love in the least. It's about him having control and being the center of everyone's attention. Well, he'll get all the attention he wants now.

Mitch's phone pings. He looks down at it, and a smile grows across his lips. He looks up at me with gleaming blue-gray eyes.

"Aye, well, here comes ya chance," he croons. "Give me the signal and we'll shut this all down for good."

It's after hours, so when the doors to the gym open, we all spin toward them. Michael comes strolling in with a few goons following. My jaw ticks at the sight of him.

"Hello, fellas," Michael coos like a snake charmer.

"You have balls of steel," I hiss.

"Yes, well, you would know. Wouldn't you, love," he replies.

"Fuck you."

"Yes, at some point we may get back there. For now, I'm just going to teach you a little lesson."

"Is that right?" Beau hisses beside me and goes to take a step forward.

I place a hand on his chest to hold him back. If anyone is going to lay hands on Michael, it's going to be me. Beau reluctantly halts.

"Sorry to hear about you losing your promotion and your job, sweet pea," Michael purrs at Andy.

This time Beau is the one grabbing me. Chris is on my other side, helping to restrain me. I don't care if he's talking shit and doesn't know that Andy didn't lose a damn thing. He doesn't need to say a word to Andy, period. My lips curls back over my teeth as I glare at him.

"Oh, come on now. He can afford not to work. Don't be so sour about it," he taunts. "You see, I'm going to keep coming for the people you love and the things they love."

"You sure you want to play this game with me?" I snarl.

"Oh, love. I warned you not to play with me. Do you see how long I've been waiting for you to come back? Do I look like I have time for these games?" he bites out.

"You're the only one playing games. What don't you get?" I toss back at him.

I clench my fists at my sides. He's a damn lunatic. The anger running through me reaches a new level.

"You're the one not getting it, but you will," he says, looking around the gym. "This place is actually very nice. I'm going to make some good money off of it. You know, I used to want to box."

He gives a dry chuckle and starts to shadow box. I tilt my head and study him. My lips turn up, and I nod at my thoughts.

Reaching to unzip my jacket, I slip it off my shoulders. Andy takes it from my hands. I think we're on the same page when I turn to him and see the gleam in his eyes. I move toward the ring in the center of the gym.

"Get in the ring, Michael," I say, beckoning him with my hand.

He laughs, his head falling back. "What is this shit?" he snarls.

He folds his arms over his chest. His goons laugh around him. They're the only ones laughing. My crew stands ready to watch me knock this fool out.

"I said…. Get. In. The. Ring," I bite out.

Mitch and Beau go over to surround him to move him toward the ring. His goons go to flex, but my guys have them surrounded, staring them down. It's clear they don't want it. They back off, abandoning their boss.

Michael's face clouds over in disgust. So much for his hired hands. He's not about that life. What did he expect? Looking at his men backing off, he rolls his eyes, before shrugging off his suit jacket. His dark eyes glare at me with more hatred than I've ever seen him aim at me.

Good, the feeling is mutual.

"Let's go. We're settling the score. I'm going to teach you a lesson," I say.

Beau shoves him forward when he doesn't start moving. Michael snarls at him but starts for the ring. My lips turn up when his face begins to show concern.

His red cheeks reveal his anger. Michael loves to be the one calling the shots, always the one manipulating the outcome. Oh, how the tides have turned.

"You're a basketball player, Kyle. Not a fighter." The smugness returns with his words.

"Are you sure about that?" I say with just as much smugness.

I never told Michael that I used to train with Beau, only that I'm part owner of the gym. I could have boxed and done as well as I have balling. Not to mention, I've been a scrapper all my life. Savanna used to say I'm naturally good with my hands.

"Leave now and I forget about all of this," Michael says with less certainty as he steps into the ring. "The gym is mine. I have the docs to prove it."

"Sure you do, pudding," I tease.

His eyes scan the outside of the ring. His face crumples, seemingly calculating the situation. I snort to myself. He doesn't have to worry about anyone outside this ring. I've got this all on my own. As long as his men don't try anything stupid, we're all golden.

"Only one leaving here is you. But first, you and I need to make some things clear," I state, rolling my neck on my shoulders.

"Oh, really? What's that?" he mumbles while he starts to bounce on his feet.

"I know you're behind the pictures, the alleged sex tape, and the all so convenient death of my piece-of-shit uncle," I hiss.

"I did you a favor. Because of me you won the championship. You should be happy I took care of that piece of shit. He was bleeding you dry, and he deserved what he got," he seethes. "You abandoned me, tried to embarrass me by dating this nobody. I've done nothing but help you. You would be nothing without me."

Rage charges me as his delusional words spew from his mouth. His egotism shows how much he truly believes all of this. That ever-present grin only serves to piss me off more.

I throw my first two-piece combination, hitting him in his mouth to knock the grin off. He staggers back. His busted lip is satisfying on so many levels.

His entitlement goes beyond material things. Michael believes he has a right to people and their lives. He needs to understand he has no rights to me.

"You see. Your problem has always been thinking I'm one of your little boy toys. You've tried to play me from day one. You saw me vulnerable and you pounced," I say.

"I saw your potential and tried to pull it out. I saw me in *you.* You have potential to be great. You were better than the others," he rants.

He charges me with a few combinations of his own, but I dodge him and the weak punches he throws. He looks like a flailing fool. He's probably regretting entering the ring by now.

"I'm smarter than the others. I'm not going to bow down to your bullshit. I'm not going to let you ruin my life or anyone I care about."

I let a right hook fly, followed by an upper cut. His head whips back; his body sways right. I dance back, plotting my next blow. When he pulls it together he looks at me, shooting venom with his eyes.

"*You* ruined your life. You walked away from *me*! You were so worried about everyone knowing the truth, knowing that you loved me. Now look, they all know," he says with sinister grin on his split lips.

"That wasn't love. You don't know how to love. You're so fucked-up in the head from your biological parents, you don't know the meaning of love. That is if any of that shit was ever true. You're a fucking pathological liar. And nobody knows anything! All you did was plant seeds, but they don't know me. You don't even know me.

"If you did, you wouldn't try to force anything on me. I make the decisions in my life and do things when I'm ready. Instead of trying to rush me, you should have taken the time to understand me," I seethe.

"You are so wrong. I know everything about you. I know exactly how you think. This thing with that little schoolteacher isn't going to last," he snarls, tossing another punch.

I dip back out of the way. He throws another, but I block it quickly. His next one misses my face, but brushes my shoulder. It's not even enough to make me flinch. I rain blows on him, backing him across the ring into the ropes.

I back away, glaring into those cold eyes. I don't know what I ever saw in him. I snarl at him in disgust.

"Let me explain something to you. Yes, Michael, I've been broken a few times. I met the devil when I was a boy, much too early in my life to be afraid of shit now. If you wanted to come for me, you should have done so with guns blazing. This is only a taste of what I'm capable of. You can get touched, Michael.

"Stop thinking you're God. You're not. Don't play with me, my family, or my man. Do yourself a favor and forget all about me. Walk away, last time I'm going to tell you," I say in a calm I don't feel.

I throw a hard punch to his jaw, knocking him on his ass. From the look in his eyes as he struggles to sit up, I know I've made my point. At least, if he has any sense he'll take heed.

"We good, Michael?" I ask through clinched teeth.

"Oh, you're good. Good and fucked," he spits.

However, his confidence is as shaken as his voice. His eyes aren't glowing with that air of control. Michael looks like he'll think twice about fucking with me from now on.

"Wrong answer," I reply. "You fucked up, Michael. Your arrogance has caught up with that ass. Unlike you, I don't bluff. You never had a tape. It was a nice play, but again, I've never slept on you. In the back of my mind, I always knew you were going to show your true colors. We're done."

"We'll see."

"Yeah, we will," I toss over my shoulder as I turn to Mitch and nod.

This is a waste of my time. I've made my point. Although, with people like Michael it will never fully sink in. The world will always owe him something because he's so damn insecure and hateful.

Mitch nods back and puts his phone to his ear. This should be interesting. I can't wait to see what Mitch has in store.

Andy

Michael's cheeks are red with rage. Bruises are already blooming on his face. Yet he doesn't move from the floor as he glares at Kyle's back. I'm the nearest to him outside the ring as I watch him closely.

It's the reason I'm quick to react when he gets up to charge Kyle. Moving nimbly, I reach into the ring and grab his ankle, tripping him onto his face. Kyle turns swiftly at the sound of the crash.

"Ow, fuck," Michael hollers.

"I'd stay down if I were you," I hiss.

"The things I plan to do to your life," he snarls. "Both of you!"

"Yeah, yeah, yeah," Beau taunts, waving Michael off. "We almost done here?"

"Aye," Mitch says simply, his eyes narrowed on Michael. "Ya should have given up while ya were ahead."

"Fuck you," Michael barks. "You thugs beating up on me will never stop me. As for you, pieces of shit, you're all fired."

If you ask me, I think his men quit well before he stepped into the ring. The only reason they are still here is because we haven't allowed them to leave. Who knew a group of athletes could look so intimidating?

"You have a big mouth," Daniel grunts.

"I'm coming for you, too, all of you," Michael hisses.

"Aye, figured that, asshole. Good thing I know where ya buried that body," Mitch retorts.

"By the way, you killed the nephew of a kingpin, dipshit," Beau spits at him. "Good luck in prison."

Michael freezes, his reaction to Beau's words registering on his face. He closes his eyes.

"You're lying," he hisses. "You're bluffing."

"You wish," Daniel replies.

The blood drains from Michael's face. This is more satisfying than I thought. Seeing that look on his face is worth it.

"You're one twisted son of a bitch," Ray mumbles.

Trusting my brother was the right thing to do. With some more digging he found Fernando's body. It was a long shot, but my brother has good instincts. He followed his gut.

The feds enter through the front of the gym headed for Michael. My smile spreads across my lips. This is what he deserves. I hope he rots in jail.

A few calls and Mitch found out there were some feds salivating to get their hands on Michael. Wire fraud, money laundering, and racketeering are just a few of the crimes adding up against him. It turned out to be a win-win.

"Thanks, Connor," one of the feds says, walking up to shake Mitch's hand. "We've been looking for something to stick on this one for a while."

"Take him, then. We have no use for him," my brother says.

"I can't believe you betrayed me like this," Michael starts to shout at Kyle as they slap the cuffs on him. "After all I did for you. I loved you and you repay me like this? So ungrateful and selfish."

Kyle ignores him, moving to step out of the ring. He comes to me, hovering over me as he looks down into my eyes. I smile up at him.

"You can't even look at me while they do this. That's how I know you still love me," Michael continues to shout. "You'll forever have to live with this. I don't deserve this. I did nothing but love you all. Each and every time, you all were the ones that tried to leave me. You will always love me."

I search Kyle's eyes. His disinterest with this scene is clear as he stares back at me. He looks thoroughly over it. I'm right there with him. It's time to start a new chapter.

"I believe I'm done here." He confirms the look I see.

"Let's go home," I say.

CHAPTER THIRTY-SEVEN

Our Future

Andy

I sit silently beside Kyle on the bed. He has been lying on his back, staring up at the ceiling since his shower after returning from Beau's gym. I haven't said a word. I'm waiting on him to finish processing it all. Michael is one sick man.

"I want to buy a new house," Kyle says, breaking into the silence.

"Really? I thought you loved this place." I turn to look at his expression. He's watching me as always.

Yet I see something else in his eyes. The anger and tension from earlier are gone. His gaze is soft, and his face is open, almost hopeful.

"When it was just me, it was cool. I mean, I thought it would be just me." He takes a pause and frowns. "It was my first place. I had all these dreams of the perfect bachelor pad."

"Bringing home a different groupie every night," I tease.

He pulls a pillow from beneath his head and slaps me with it. I burst into laughter. It feels good to be able to joke around with him. Things were strained at the end of our time in Greece. I snatch the pillow and wrap myself around it, shifting in the bed to face him. He reaches for my left leg, placing it to over his stomach.

"Truth be told, I just wanted a safe place to get away after a long day. A spot to call my own. Shut out the world and think by myself," he replies.

"Okay, so you want something different for Mas now. I can see that."

This place is beautiful, but it's not the type of place I would think of to raise a family. When I first started to come by, I used to worry about Mas running around in here. The stairs freaked me out, with their openings and wide railings.

"No, I want something different for *us*," he says pointedly.

He pulls the pillow from me, tossing it aside. Lifting to place his back against the headboard, he then shifts me to straddle his lap. His hands go to massage my back.

"When you say us, you mean you and Mas, right?" I say cautiously and swallow hard.

I feel like I can't breathe. I don't want to get my hopes up, but it's hard not to wish for more. I know good and well Kyle doesn't want to expose Mas to our relationship. It's something I've compromised on. I knew what I was getting into. I'd never force him to change that.

If he ever changed his mind, it would have to totally be his decision. Yet I can't say there haven't been nights that I sleep alone in my bed in my apartment longing to be next to him. It's so much worse when I know he's here in the state. So near, but seemingly so far away.

He cups my face in his large palm, his warmth filling me. I take in the nervous look on his features. His thumb brushes over my lip, stopping in the center of it on the return pass. He applies slight pressure, watching the action as he does it. His eyes lift to mine again, and I see a new determination.

"Us means us. You, me, and Mas. My family," he says.

"Y… you want me to move in with you and Mas?" I stammer out.

"Yeah, Mas, and I want you to move in with us. I was hoping you'd be cool with that. Emma scheduled an appointment for us to go house shopping next week," he replies.

"You're sure this is what you want? What about Mason? He's only seven. We can wait. Give him more time to understand," I say.

My heart is in my throat. I want to say yes and give him the blowjob of his life, but I don't want to be selfish. This needs to be right for everyone involved.

"That kid took over for the tour guide in Greece. Corrected him on several occasions, giving him references to read and watch. Do you really think Mas doesn't understand?" he scoffs. "I've been underestimating my nephew. He knows. He told me the day we spent on the beach."

"Really?" I ask, my brows drawing in. "We're always so careful."

"And, babe." He gives me a pointed look. "Have you paid attention to how we gravitate toward each other? I had to be honest with myself. After Mas told me he noticed that we have a different kind of relationship, I watched. To someone who's not paying attention we may hide it well. And still... the way we love each other fills a room. My love for you is undeniable. I can own that now."

My mind is reeling. This is happening. I rub my hands on my thighs, while Kyle still has a hand on my back rubbing circles. I'll admit he's keeping me from spiraling into a panic attack. This relationship has just become real. I've been living a fairy tale for over two years now.

"Say something," Kyle says in a deep whisper.

"I don't know what to say. I don't think I'm awake," I reply honestly.

He draws my face to his, searing my lips with a passionate kiss. He bites down on my bottom lip before he pulls away. The look in his eyes sends a flame burning through my belly.

"You're awake. I can give you more proof if you like," he says, a lopsided grin on his lips.

"Yes," I blurt out.

"Yes, to what? Moving in or more proof," he asks.

"Both," I breathe, grasping his face and kissing him again.

I'm a bit thrown when he allows me to take over the kiss. He yields to my invasion of his mouth, sharing in the kiss, but not dominating it. I think to pull back at first, but my instincts when it comes to Kyle drive me forward.

I reach for his shirt, pulling it up over his head. My fingers are back over his waves as soon as the shirt is discarded. Again, he allows me to guide the kiss, taking direction from me. It's an empowering feeling. However, at the same time it's a humbling one.

This man has a need for controlling his environment and experiences. His ability to control his life is something that I love about him. It's a part of his charisma and charm. I learned early on in our relationship the buttons I could and couldn't push. This shift is a new level in our bond, and that fact is not lost on me at all.

I break the kiss to move my trembling hands to my shirt buttons. We watch each other as I slowly free myself of the fabric. I clasp his hand, placing it over my heart.

"This beats for you. I was born to be with you. Wherever you go, I go," I say.

He nods, lifting his other hand to stroke my face in the tenderest caress. His eyes speak a thousand words, all of love and trust. He was right—the way we love one another is enough to fill a room. Or better yet, an entire home.

"I've never needed to broadcast who I am. I just needed the right person to help me carefully unfold the many layers. Someone safe, someone loving, someone for me," he says. "Someone like you."

Our lips are locked again, but I can't tell which one of us initiates the kiss. We cling to each other like lifelines. I pour all of my love into the connection. He is just as much my safe place as I am his. We're the balm for each other's scars.

I pull back when, again, he's allowing me to take the lead. Searching his eyes, I find the unspoken answers. I'm filled with a profound level of love for him.

Kyle is handing me a gift, and I intend to cherish and worship it. We slow things down, taking in the connection and elevation in our relationship. No words are spoken; none are needed. We remain in the moment, sharing an intimacy not meant to be shared with anyone else.

Kyle's trust in me sets my blood on fire. However, this is something we both approach with care and love. The entire experience leaves me breathless and filled with mixed emotions.

Kyle

Coming down from my climax, I stare up at the ceiling. My mind is conflicted. While that was amazing—I mean, a spiritual connection was evident, and Andy took his time with me—I wouldn't say that was the best sex of my life. I did come. That's not the issue.

I'm not sure if it's my aversion to anal or Andy's timid and cautious touch. Something was... it didn't take me all the way there the way our sexual connection usually does. I can't say it was traumatic. It was just... I can't find the words or thoughts to sum it up.

We're always honest with each other, especially when it comes to sex. However, I don't know how to tell him what's on my mind, while sparing his feelings. The last thing I want is for him to get in his emotions, allowing those insecurities to surface.

"Can I be honest?" Andy says nervously.

"Always," I murmur.

"That wasn't what I thought it would be. I mean, the connection was there. That part was amazing. I'm just not.... Thanks for sharing that with me. But... yeah, I'm not sure I liked it," he says cautiously.

I tighten my arms around him, looking down we come eye to eye. With a smile on my lips, I peck his. We both burst out laughing, tears rolling out the corners of our eyes as we lie there. I'm glad he said something.

"Yeah, I feel you," I say through my laughter.

"It's not you," he starts. "I—"

"We're cool. Might be something to work on or revisit at another time," I reassure him.

"Maybe," he says, not sounding too convinced.

I laugh some more. I love the honesty we have. With the past now officially out of our way, we can move forward into our future. We'll figure out what's right for us. As long as we do it together, I'm good.

CHAPTER THIRTY-EIGHT

Closing the Past

Kyle

I wipe the sweat from my face as I climb the stairs from the basement. I've been working out while Andy and Mas went out for ice cream. Emma is taking a much-needed vacation before life gets crazy around here. I'm grateful for all of the time she's put in with me and Mas.

Emma's vacation has also given Andy and me time to see how we'll all adjust to Andy living with us full-time. So far so good. If I were to be honest, Mas seems to be happier than ever. Rumor has it he even has a little girlfriend at camp. He's been asking for an extra snack every morning.

So much for me shielding his innocence. That kid is seven going on twenty-one. I think I'll settle for protecting him and his happiness rather than covering him from the world. He's wise beyond his years and teaches me something new every day.

The doorbell rings as I get to the top of the stairs. A smile comes to my lips. Andy must have forgotten his key. Mas was talking his ear off when they left. I watched him have to double back for his wallet.

I jog to the front of the house. When I open the door, my smile falls from my face. I go from zero to hundred in seconds. I was peaceful and content. Now, I'm raging mad, praying Andy returns soon to calm me down.

"Please, I just want to talk," Aunt Bethany pleads when I go to slam the door in her face.

"Have your lawyer call my lawyer," I say, continuing to shut the door.

She steps in the doorway barely quick enough to keep me from closing the door. Her eyes look up at me pleading. I only pause because a memory of my mother singing and dancing around the living room enters my head.

I frown and hold the door open enough for her to enter. She moves slower than I'm used to. Instead of making her way to the living room, she takes a seat in one of the gold-and-white decorative wingback chairs I have in the foyer. I lean up on the door with my arms folded across my chest.

I take a few minutes to observe her. She looks winded. Her skin is uneven, and she looks smaller than she was the last time I saw her. I'll be real. She doesn't look well at all.

Aunt Bethany pulls a handkerchief from her purse and starts to dab at her forehead. Guilt rises. Savanna and my mama would still want me to be civil to this woman. I clear my throat, pushing off the door.

"Can I get you something to drink?" I ask.

"Please, baby. Some water," she says softly.

Her words paralyze me for a moment. I remember when she was this gentle with me as a boy. There were times when we first arrived in her home that she was comforting and loving.

I shake it off and go to get her a glass of water. I rinse a glass, stopping to grab the edges of the sink. I drop my head between my shoulders and take a minute to collect my thoughts. I feel like an elephant has taken residence on my back.

As much as I want to hate that woman out there, she's my aunt. The last blood relative I have outside of Mas. She looks as bad as Savanna did near the end. I can't ignore that as much as I would like to. Pain rocks my body as I think of all my sister went through. I made sure she had the best to ease her pain.

Aunt Bethany has nothing. From what Mitch says, they haven't released the insurance money yet. Until seeing her like this today, I told myself I didn't care. Now, I can't say that with a straight face.

"You always did take your sweet time," I hear behind me.

I turn to find my aunt sliding onto one of the barstools at the kitchen island. I move to put water and ice in the glass from the refrigerator door. Placing the glass in front of her, I take the seat next to her.

"I didn't come here to upset your life any more. I'm in no shape to take that child from you. I didn't want to go through with it in the first place. When I found out Rodney gambled the deed to the house away and I couldn't pull the money I needed from it, I was crushed. Then that man showed up offering us all kinds of help and information—" She breaks off to give a dry cough.

She lifts the glass with a shaky hand to take a sip of the water. Her hands are so frail.

"Don't," she whispers. "I don't deserve your pity."

"Why are you here?" I ask.

"I did my sister's children so wrong," she says on a small sob. "I didn't want to believe the things you two said. Rodney was the only man I ever knew. He sweet-talked me right out of my mama's home. Mama told me he was the devil in a dress suit. I was grown and knew it all. I wanted to be married like my big sister.

"Your daddy was so good to her. He worked so hard for you all. The night they were killed in that car accident, your father was going to tell her he got a promotion that was going to allow him to be home more, to spend more time with you kids. I knew because he'd come to me, planning something special and asked me to babysit.

"I was so jealous. I had a husband that took me to church every Sunday. He was adamant about our following the Lord, but when he wasn't home, I knew he wasn't working hard like your daddy. I was so guilty when your mother died.

"I couldn't have kids of my own, so I thought the Lord was punishing me for my jealousy by making me raise my sister's kids. You two were so perfect. It was killing me to sing you to sleep at night, braid your sister's hair." She stops for another coughing fit.

"So you let him abuse us because you hated us?" I say to my hands in my lap.

She sips the water quickly, then shakes her head.

"No, no, no. When I tell you I didn't know, I truly didn't see what was going on. I knew he was stepping out on me. When your uncle started bringing me weed and alcohol, I thought he was just trying to distract me from the woman down the block he'd gotten pregnant. At that point, I was so low, I never thought it was to take my focus off of you two.

"He'd feed me that shit, then tear me down and tell me to go to church to repent for my weak and sinful ways. I hated that man, but he always gave me enough of everything to be content. I never learned how to be on my own. I never had a job. I never paid a bill in my life until the month after that man was murdered. I had two children to look after. I couldn't leave him." She stops as tears roll down her face.

"You really didn't know?" I ask with disbelief dripping from my words.

"I should've seen the signs. Now, when I think back, I know I should have.

"I wasn't going to take you two at first. I didn't feel I deserved you. He had me sold on the dream of finally having the children we always wanted. He had an entire family down the block. I thought if we were the perfect family he'd choose to take care of us, not them. It's why I started being so hard on you two. I was so selfish," she sobs.

"I won't deny that," I mumble. "Why believe me now? Is it because he's dead?"

"That day... when you told me what he made you do. I... I wanted to believe you were lying. I went home and prayed that you were lying. It was in the middle of praying that I lost my mind and started tearing the bedroom apart." She gives a bitter laugh.

"Be careful what you ask the Lord for. I found a hidden hole in the wall. That son of a bitch had pictures of you as a little boy, naked. My sister's precious baby boy. That motherfucker was touching you from damn near the time you entered my home. Then I found pictures of your sister and others—other children, women, men—"

"You can stop." I hold my hand up.

"I need to tell you this," she presses. "I never agreed to take Mas. I never signed those papers to take him from you. Rodney went behind my back and did all of that. The day I found all of that shit, I gave up trying to save my life. I had no use for that money. This is the least of what I deserve. But that son of bitch wasn't going to be left on this earth to bother you for another minute. I had planned to pour bleach down his throat in his sleep.

"What time do I really have left? I would have gladly finished my days in prison. That still wouldn't be enough to right what I did or what I allowed to be done. But that smug-ass lawyer came back and said he'd take care of Rodney. All I had to do was get him to the location he gave me," she reveals.

"But why would he do that?" My brows furrow.

"I think Rodney was threatening him for more money or to get the money that was promised to me if I went through with taking Mason," she replies.

"Okay," I say, looking up from my hands. "But why shame me for being gay? Why'd you take me to that church and make me feel like I was the most disgusting human on earth?"

"Damaged people damage people. I thought I did something to mess you up. I had failed my sister and her children. I truly believed God would fix you—"

"I wasn't broken!" I bellow. Tears stream down my face. "Being gay wasn't what needed to be fixed. I didn't need God to make me straight. I needed to get away from your husband. For so long in my life, I didn't want a man or a woman. I couldn't stand to be touched. That has nothing to do with being gay. It had everything to do with being raped and molested repeatedly."

I point to myself and continue.

"I'm a praying man. I talk to God daily. Never once have I felt in my spirit that He doesn't love me because of who I love. You had that pastor try to break my soul because you *thought* I was gay. You never asked me, you never talked to me about it. I told you I wasn't because I didn't realize that I was. I was thirteen! I'd been confused about sex and relationships for years. Had you talked to me, you could've helped me understand my way through it all.

"You took that monster's word for it. Your husband fed you that shit to taunt and abuse me and you threw me to the wolves to quote unquote *fix* me," I say angrily.

"And I will forever be sorry for that," she murmurs through her own tears. "We always take the most beautiful things and destroy them. I did that with God, you, and your sister. You've built a beautiful life for yourself. You were there for Savanna when she needed you, and you're doing a wonderful job with her boy.

"That—" She points to my heart. "That's a blessing from God himself. You have a heart of gold. You always have, you always will. I didn't come here for forgiveness, but I wanted you to know I'm sorry—"

"Well, you've said it."

She purses her lips and nods her head. Lifting her handkerchief she wipes her eyes. I don't know how to feel. I have so many warring emotions going on inside me.

"You've always been just like your mother. I never learned my lesson. I envied a child, and because of that I lost the opportunity to be the mother I always wanted to be. That's the real reason I treated you so poorly. This is a house of my own creation." She laughs bitterly.

I feel my brows wrinkle and my head jerks back. The one emotion that becomes prevalent is pity. Not because she's dying, not because she's sick. I pity her because she's sitting here admitting that many lives were ruined because that narcissistic spirit lives inside of her.

"Thank you," I hear myself say.

She looks up at me, confused. I, on the other hand, have never seen things clearer in my life. I feel like I'm seeing life for its true meaning as I sit here.

"For?" she asks.

"Showing me that it's not about me. There are bigger things in this world, people who need us more than we need to please ourselves. Mas deserves better than me protecting me or me pleasing me. Thank you," I say.

"I know I had nothing to do with it, but you're a great man, Kyle. Nothing and no one can take that away from you," she says and stands. "Whoever you find to love will be blessed to have you."

"I know I am," I hear Andy say.

I turn to see him standing a few feet away. I get up to walk over to him, wrapping an arm around his waist. I place a kiss to his forehead before turning back to my aunt. I'm surprised when I don't find a look of disgust on her face.

"I've said my piece. I won't disturb your life anymore," she says.

"Aunt Bethany, wait," I huff.

Maybe we can find a treatment for her that will help. I can do some research and make a few calls for her. I go to tell her as much, but she raises her hand.

"I've been sick for years. I won't waste your time or your money. I didn't come here for that. All I ask is you don't let them bury me anywhere near that man. If my punishment is to see him in hell, so be it, but I will not have my bones lying next to that piece of shit," she mumbles.

"You sure have been cursing a lot the last two times I've seen you," I tease.

"I'm sure you've heard worse. Besides, who's gonna spank me? My mama been long gone," she says with a ghost of a smile. The small smile wobbles before she places her next request. "Can I say bye to the baby?"

"Sure." I nod. "You can say hi."

CHAPTER THIRTY-NINE

Reveal My Heart

Andy

As much as Kyle's Aunt Bethany hurt him, he still had empathy for her. This loss has rocked him. She died a few days after she appeared at the house to see him. When he received the call, he sobbed like small child.

He has shut down a bit since. I've been waiting him out, which is why I was thrown when the guys arrived this morning and said that Kyle had asked them all to come over. In fact, I was hurt. I thought when he was ready to open up it would be to me, not his group of friends.

I've tried not to let it show, but I don't think I'm doing a good job of it. Everyone is in the living room waiting for Kyle to come out, and I've been in the kitchen pacing. I asked the chef to make us all breakfast, and I've remained in here pretending to help.

"Yo, And," Kyle calls from the living room.

"Yeah," I reply.

"Come here."

I roll my eyes but turn for the living room. I enter the spacious room where I left everyone after letting them in. I stop in my tracks. I'd been so angry I didn't notice everyone had arrived in white linen shorts and buttons-up shirts.

How did I miss that?

Now, they are all standing around the living room with light green roses in their hands, holding them over their hearts. They look like white knights, a legion of gorgeous forbidden angels or gods as Mas would call them. Confusion covers my face. I look from side to side, searching for Kyle to figure out what's going on. Blitz's bark grabs my attention. I turn around to find Kyle, Mas, and Blitz standing behind me. Both Kyle and Mas have green roses in their hands.

"These are my brothers, my family, the people I trust most in my life. When I need to build, I sit down with them. They help me make my best decisions. If I fall I know I can count on one of them to lift me up. There was a time I was good with that—only having my brothers as my counsel.

"Then life decided I was ready for more. That I was ready to expand my family, to grow my circle of trust. When Mas asked me when we were going to be a real family, I didn't know what to tell him. I thought about it long and hard.

"The answer I came up with is… we already are a real family." He says the last part as he digs into his pocket and pulls out a box. "Mas also gave me some great advice. He told me I should ask you to marry me. I think the kid is a genius—"

"Kyle," I choke out like a warning.

"Hold on, baby. I'm not finished. I thought his advice was genius, so we went out ring shopping. Then I called my counsel, my brothers, and my family." He takes a pause in his words.

I wrap my arms around my middle to hold myself together. My family starts to enter the room all dressed in white, holding the same green roses as everyone else. My mother, my dad, and my siblings. Daphne and Emma are right behind them.

"You see. My life has been filled with abundance since I met you. I didn't realize it until I looked around at all my blessings. Green roses are a sign of abundance, of constant rejuvenation of spirit, the renewal of life. You bring me a constant renewal. Every time I look into your eyes, I feel rejuvenated." He takes another pause, handing Mas the rose he's been holding.

Everyone comes forward one by one, starting with Mason, placing the roses at my feet. Kyle begins to fill the space with the perfect melody as he croons with that rich deep voice of his. I start to laugh, a big smile taking over my face as he sings about not wanting to be right if loving me is wrong.

He once said that our love could fill a room. I can definitely feel the love everyone is sharing with us. When everyone has placed their rose down and cleared the way, Kyle is standing before me.

He lifts a hand to swipe a tear from my cheek. Still singing in that soulful voice, he locks eyes with me. Belting out the last note, he drops to one knee before me.

"I want to make my decisions with you. I want to come to you when I'm thinking about building in my life. I want to raise Mas with you and be the family we were meant to be. Andy, will you marry me?" he asks, opening the box in his hand to reveal a ring.

"Yes," I try to say through my clogged throat.

Kyle slips the ring onto my finger, lifting to his full height to cup the back of my neck and kiss me just the way he did the very first time. Only this time, I know who I am. I'm confident in the person that stands before him, and it's all because of his love.

"Now that's how ya do it," Mitch cheers.

We break our kiss as the entire room bursts into cheers and laughter. Kyle wraps his arms around me, hugging me hard enough to crush me. I embrace him just as hard.

"I have an announcement to make," Kyle says to the room. "I'll be retiring from the NBA. Andy and Mas are more important to me. I think it's time I do something else."

I pull away and look up at him. I know my face has to reveal my shock. He shrugs as if it's no big deal. I know it's not that simple. He loves to play. I can't believe he's making such a huge sacrifice.

He dips his head to place his lips to my ear. "I love you and Mas more. It's time I focus on the things that matter most," he says, kissing the shell of my ear.

"As long as you're happy," I say, searching his face.

"You said yes. I'm good," he says with a sparkle in his eyes and a sexy smile on his lips.

Kyle

It's been a good day. I took my aunt's passing hard, but it also made me think about how short life is. I planned today as the start to the rest of my life. I was glad all of our family could be here with us. These are the people that have been there for me and Andy without question.

I look at Andy across the yard, sitting with his family and Mas. It's like a scene out of a movie. The scene is picture-perfect, but it's the smile on Andy's face that's enough to push this day over the top. All roads have led to this. Sure, there were cracks in the path, a few detours, some scrapes and bruises, but they were all worth it in my opinion. They're my battle scars and I own them, no one else.

I turn back to my friends sitting around me. It's that time. Our mandatory check-in. Javier pours the brandy he brought with him into tumblers, passing the glasses to the left until we all have one in our hands.

I count myself blessed for the millionth time today. These men dropped everything to be here for me. That's more than I could ask for.

"To our brother's new beginnings." Javier lifts his glass to salute.

"Salud," we say in unison and take a drink.

"This is bittersweet for me," Ray says.

I turn to him, already knowing what he's talking about. Ray has been holding out hope for years that we'd get to play together.

"You should be happy he's retiring. He can stop busting our asses," Chris says teasingly.

"Man, that's what makes it bittersweet. On one hand, I know I can win a championship now. On the other hand, I was hoping to someday do it with him," Ray says, looking down into his glass. "It would have been nice if we all could have pulled off getting on the same team."

"You know that wasn't going to happen unless you were willing to come to my bum-ass team. They paid too much for me. Nobody wants to buy out this fucking contract. I'm going to have to take a pay cut if I want out," Chris mumbles.

"Man, what you talking about? Your team made the conference finals. We didn't get out of the first round," Ray huffs.

"Yeah, we made the conference finals, but it wasn't because that team is any good. I'm just saying. The team we have now will never be a finisher. We get by on dumb luck," Chris says and sucks his teeth.

Everyone falls silent for a moment. We could sit here and debate what sucks about our teams, but it's not why we're here. If we go down that road, we could go on forever.

"What's the plan?" Beau asks, breaking the silence.

"Find a new place for us to live, plan a wedding, and open a safe place for orphaned kids," I reply.

All of my friends sit forward in their seats. I know I have their full attention. We all have been through rough childhoods.

"You've thought this out, I see," Jordan says.

"Yeah, I was going to talk to Beau. We still have one lot we haven't broken ground on yet. Permits have been screwed up, and the crew had some issues—maybe with good reason. It's big enough for what I have in mind," I say.

"Sounds like a plan. We tripled our targeted projections for the other lots. I say we go for it. We can get some plans drawn up and get started on the logistic of running something like that," Beau replies. He already has his phone out. I'm sure he's making notes or sending texts out to get the ball rolling. I appreciate that.

"I was thinking… if you guys are interested in raising the money like we talked about, we should move forward with opening the school. Give the kids a home and safe place to learn."

Silence falls again. I can see the distant looks that cover a few faces. Safe homes and places to learn weren't a given when we were coming up. We could all tell stories.

"I like that," Chris says into his glass. "I like that a lot."

"You think Andy would want to take on the school? You know, become the principal there?" Beau asks.

"I don't know. Maybe," I muse.

I don't know why I hadn't thought about that. I make a mental note to make the offer. He loves his school, but you never know.

"Whatever you need, I'm in." Javier lifts his tumbler.

I smile. Javier's connections will prove invaluable. Beau's fingers fly over his phone some more. I can already see this coming together. It feels right. Everything is falling into place. This is exactly what I need to do.

"Man, life sure can throw you a curveball. I never thought one of us would be getting married." Jordan smiles.

"You're telling me." I laugh.

"Dude, I mean, don't get me wrong. I wouldn't mind finding someone to just kick back and chill with," Jordan adds. "I'm getting tired."

"I know what you mean," Javier says glumly. "I'll be retiring soon. It feels like I should be retiring my antics at the club as well."

"Seriously," I interject, tilting my head to look at my friend more closely.

That usual spark is missing from his eyes. He does look more taxed than usual. I start to look at all of my other friends. They all seem to be in deep thought.

"How's Joey?" I ask Chris.

That question brings a smile to his face. There was a time that I thought those two would be married by now. Joey and Chris have known each other since they were little. They're like night and day, but they're perfect for each other.

"He's good. Real good. Don't tell him I forgot to tell you he said hello." Chris grins.

"I'm so telling," I tease.

Mason's laughter pulls my attention. I turn to see him sitting next to Andy, leaning against him with his head thrown back. From this angle, I can see the joy on his face.

"You did good," Daniel speaks up. "He loves Mas as much as you do. That kid truly believes you two could hang the moon for him if he asked."

"For him, I'd find a way," I say.

"We know," Beau replies, slapping a hand to my back. "Trust me, we know."

CHAPTER FORTY

Dreams Do
Come True

Kyle

I stand beside Andy, with a sleeping Mas in my arms. He wore himself out with all the excitement. We're seeing the last of our guests off for the night. We've done breakfast, lunch, and dinner together in celebration of the engagement.

I think everyone's a bit worn out and ready to call it a night. The guys are gone expect for Beau, who's sticking around to help Emma clean up in the backyard. They'll probably be crashing here for the night.

"That was such a lovely proposal," Andy's mom sings. "Ya out did yerself, Kyle."

"I'm *so* jealous," Tara sighs out, with a dreamy look in her eyes. "I guess I'll finally have to change my screensaver. It feels so dirty to have my brother's husband on my phone."

"Don't move so fast. You never know when we might need a beard," Andy jokes.

"Nah, that's not going to be necessary," I say, staring Andy in the eyes.

His brows dip. I can see the questions dancing across his face. I give him a lopsided grin and wink. We have a lot to talk about. I wrap my free arm around his waist, pulling him into my side.

"Youse guys have a lot of planning to do," Andy's dad says. "I'll be waiting with my checkbook open."

Andy's head spins toward his dad. His face is more stunned now than it had been a moment ago. I feel his body stiffen at my side, he's holding his breath. I start to rub his ribs to soothe him.

"You don't have to do that," he pushes out.

"Aye, of course I do. I figured it's my job since Kyle was the one to propose. You boys let me know what youse need. I'm taking care of it," Oscar replies.

"Seriously?" Andy utters.

"Aye, I still ache that you didn't feel ya could come to me for ya surgery. I would have paid for the best for ya. I'd sell my arm to give ya the world if ya asked.

"I've worked hard to give youse all anything ya need. Even knowing what the grands left the lot of youse. Yer never a burden, And. It's just money. Knowing yer happy is priceless. Ya wouldn't have to ask me twice, ya wouldn't," Oscar says, his eyes beginning to mist and his voice clearly getting emotional.

He places a hand on Andy's shoulder, bringing him in for a hug. They stand in a tight embrace for a long moment as the rest of us look on. Honoria moves in to wrap her arms around them when both of their shoulders begin to shake. Mitch, John, and Tara all join in on the family hug.

Not for the first time I admire the connection and love the Connor family shares. I've longed for that all my life. As if I'd said the words out loud, Mitch and John open up the circle, holding their arms out for me and Mas to be brought in.

With both arms around my nephew, I step into the group, accepting our place in this family. Mas stirs a little, but he doesn't wake. My heart is overwhelmed as I think of all the love my nephew has gained. This isn't just my new family—it's his. He'll always be loved.

Everyone starts to break out of the hug one by one. We all stand around with smiles on our faces, a few cheeks moist from tears. I'm happy that they're tears of joy.

"We'll be getting out of ya way for the night," Honoria says. "Oscar, let's go. They need to get the wee lad to bed, and I'm sure they want to celebrate."

Mitch and John groan, while Tara and I laugh at Honoria's mischievous smile and the wiggle of her brows. Oscar gives a crooked grin as he shakes his head at his wife and wraps an arm around her shoulders.

"I'll be back tomorrow afternoon. Promised my nephew I'd take him to a game," Mitch says with his chest poked out. "I really have a nephew. Yer showing me up, And. Not sure I like it, I'm not."

"Get over it," Andy tosses back.

"Congratulations." Mitch pats his cheek. He then takes two fingers, gesturing between his eyes and mine a couple of times.

"Remember, I'm still watching ya. If ya break my brother's heart, I'll batter ya."

"Ya have nothing to worry about," Andy huffs. "Ya should be more concerned with the one yer stringing along."

"Good night, good people," Mitch says and rushes for the door.

We all burst into laughter. He's out of the house like someone set fire to his ass. I heard about Mitch and his antics. I'm sure there's an interesting story there.

"I'll give you two a few days before I show up to help plan the wedding," Tara says with stars in her eyes. "This has to be epic."

"*No,*" Andy groans.

"Oh yes," she sings. "I've been waiting for this day."

"Get out," Andy teases, pushing her toward the door.

"Love ya." She turns her head to kiss his cheek, then follows her parents out the door.

"Proud of ya, And," John says, pulling his brother into a hug. He turns to me. "Thanks. Yer exactly what I always wanted for him."

With that John turns and leaves. Andy and I move to stand at the door to watch everyone get in their cars and drive off. The reality of the day sets in. We're engaged. There's a wedding to plan.

"You're not having second thoughts, are you?"

I look down at Andy to see him watching me closely. I brush a hand across his cheek and shake my head. I nod for him to follow me as I turn for Mason's room.

We work together to get Mas into his pajamas and tucked into his bed. When he's all snuggled in, we stand watching him for a few minutes. He looks so peaceful without a care in the world. Just as he should be.

"Come on," I say to Andy, lacing my fingers with his and leading him out of the room.

I know Beau and Emma will either let themselves out or make themselves at home. I'm not worried about either of them. What I do want is to finally have some alone time with my fiancé.

Once in our room, I seal the door behind us, shutting out the rest of the world for a few hours. I've grown accustomed to having Andy living here. It feels like it's where he was always supposed to be.

"Are you happy?" I ask, pulling his back to my front as I walk him to the center of the bedroom.

He snuggles back into my warmth. I try to ignore his ass brushing against me. Dipping my head, I nip his neck gently.

"Very. That was amazing. I wasn't expecting any of it," he replies.

"I had planned to do it sooner, but… you know," I murmur into his neck.

"You threw her a beautiful service. Again showing how big your heart is. I know that wasn't easy for you," he says.

"It is what it is. I did what I thought my mother would have wanted. She was her little sister. We all lose our way sometimes," I say with a shrug, flicking my tongue against his neck.

He runs his palm up my arm, my eyes close, and I inhale him. I'm content with the silence that falls over us as we stand there. My mind plays over the day. A smile takes over my lips when I remember Andy's face as I proposed.

It couldn't have been a better reaction. I start to hum a song that pops in my head. It was playing this morning as I waited for everyone to arrive: "Good Man," by Ne-Yo.

I lick the back of Andy's neck in between crooning the words in his ear. He reaches up, holding me to him. My eyes open, and I grin at the goose bumps I see rise on his skin. With the song in my head I start to dance against him. I move his body with mine.

We lace our fingers as we rock together. I chuckle when he shivers against me. I decide to stop teasing him. I kiss the top of his head, resting my chin there. I hum as we continue to slow rock. It's a much-needed moment for us. To just be.

I close my eyes again, relishing life itself. Andy's words from earlier play in my head. I stop humming to reply to his earlier question.

"I wasn't having second thoughts. I was wondering what kind of wedding you were thinking about. What do you want?" I say, kissing his neck.

"I was thinking about something on a private beach. Nothing too big. Just our family," he says thoughtfully.

"Are you sure? If you want something else. Something more open—"

"Nope. I appreciate your willingness to do that for me, but it's not necessary. It's not what I want at all. Remember, before you, I wasn't completely out there in the open. I'm not going to jump out there now. I like where we are. My job hasn't changed. I don't think some of that school board is ready for this," he says.

"Okay, as long as you know we can do whatever you want," I offer.

He turns to me. His blue-gray eyes filled with the kind of mischief I love. His lids hood as his eyes roam over me.

"I have something I want," he says in a low sexy voice.

My mouth kicks up into a smile, my teeth sinking into my lip. I'd be lying if I said I haven't thought about putting the perfect end cap on this night. Andy's hair has grown longer than usual. His locks have been falling in his eyes all day. It's sexy as fuck on him. I've been wanting to get my hands in it for hours.

I start at the buttons of my shirt, releasing them slowly. Andy steps out of his shoes, not taking his eyes from me. I shrug off my shirt, coming out of my shoes as well.

As he reaches up to push his hair back from his face, the ring I placed on his finger winks back at me. I halt, my brows drawing. This is my life. This man before me is mine. Andy's eyes start to look concerned. I step toward him.

"You're mine," I murmur, allowing my hand to take a pass through the front of his hair.

"Yeah, I am," he replies, gaze softening, his hands going to my stomach and slowly moving up.

As I look into his eyes I realize how clear my mind is. I'm not stressed about a team, a championship, people seeing me, my nephew's safety. I know Mas is safely tucked away in his bed, and the rest of that shit doesn't matter.

In this moment, all that matters is the man standing before me. I reach for the hem of his shirt and slowly drag it from his body. I watch closely and grunt in satisfaction when Andy doesn't subconsciously start to hide.

He stands before me knowing he's mine, knowing that I cherish him for who he is. I wrap my fingers around his throat, tipping his head back. I bite his chin, licking away the sting I know I've left. I take his lips and make slow love to his mouth, my fingers flexing around his throat.

Andy's fingers move to claw down my back. I hiss into his mouth. I release his neck to reach for his thighs, pulling him onto my waist. He wraps his arms around my neck, cradling my head in his arms.

We lock eyes and stare at each other. The heat in the stare is enough to make me combust. We let our eyes do the talking and lovemaking. We both divulge all of our feelings for each other. Words would be a hindrance to the chemistry we have.

I glide my hands up his back beneath his shirt. His eyes slide closed, and his head falls back slowly. I move across the room to the closest flat surface. His head lifts back up, and his eyes open just before his back meets the wall.

We both grunt with the connection. I keep my eyes on his as I lower my head to nip his shoulder. I kiss a trail to his left nipple. When I get to it, I give it a bite. His back bucks off the wall. I smile against his skin, flattening my tongue again the flesh to soothe it.

I kiss my way over to the other side. Again, I bite and soothe. His fingers are locked around my neck. I tease his side with the fingers of one hand. The other hand, I plant beside his head. He turns his face and licks my wrist.

I lift my head to look at him. My features tighten with lust. I move in to kiss him again. Reaching between us, I pop his jeans open. Instead of sticking my hand inside them, I drag my hand up his chest. Placing two fingers beneath his chin, I tip his head back to attack his neck again.

My shorts fall from my hips. I pull away to see Andy smiling back at me. I step out of the fabric he just released from my body and kick it aside. I tell him to hold on with my eyes. It's a silent command that he understands right away.

I hook my fingers in his jeans and drag them down his hips. He releases his legs from around me. I keep him pinned to the wall while we work together to get the pants off. I toss them aside and bring his sexy limbs back around my waist. He starts to grind against my erection.

I place both hands on the side of his head and start to slow grind into him through my boxer briefs. His bare arousal presses up to my covered one. We're in that intense stare again. Andy's tongue peeks out his mouth to lick across his lips in slow motion. It's so sexy I harden more.

I grab a hold of that hair that's been begging for my attention. Tilting his head to the side, I lick the side of his face. He groans, rocking against me harder. I lick his lips, suck the lower one into my mouth.

We're in no rush. I know I'm not. I want to devour him slowly. I'm pacing myself, for the best is yet to come.

We continue to grind against each other. I feel that familiar tightening in the pit of my stomach. I'm near ready to blow, but I don't increase the pressure or my movements. Instead, I start to travel down his body with kisses once again.

His legs unwrap from around my waist, placing him on shaky limbs. I continue my path until I'm on my knees before him. I grasp his waist, pinning him in place as I make circles on his left hip bone with my tongue.

My lips caress his skin, moving slowly across to his right side. I ignore his arousal that's bobbing for my attention. I'll get there soon enough. I look up at Andy as my lips and tongue tease and taste his hips and torso. I go everywhere expect for where he wants me most.

My hands slide around to cup his ass. His cheeks flex in my palms. I give a good squeeze, still watching him. I note the shift in his breathing. I'm enjoying the look of desire mixed with frustration.

Burying my face in the silky strands around his arousal, I inhale. He smells like my body wash and cologne. I remember chasing him out of the bathroom this morning when I found him in my shit. I groan. I like it. He smells of me and notes of what makes him, him.

I reach for his hand, placing it over his length. I nod my silent command, in between placing kisses over his waistline. He clasps his fingers around his girth and strokes. I ghost my face from one hip to the other, repeating the path again with my tongue. I keep teasing. Denying contact, taking a taste, denying him again. The flex of his stomach reveals this is getting to him.

I start to nip up and down his right thigh, taking the trip several times. My tongue dances across his skin, avoiding his stroking hand. Traveling across his waistline again, I start to nip, blow, suck, and lick on his left thigh just like the other. Reaching up, I give his nipple the attention I know he loves. Pinching just enough to leave a bite, then soothing it with my thumb.

Suddenly Andy changes the script. Placing his fingers beneath my chin, he draws my eyes to him. Gently, he brings me to my full height with his fingertips guiding me. His head tilts back to look up at me. Dipping my head just inches from his, I breathe him in.

My tongue peeks out to flick against his lip, causing his breath to hitch. His entire body shivers before me. I nip his bottom lip, then the top one. When Andy tries to lean in for a full kiss, I pull just out of his reach.

His eyes blaze with desire and determination. Pushing at my chest to give him a little more room, he drops to his knees before me. I don't get a chance to react before he has me in his mouth.

He looks up through his lashes, and our eyes connect. I bite my lip and let my eyes roll. The sound of him giving me head alone is enough to make me take a pause to relish it for a moment.

Damn. This motherfucker and that mouth.

My thoughts echo in the moan that vibrates from my chest. I lock my fingers in his hair, massaging his scalp as he sucks me like a prize-giving lollipop. My hips start to buck forward.

He's driving me insane, but this is not how I wanted this to play out. I want to give Andy pleasure. Mimicking his earlier action, I place my fingers under his chin, move my hand to gently cup his jaw, and pull free.

"Spit on it," I say.

He does several times before I bring him to stand, his eyes intent on me. His cheeks are red and his eyes bright. I crowd him against the wall again. This time when I lift him onto my waist, I guide him onto my waiting arousal.

The slow gasp of air he takes is the sexiest thing I've ever heard. It's like he just breathed me in. I plant my palms on the wall, and his hands go to my shoulder. I move into him with slow deliberate strokes.

I kiss the tip of his nose, then brush mine across the bridge of his while rocking into him. The energy that hums over our skin charges everything around us. His hands move to the sides of my face, bring my lips to his. I breathe into his mouth as I increase the pace just a bit.

The lock of our lips takes me to a deeper level. Wrapping my arms beneath his thighs, I move from the wall, bend my knees, and start to bounce him on my dick. Andy's head falls back in a silent scream. I can see the strain from him confining the sound.

I place my lips next to his ear, but no words come out. All the nasty shit I want to say just doesn't fit this moment. The connection is deeper than a few crass words. I just allow my breath to fan his ear, sending tremors rocking through him.

I turn for the bed, walking us to it. Andy nibbles at my lips, as I climb onto the bed with him. I'm still seated inside him. I reconnect our eyes. My hands caress up from his ass, over his thighs, stopping behind his knees. I push his legs back, watching his eyes widen.

I bite into my lip and groan as I feel him tightening around me. It feels so good. I have to take a pause as my heart pounds. I close my eyes and gather myself.

Andy

I never thought sex with Kyle could get any better than the lovemaking I've experienced with him in the past. He's proving me so wrong. This is over-the-top. Every cell in my body is screaming his name.

It has to be the knowledge that today marks the first day of the rest of our lives. The future is officially ours to hold. No crazy ex. No scarred past suppressing life itself. No insecurities to block the purity of the moment.

There's nothing to keep Kyle from spending as much time with Mas as he likes. He can be a good uncle without having to worry about running off to a game. We can build the family we want, and it all starts here. Today, with us.

Making love like this seems like the perfect note to the perfect song. Each kiss, each caress, each stroke is life to our relationship. It's one thing to feel Kyle—it's another to understand him. Tonight we are understanding each other.

The look on his face right now isn't helping to calm my racing pulse. He looks like he's in complete ecstasy. My eyes dance over his handsome face while his are closed. His jaw works. Those full lips look so edible. He has an iron grip on the back of my knees.

I feel him pulsing inside me and I want more. I clench my ass and his eyes fly open. I grasp my ankles, drawing my legs farther into my chest. A vein pops in his neck as he grinds his teeth. He starts to move again.

He bites his lip in concentration. I can see in his brows how much he's trying to control himself. He's so beautiful. I look between us to see his dark skin against my paler color. We make a sensual blend. I can't take my eyes away. I watch as he moves in and out of me.

My eyes only tear away when he starts to work his body into me harder. He's like a dancer, rolling his body and working his legs and back. He dives into me, giving me all of him.

Still, neither of us has uttered a word. Our eyes and bodies are doing all the necessary talking. Right now, his eyes are telling me he's about to come. He dips his head, taking my lips.

He swells inside me. Our lips slide against each other. I can't get enough of tasting him—any part of him. I wish he would have let me finish earlier. I start salivating at the thought of him in my mouth.

He didn't finish then, but I have no question that he does now. With a growl into my mouth, he spills into me. I close my eyes and revel in the feel of his seed warming my insides.

He places kisses all over my face. I smile lazily, content with the world. I'm good on not coming too. However, I should know better.

He pulls from my body, and moments later his mouth is wrapped around my length. I buck off the bed. My toes curl into the mattress, and my head sinks back into the pillows. Once again, I'm trying not to call out, knowing we're not home alone.

It just feels so damn good. I pull a pillow over my head and bellow into it. My legs start to shake. My hips are rocking of their own according. I'm turning mindless beneath him. Kyle's skilled mouth leaves me twisted in knots.

My arms clamp the pillow over my face as I spill down the back of his throat. I come so hard I'm seeing stars. I'm boneless as I melt into the sheets.

If this will be my life, I'll take two please.

I laugh out loud at my own thoughts. Kyle tugs the pillow away to look down at me curiously. I grin back at him like as idiot.

"Something funny?" he mumbles.

"Was just thinking, if you asked me to marry you again, I'd say yes," I reply.

Kyle looks at me like I'm crazy. Shaking his head, he lies on his back, scooping me into his arms and onto his chest. I caress his stomach, giving a long yawn.

"I don't know why you're settling in as if I'm done," he says, running his fingers through my hair.

I can hear the humor in his voice. I turn my head up as it rests on his chest. I toss my leg over his torso and start to get more comfortable against him.

"Why in the world would I ever think that?" I tease.

"Have no idea," he says. "You ought to know better."

I give him a lazy grin, lifting to give him a peck on his lips. He slaps my ass and I burst out laughing. I love the smile on his handsome face.

"Mr. Tyson, is this the behavior I have to look forward to?"

"Did you get into something you can't handle?" he says.

"Nope, we're going to be an old married couple now. That means slow, lazy sex from now on," I throw back. "When it's done, it's done."

"First of all, who's old?" he says and yawns. "Damn. Okay, it's been a long day, but we're not making a habit of this one-and-done shit."

His snores follow not too long after his words. I smile and drift off to happy thoughts.

This is what life should be like.

New Beginnings

Kyle
A year later....

"This... my friend, was worth the blood, sweat, and tears," Javier says as we look out over the playground at the children's complex.

This place is amazing. Beau really took my idea and turned it into a wonderland I could never have dreamed of. It's more than an orphanage. Everything is state of the art. The place was built to encourage these kids to feel at home but also to explore who they are and their interests.

We have a music center with studios, equipment, and instruments. There's a sports center where they can play any sport their hearts' desire. A media center for film, writers, and so much more. A state-of-the-art kitchen where they can cook with the chefs if they'd like. We left no stone unturned.

"It is," I reply. "Look at them. I've been here for every single intake and arrival. I've seen their sad and scared faces when they get here. Now look."

"Safe and happy, just what you wanted," Jordan says from my other side.

"Yeah."

He just took the words from my mouth. We screen every single worker through at least three different systems. Mitch oversees the final approval. I've worked with the staff up close and personal. If I get a bad vibe, I let them go without question. Everyone comes in on a hundred-and-twenty-day probation.

These kids will always be safe on my watch. I also promised myself they will always have the best. We take the broken, bent, and unwanted kids. Here they will learn to heal and be loved.

"I think Mas thinks he has forty new siblings," Beau muses.

"I thought it was just me," Andy says with amusement coloring his words. "He loves this place. I think it's good for him and the other kids. They gravitate to him."

"With the exception of one." Beau throws his head back and laughs.

We all laugh. My poor boy.

"Nah, they're going to be best friends. Just you watch," I say, still laughing.

"If you say so," Beau says, with doubt.

"I'm with Kyle," Andy agrees.

Cheers erupt on the basketball court, pulling our attention. My lips kick up as the subject of our conversation hands out high fives. I look to the left of the scene to find an intent Mas hovering on the sidelines. Yeah, Mas has a best friend in the making.

"Personally, I think this has been good for all of us. Didn't know I wanted to be a papa until I gained a bunch of niños." Javier laughs.

"Tell me about it. I find myself headed to this place more than my own home," Jordan adds. "They keep me out of trouble."

We all turn to look at Jordan. I think we're all thinking the same thing. He has been staying out of trouble lately. I haven't seen him on the cover of the tabloids in months.

Um, interesting.

I think we're all growing up. I know I have. Our wedding is next month, and we've just finished unpacking the penthouse suite of the main building on the children's complex. Beau decided to add in suites in case we ever needed to stay on-site.

Andy and I decided this was where we wanted to live and had the penthouse designed for our family. I think it was the best move for us. It feels just like home.

"Are you ready for the first school year?" Jordan asks Andy.

"Yeah, I think I am. The school looks great, and the staff is rounding out nicely. I like that we decided to open registration to the complex tenants," Andy replies.

"I'm still on the fence about that shit. If those little privileged assholes start fucking with our kids, they're out," Beau grumbles, speaking to my own thoughts.

We went back and forth on the topic a few times. A few of us weren't too sure we wanted kids at the school that might look down on the kids from Savanna's House. Andy was adamant that the school should be open to others.

He has a vision for it all, and I decided to trust it. It's his thing after all. Andy has taken on the school as headmaster. While he, Tara, and Emma have been very serious about this wedding, Andy's been even more serious about the direction of the school. I have faith in all he's done for the school and these children. I think they all have become ours.

"Yup, they have become all of our niños." Javier chuckles.

"It will be fine. I've talked with the parents, and I've designed the program to be inclusive. I'll be watching," Andy reassures.

"You guys need anything?" Jordan asks. "I'm heading out on the road for a bit this week, but if I can help with the new place, the wedding, babysitting during the honeymoon, whatever you guys need, let me know."

"Thanks for the offer," I reply.

"I think we have it all covered. Mas wants to stay with my parents for the two weeks," Andy says. "We finished up with the place. I'll be back in time to get the school open and running. We're pretty good."

"Well, the offer is out there," Jordan says.

"Fellas, it is always good to be in your company. This is a good thing we've done here. I'm going to hit up the deep pockets to keep it going. Call me if you need me," Javier croons. "Adiós, mis hermanos."

"Later, man," I say, pulling him into a one-armed hug.

"I'm heading out as well," Beau says. "I need to get down to the gym."

We embrace next. I'll see him later when I drop Mas and a few of the others off at the gym for their classes. Emma usually does it, but she's been avoiding her new crush in the last few weeks. The Daltons have been making life quite interesting lately.

"I'm going to join the street hockey game in a few," Jordan says as he stretches.

"Cool." I nod.

Andy and I are the only ones left on the little hill we've been standing on looking over the playground. I take in a deep breath. This right here is well with my soul. Savanna would be happy.

I turn my head to the right when Andy's laugh meets my ears. His face is alight with amusement, and his eyes are sparkling. He's still as gorgeous as the first day I ever laid eyes on him. My lips curve in the corners when I note he's wearing a short-sleeve shirt and shorts.

We've come a long way, baby.

"What's so funny?"

"Mas once referred to us all as gods. His superheroes, he called all of his uncles. I just find it funny how we've gotten into the habit of standing up here to look down on the place. It's our Mount Olympus," he explains happily.

I join in on the laughter, looking out over the complex. Who knew this would all lead here? Although, I'm not too sure on the superhero part. I'm still worried about making all the right choices concerning Mas.

"That kid is something else." I grin.

"I think he's going to give us a run for our money," Andy says, not sounding the least bit put off.

"Twenty-eight days. Are you ready to become Mr. Tyson?" I ask, reaching out to bring him closer.

Andy leans into my side, wrapping an arm around my waist. We melt into each other effortlessly. This is who we've become. We don't throw it out there into people's faces, but we don't hide anymore. Our love is our love.

"Kyle, I've been ready to be yours since the day I was born. I'm finally complete," he replies, and it's all that needs to be said.

I kiss the top of his head, squeezing my arm around his waist. I feel the exact same way.

ACKNOWLEDGMENTS

Hello! Thank you so much for spending some time in my head. I love to share the worlds that live in my brain, and you taking your precious time to read them means the world to me. It is my hope that you enjoyed Kyle and Andy's story as much as I enjoyed working on it.

I want to thank all of those that have supported me as both Royal Blue and Blue Saffire. The encouragement means so much. I love writing love, and every chance I get to craft a story from the heart it's like breathing. I leave a piece of me in every book. I thank you for loving those pieces enough to keep cheering me on.

I want to thank my husband for being the voice of reason with every step I take. He is the balancing scale to my swinging pendulum. My peace, my equilibrium.

I want to thank God, my true cowriter. Again, energy is everything. Grace and Favor paves our way to all things good. Forever grateful and giving praise.

ABOUT THE AUTHOR

The color blue is known for trust and healing, as are the words of author Royal Blue. Blue started writing books to heal herself after losing her mother to breast cancer in 2007, followed by a miscarriage only eight months later. Books and words were one of the things that held her together.

As a young girl, Blue's mother introduced her to the world of love and music through movies like *Seven Brides for Seven Brothers, Bye Bye Birdie*, and *Neptune's Daughter*. Once she got her hands on books that sucked her into the magic that pages bring, an authoress was born. A story here, a few songs there, but she actually didn't complete a manuscript until 2009.

However, books were piling up and collecting dust as fear clung and whispered evil thoughts. Yet, fear was silenced in 2015. Needing to write in order to breathe and wanting to share, Blue Saffire, Royal's alter ego, rose from the ashes and entered the world.

The self-proclaimed hermit was born in Far Rockaway, NY, but is now a Long Island resident with her loving and supportive husband. The two work round the clock creating music and characters. There is no shortage of laughter or creativity in their home.

Never in a million years did she think the passion that saved her sanity would allow her to walk around with blue hair and spend her days dreaming of hot men to put on paper. After all, an MBA in Marketing and Project Management, as well as a MED in Curriculum Design and Instructional Technology, tell a very different story. Although, it's safe to say Royal would rather be doing something Blue with her time.

Email: AuthorRoyalBlue@gmail.com

Website: AuthorRoyalBlue.com

Twitter: @authorroyalblue

Facebook: https://www.facebook.com/authorroyalblue/

Instagram: @authorroyalblue

Wait, there is more to come! You can stay updated with my latest releases, learn more about me, the author, and be a part of contests by subscribing to my newsletter at
www.RoyalBlue.com
If you enjoyed Kyle's Reveal, I'd love to hear your thoughts and please feel free to leave a review. And when you do, please let me know by emailing me AuthorRoyalBlue@gmail.com
or leave a comment on Facebook
https://www.facebook.com/authorroyalblue/
or Twitter @AuthorRoyalBlue

Other books by Royal Blue
Beau's Redemption
Jordan's Commitment...*Coming 2020*